His kiss literally took Kate's breath away

After a moment, she had to turn her face from his and gasp.

"Am I going too fast?" Nick whispered thickly. "I'm sorry. It's just that I've been lying awake thinking about you for days now."

Kate turned her head back and gazed up at him through her lashes. "I've been thinking about you, too."

He kissed her lips again and smiled. "Then it's time we did something about it, wouldn't you say?"

He kissed her again, generating a flame between them that made Kate melt and cling. "You're so lovely," he murmured.

"I bet you say that to all the girls you rescue," Kate retorted huskily.

"Kate," he said earnestly, "believe me. Since meeting you, I haven't given any other woman a thought."

ABOUT THE AUTHOR

"When I first started the Byrnside Inheritance, I felt a little like Christopher Columbus setting off into uncharted seas," says Jane Silverwood. "It's been an exciting and satisfying voyage of discovery for me. I hope readers will have the same feelings about these three stories and their characters." *High Stakes*, the first book of the trilogy, is the author's fourth Superromance.

Books by Jane Silverwood

HARLEQUIN SUPERROMANCE
282–THE TENDER TRAP
314–BEYOND MERE WORDS
375–HANDLE WITH CARE

HARLEQUIN TEMPTATION
46–VOYAGE OF THE HEART
93–SLOW MELT
117–A PERMANENT ARRANGEMENT

Don't miss any of our special offers. Write to us at the following address for information on our newest releases.

Harlequin Reader Service
P.O. Box 1397, Buffalo, NY 14240
Canadian address: P.O. Box 603,
Fort Erie, Ont. L2A 5X3

High Stakes

JANE SILVERWOOD

Harlequin Books

TORONTO • NEW YORK • LONDON
AMSTERDAM • PARIS • SYDNEY • HAMBURG
STOCKHOLM • ATHENS • TOKYO • MILAN

This book is dedicated
to my mother

Published January 1991

ISBN 0-373-70434-8

HIGH STAKES

PROLOGUE

JAKE CAINE'S MERCEDES CONVERTIBLE moved past the twelve-foot brick wall that guarded Owen Byrnside from the world. As the wrought-iron gates swung closed behind Jake, he glanced up at the rearview mirror. Through it he could see the crest on the gate. It was the logo featured on all the Byrnside publications—from magazines to books, to tapes and CDs—a swooping falcon with outstretched claws and a cruelly curved beak. *Looks a lot like the old boy himself,* Jake thought.

Smoothly his car purred along the road that curved through the park. In this crisp New England weather the scene was particularly striking. On either side of the winding track, stately oaks and elms bordered acres of neatly clipped grounds. Shrubbery, presently laced with an early March snowfall but in the summer months kept immaculate by an unseen army of gardeners, dotted the gently rolling hills and valleys.

A final tree-lined curve, and the mellow gray stones of Taleman Hall rose out of the landscape. Though it hadn't been standing more than three decades, with its crenellated towers and keystone windows, it had been designed to impress and built to last. And in the first the architect had succeeded. After pulling his car into the circular cobblestone drive, Jake gazed up at the sprawling roofline. Then he raked a hand through his thick brown hair, collected his leather briefcase and extricated his long-legged body from the car.

Twenty minutes later he stood at the foot of an enormous canopied bed gazing into the withered but still fiercely commanding visage of Owen Byrnside himself.

"Three of them, you say?"

Soberly, Jake nodded. "And little more than a month after they left, the Broadstreet Foundling Home burned to the ground. All the records were lost."

"Lost!" Owen cursed colorfully. "Then how in hell—"

Jake unsnapped his briefcase. "Fortunately, I was able to trace one of the nurses who worked at the home during that period, a Miss Ada Kindle. She's retired now and getting on in years. But she remembers that night."

"The first of April twenty-six years ago? How is that possible?"

"Because it was April Fool's, and because three female infants were left at the Broadstreet's door within two hours of one another. That was a most unusual occurrence."

"I should hope so." Owen Byrnside's veined hands were clenched on the embroidered sheet that covered his laboring chest. "And to think that one of them may have been my flesh and blood, my granddaughter!" The possibility was apparently too much for him. He began to cough violently. As soon as the hacking started, the uniformed nurse hovering in the hall rushed in.

While she fluttered about administering water and checking Owen's pulse, Jake turned toward the window and gazed out at the decorative pool beyond the stone balustrade. Silently he reflected on the many painstaking weeks he'd put into this search.

At first, taking an anonymous letter seriously had seemed ridiculous. Who would believe that Christopher Byrnside, Owen's wastrel son, who decades earlier had disassembled himself and his sports car on a lonely country road, had managed to sire a mystery child? Even more improbable, if that mystery child really existed and could be found, she was the heiress to a worldwide publishing and recording empire. Yet, after he'd received the letter, Byrnside had insisted that they mount an investigation.

"You say there were three infants abandoned at the damn foundling home that night? All right, but what makes you think that one of them may have been left by Gloria Dean?"

Jake's attention was jerked back to his client, who had peremptorily shooed his nurse away.

"The date, and the fact that one of those babies was wearing a gold locket. From what I've been able to learn of your son's lady love, she had a flair for the dramatic. That locket would be just her style. Ada Kindle doesn't remember which one of the babies wore it. But it was a distinctive piece of jewelry, so she does remember what it looked like." Jake paused and then handed Byrnside a piece of paper. "That's a photocopy of a pencil drawing she made for me."

As he studied the reproduction, the old man's pale blue eyes glinted in a sudden almost pathetic eagerness. "Christopher got that locket from his mother." Owen's scrutiny shifted to a gilt-framed painting on the wall opposite his massive bed. It was a portrait of a lovely woman with soft brown curls. As he gazed at it, his expression grew pensive.

"Our son's death was the bitterest disappointment in our life together. I don't know—perhaps the empire I built was my way of compensating for that. If so, it was all in vain. I'm a sick man, Jake. The doctor says this bum ticker of mine could give out any time now. And as I've lain here in this damned bed thinking about my life, I've realized that nothing can make up for dying without an heir. No, not the money, or the power, or the good works, either! I want to know that I'm leaving behind me flesh and blood—flesh and blood that is my own. I need to know that!"

The old man's expression hardened, grew fierce, and he turned on Jake a concentrated, unblinking stare. "Find this young woman, Caine! I don't care what it takes. I don't care how far you have to go, or how much you have to spend. As of now, you have my every resource at your disposal. Just find her!"

CHAPTER ONE

NICK HAD JUST STUFFED his shaving gear into the leather satchel that was his only luggage when he heard a light footfall outside in the corridor. Warily, he raised his head.

A polite tap rattled the door and then an appealing female voice murmured in French, "Maid service. I have some fresh towels for you, monsieur."

Silently, Nick stalked toward the door. Blast, what now? He'd just finished delivering a colt he'd trained at his horse farm in Ireland. With his business in Paris finished, he was anxious to be on his way. Stationing himself to one side, he said, "Thanks all the same, luv, but I'm just about to check out, so I don't need fresh towels."

"Oh, but I was told to bring them to your room. Please, I must do as I'm ordered or I lose my job."

Nick reached across and turned the lock.

A curvaceous young woman in a maid's uniform strolled in closing the door behind her. She carried a stack of towels and wore a smile calculated to make the hotel's male guests whose beds she turned down very happy indeed. "I'll just put these on the nightstand."

"All right, then." Bemused, he watched as she dropped the fluffy stack next to his satchel. Then, shooting him another dazzling smile, she swayed back toward the door. When she opened it, two burly men burst in, rushed past her and grabbed Nick.

After he'd finally given up struggling against them, he looked from one broad, leering face to the other and cursed his gullibility. He recognized them both. They were Ben Murtle's thugs. "What do you want?"

"You, little man," the shorter of the two sneered in his nasal cockney accent. He was only around six foot. His partner had to be six-four and was built like an oversize beer keg on stilts. "We're not sure you're going to do what you've been told, Conti. So we're here to give you a little preview of what's in store for you if you're dumb enough to climb aboard Seasonwine at Aintree. Show him what I mean, Denny. But don't hurt him too much. I want to have some fun with him."

Grinning, the goon named Denny aimed a solid punch at Nick's solar plexus. It landed him a hammer blow, knocking the wind out of him and making him grunt in pain as he doubled up.

"Now make sure he doesn't go anywhere," Denny's partner ordered. "I'm going to go run some water in the tub."

"Chuck's planning some real interesting experiments with you," Denny snickered into Nick's ear as he wrapped his thick arm around his neck in a bizarre parody of a lover's embrace. "How long do you think you can hold your breath, pretty boy?"

Not nearly long enough, Nick suspected. Despite the emotions roiling in his stomach, he forced himself to stay limp in Denny's musclebound grasp. In his experience, men who were built like grizzly bears tended to underestimate their shorter, less beefy brethren. And sometimes, if you were quick enough and knew something about the martial arts, that could work to your advantage. At least, Nick hoped it could.

Suddenly he struck like a rattlesnake, sinking his teeth into Denny's forearm deep enough to draw blood. As the hoodlum yelped and loosened his grip, Nick jabbed an elbow into his rib and hooked a foot around his ankle. Denny crashed to the ground, and Chuck came running out the bathroom door, arms extended like a gorilla on the attack. But he was too late. Nick had hurled himself at the window and, protected from the worst of the broken glass by his leather jacket, was already halfway down the fire escape.

Luck stayed with him and he managed to flag down a cab the instant he emerged from the alleyway. There had been airplane tickets to Rome in his luggage. Now they were in the hands of Chuck and Denny, who'd probably stake out the airport as soon as they found them. On the spur of the moment Nick decided to take the train.

"Gare du nord," he told the driver. *"Vite, vite."*

As the Citroën wove an erratic path through Paris's snarled traffic, Nick kept busy looking out for pursuing vehicles and mentally reviewing his situation. Murtle was just a flunky. Lou LaFiore was behind this, behind all the other threats, too. Nick was sure that Lou's crazy jealousy had caused the skull-basher at Aintree two years ago, and though Nick had once worked for the man, he remained something of a mystery. For one thing, he had several residences and could be hard to pin down. But Nick had learned that he would be doing business in Rome for the next few days. *Somehow,* Nick thought, *I have to connect with him there. I have to make him call off his vendetta.*

"Pardonnez-moi, but don't I recognize you, *monsieur?"*

"I beg your pardon?" Startled, Nick jerked around and caught the driver eyeing him through the rearview mirror.

"I 'ave seen your peekture in the paper. You are the rider coming out of retirement to race Seasonwine again, no?"

"No," Nick lied. He reached for his sunglasses. Under other circumstances he would be flattered. But right at the moment recognition was just what he didn't need.

The cabbie's face fell. "But you are the image of Nick Conti."

"Sorry to disappoint you."

The man shrugged. "I only wanted to wish you luck. They say it will be the race of the decade."

"They say that about every big steeplechase."

"Ah yes, but this one is unique."

Nick didn't comment. Inwardly he was hearing that last whispered warning he'd received over the telephone. "Remember what happened to you last time you rode Seasonwine? Either you resign in one piece, or we'll fix it so there isn't enough left of you to ever climb on the back of a nag again."

The cab pulled up in front of the train station and Nick, grateful that his wallet had been in his pocket at the time Denny and Chuck burst into his room, paid the driver. With his sunglasses firmly hooked to his ears and the fleece collar of his leather jacket pulled up, he bought a ticket to Rome, picked a newspaper out of a stand and then went onto the platform to wait. Pray God no one else recognized him before he boarded that train!

To protect his back, he leaned against a wall and then, watchful behind his dark lenses, unfolded the newspaper. For the next half hour all kinds of people wandered past. But none of them looked as if they might be one of Murtle's hit men—or women, he added to himself as he remembered the maid. He'd always been a fool where women were concerned. In fact, he owed most of his troubles in life to that weakness. But no more. Until he settled this thing with LaFiore, he intended to trust no one.

At last the train bound for Rome chugged onto the track and the crowd thickened. A group of nuns swirled past followed by two elderly businessmen in homburgs and pinstripe suits. He had been eyeing them suspiciously when his attention was distracted by a commotion a few yards to his right. At the center of it a redheaded young woman had just dropped a heavy suitcase in order to chase after a pair of wild-eyed youngsters.

Groaning inwardly, Nick yanked the newspaper back up in front of his face. He'd recognized the kids. Of all the unfortunate coincidences! They were Lou LaFiore's unruly twins.

He was too late. "Nick!" they shrieked, their piercing voices echoing down the length of the concrete siding like bat squeaks. "Nick Conti! Can we have your autograph?"

Nick dropped the newspaper and strode away, hoping to lose himself in the crowd before they identified him to the entire world.

THE TRAIN had been rolling across France for three hours when Kate tiptoed out of their compartment and then cautiously locked the door behind her. For more than a minute she stood, tugging undecidedly on one of her bright curls. Was it really all right to leave the boys alone for a few minutes? What if they woke up? But eight-year-olds were no longer babies, she reminded herself. Surely they would be all right. And, God knew, she needed a moment to herself to draw a free breath. Another day like the two she'd just had and she'd be ready for a rest cure in a mental institution.

Kate alerted the porter that if there were any problems she could be found in the dining car for the next twenty minutes. After giving him a generous tip to keep an eye on their compartment, she made her way down the narrow, carpeted corridor. With quickening steps she walked through the three sleeping cars that separated her from the oasis where the night train between Paris and Rome served food.

When they saw her coming, the waiters there went pale—and small wonder after what the twins had put them through earlier in the evening. Here and there on the red carpeting Kate could still detect stains from the platter of fettucine Alfredo the boys had overturned.

"You are alone, *madame?*" the maître d' queried, gazing nervously behind her.

"Yes, the children are asleep," she assured him in stilted French. "I'm so sorry about that little trick they played on you. I can't imagine what possessed them to pour water down your socks. I gave them a good talking to."

He eyed her coldly, and she knew he was thinking that if they were his he'd do a lot more about their behavior than just talk. So would she if she had a little more time with them. Since taking on this job, she'd more than once had the urge to tan Rudy and Randy's backsides.

"Your children are unusually lively," the maître d' commented. "Perhaps you should consider purchasing an airplane ticket the next time you travel."

"I couldn't with the boys. They get airsick."

"How unfortunate." He tapped a stack of menus balanced in the crook of his arm. "There are several tables available. If you'll just follow me..."

A few minutes later Kate sat sipping from a cup of tea and nibbling toast as she gazed out the train's dark window. What parts of the French countryside was she missing, she wondered. At this very minute the train might be passing vineyards, romantic little towns. Perhaps the roofs of centuries-old châteaus or the spires of medieval cathedrals were visible in the distance . . .

"Mind if I join you?"

Kate turned away from the window and saw a leanly built man in a buttery leather jacket smiling at her. She recognized him at once. It was the man on the platform, the one the boys had chased.

"I . . ." But he was already pulling out the chair opposite her. "Please do," she said dryly for, in fact, he already had. As he turned to the waiter to order, a quick glance around the car told Kate that there were two empty tables. So it was no coincidence that he was choosing to sit down with her. He must have seen her with the boys, she thought, replacing her guidebook in her purse. Yet at the time he hadn't given any sign of recognizing them. After he'd disappeared into the crowd around the train, Rudy and Randy had told her all about him. "He used to ride our dad's racehorses," Rudy had exclaimed. "He's a famous steeplechase jockey."

Kate hadn't caught much more than a glimpse of him earlier, but what she'd managed to take in had been intriguing. From the few times she'd watched the Kentucky Derby on television she'd gotten the impression that jockeys were boylike individuals. This man, though perhaps no taller than five feet eight or nine inches and built along wiry lines, had a virile muscularity about him that was not boylike in the least. Now, as she studied his cleanly chiseled profile, she saw that he was even more attractive than she'd supposed.

At that moment he turned and flashed her a smile that would have been engaging if it had reached his eyes. But as those cool blue orbs studied her, a faint chill ran up

Kate's spine. "Allow me to introduce myself," he said. "I'm Nick Conti."

"How do you do. I'm Kate Humphrey."

"Pleased to meet you, Ms. Humphrey. I hope I'm not intruding on a private meditation. There's not much to see through that window at this time of night. But you were staring out it as if the scenery were fascinating."

"Only in my imagination," she answered carefully. "This is my first time in Europe."

He nodded. "I thought that was an American accent I detected."

"That's funny. We Americans think that it's you British who have the accent. You are British, aren't you?" she added. His last name certainly wasn't, and she couldn't quite place his intonation, either. It was faintly British, but there was a smoky European flavor to it, also—as if he were equally at home in a variety of languages. He sounded rather like the sexy ployglot hero of a spy movie.

He looked faintly amused. "Like everything else, it all comes down to point of view. I was born in England, yes. And I was right about your accent being American, wasn't I?"

"It's a midwestern twang, actually. I'm from Columbus, Ohio."

"Then you're a long way from home." He stared at her assessingly. "Bound for Rome?"

"Yes."

"So am I. As a matter of fact, we may have a mutual acquaintance there, Louis LaFiore."

She inclined her head. So he had seen the boys and had eluded them deliberately. It was understandable, she supposed, considering how trying the twins could be. But then why had he elected to sit down at her table and question her about her destination? What was this all about, anyway?

The waiter brought his drink, which Kate was surprised to note was just tea like hers. "As a matter of fact," he continued after filling his cup and taking a sip, "I'm planning to pay Louis a bit of a visit myself."

"What a coincidence. I'm taking his sons, Rudy and Randy, to him."

"Yes, I saw the three of you on the platform in Paris."

"Really?" She cocked her head. "You didn't seem to. Couldn't you hear the boys call you? They were very disappointed when you didn't turn around."

"Sorry, at the time I had rather a lot on my mind. However, now that things have calmed down a bit, I must admit to some curiosity. How do you happen to be in charge of Lou LaFiore's young hell-raisers? Are you their nanny?" His watchful gaze drifted over her face and hair, and she felt herself getting slightly warm.

"Only on a temporary basis," Kate replied stiffly. "I've been hired by Jillian LaFiore to escort her sons to their father while he's in Rome. Excuse me, but I have a splitting headache." While she fished a couple of aspirin out of her purse and then washed them down with the tea, she glanced through her lashes at her puzzling tablemate.

With his blue eyes and dark, wavy hair, he was the kind of man that women noticed. Though he wasn't tall, his height in no way diminished his masculinity, which fairly crackled across the table at her.

Looking tough and assured as he took a sip of his drink and then put down his cup, he said, "I'm not surprised you've got a headache." Suddenly he grinned, and as she observed the way the corners of his deep blue eyes crinkled, she felt a warning little flutter of attraction in the region of her stomach.

"Where have you got the little devils stashed?"

"Asleep in our compartment, I hope."

He glanced at her bare ring finger. "How did you happen to hook up with them?" Once again his gaze flicked over her face. "Somehow, I can't believe that you shepherd kids around as a regular thing."

"No," she admitted, inclining her head slightly to acknowledge the implied compliment. "I just took this job to get in a little travel and earn enough money to take myself home."

"You intrigue me. Why do you have to earn your way back to the States?"

"Because I lost the job I had in England."

"And what might that have been?"

"I was the pianist with a jazz trio. When we all got the sack the trumpet player and base man collected their severance pay and boarded the next plane across the Atlantic."

"But instead of going back home to the U.S., you stayed on?"

She nodded. "I've always wanted to travel around Europe. This gig in London was the answer to a dream. I hated to just give up on it, so I thought I'd see if I could pick up work. That was a mistake. The English don't appear to be in the market for female jazz pianists just now."

He glanced at her wreath of curls. "Maybe if you dyed your hair green and painted your face with crayons."

"Oh, I think my hair is garish enough as it is."

Instead of commenting on that he said, "So when all else failed, you decided to hire yourself out as a nanny? Good thinking—the English are always in the market for those. I gather you haven't known the LaFiore boys for long, then."

"Just four days—though it feels like much longer."

Chuckling, he set his cup down and leaned back. "That I can quite understand. It's been a while since I've seen them—not since their parents' separation, actually. But as I recall, fifteen minutes in their company felt like forever."

Despite his joking remark, his eyes had narrowed again. *What on earth is going on in his mind?* Kate wondered uncomfortably. As far as she was concerned, he'd treated her oddly from the moment he'd approached her. She didn't consider herself vain. But she had noticed in her twenty-six years that most men seemed to enjoy her company. This one behaved as if he suspected her of something.

Was he fencing with her this way because she was only hired help? she asked herself. It wasn't likely that she'd know such wealthy people as the LaFiores on anything other than a temporary and impersonal basis. When the employment agency had sent her to Jillian LaFiore's house in Eaton Square, she'd been quite awed by its luxury. The twins' beautiful blond mother, however, had angered her.

"I don't want to sound heartless, Miss Humphrey," she'd said during their brief interview. "But I have my acting career to think about now. I'm going on tour for the next six months, and I simply won't be able to devote the sort of care and attention to my little ones that they deserve. It's time their father did his share. In fact," she'd gone on after taking several staccato puffs on her cigarette, "I'm insisting on it." She'd begun to stride up and down on the white shag carpeting, her three-inch heels sinking in precariously. "He's always sending them expensive gifts and saying how much he wants them to visit him. Well, now's his chance to make good."

Though Kate hadn't yet met Rudy and Randy, her heart had gone out to them. Because of her own background—

she'd been abandoned at birth and then adopted by an older couple who'd died when she was still a teenager, leaving her to be passed from one foster home to another—she had a special soft spot for the world's rejects. *Poor kids,* she'd thought. *Their mother is too busy playing glamour girl to pay attention to them, and who knows if their father really wants them.*

But that had been before she'd met the terrible twosome. Now she wasn't sure whether her heart went out to them or to the string of previous nannies they'd already sent running for their lives.

While he continued to study her, Nick Conti swirled the liquid at the bottom of his teacup. "Is Lou meeting you in Rome?"

"Yes, he is—or one of his employees is. Anyway, I believe it's all taken care of."

"Good. It can be quite hard to manage in a foreign city."

Tell me about it, Kate thought. Paris, the city of her dreams, which she'd expected to savor like rare wine, had been a battle of wills. Rudy and Randy had enraged the hotel manager by tossing water balloons down on the street below their room, tied knots in all her panty hose and run amok in the Louvre. She'd made them apologize for their behavior and kept a tight rein on them at Versailles, but enough was enough. She was quite ready to turn them over to their father.

"You've finished your tea," Nick Conti said. "Will you allow me to get you another?"

"No, thank you very much." Firmly, she set the cup down. "It's really time I was was getting back, so if you'll excuse me..."

"Of course."

He stood up just as Kate did the same, rattling the crockery on the table. Maddeningly, she felt herself begin to blush.

"Thanks for letting me share your table," he said.

"Not at all. It's been nice chatting with you."

"Happy landing when you get to Rome."

She gave him an inquiring look. "Oh...oh, yes. Happy landings to you, too."

NICK WATCHED as Kate threaded her way down the narrow aisle and through the door. And, he noted, his wasn't the only male head turning her way. In her black miniskirt and bright yellow linen jacket the long-legged Ms. Kate Humphrey cut a rather dashing figure—far to dashing for a nanny.

When she was gone, Nick settled back, ordered another cup of tea and sat nursing it thoughtfully. Now, what was he to make of her? he asked himself. Had the lovely Miss Humphrey really been what she'd claimed? Or was her relationship with Rudy and Randy's dear old dad a bit more complicated. Knowing his ex-boss's eye for the ladies, Nick suspected the latter.

Regretfully, Nick took a moment to picture her halo of dark red curls and heart-shaped face. He'd always had a soft spot for tall redheads with turned-up noses and slightly funky taste in clothes. If circumstances were different— But they weren't, he reminded himself.

This was a matter of life and death—*his* life and death. Kate Humphrey was probably what she said. But she could easily be playing on LaFiore's team the way the maid back at the hotel had been. How thoroughly had Jillian checked her new nanny's credentials? he wondered. Knowing Jillian, probably not at all.

Decisively, Nick got to his feet, threw down a bill for the drinks and tip, and then strode to the exit opposite from the one Kate had taken. He had a lot of things to do, and now one of them included keeping an eye on Kate Humphrey and her charges. Tomorrow was going to be an interesting day—very interesting.

ON THE OTHER END of the train, Kate poked her head into the compartment she shared with little Rudy and Randy. Except for their regular breathing and the rhythmic rattle of the rails, all was silent. *Thank heaven,* she thought. They were asleep and, from the sound of it, would stay that way until morning.

For a moment she hesitated and then withdrew. After checking in with the porter again, she headed toward the lounge. Before bedding down, she wanted to sit for a moment and reflect.

Her conversation with Mr. Nick Conti nagged at her. There had been something very unsettling about it.

Distractedly, she reviewed what had been said. There hadn't been anything casual about their exchange, she mused. For one thing, he'd been the party conducting the cross-examination—even though there were dozens of questions she might have been tempted to ask him. Why, for instance, would a man who'd nearly been killed in a steeplechase come out of retirement to risk breaking his neck all over again?

On the subject of horses, the only thing Kate knew was that up close and personal, she didn't like them. But stories about the upcoming Aintree classic had been in the papers for several weeks and now that the date for the prestigious and historic steeplechase was fast approaching, it filled the sports news on the television as well. Kate had been told all about it at the Brasswells.

Geraldine Brasswell had been Kate's landlady for three months, ever since she'd come to London to work at The Yellow Heel. A motherly sort of woman, Geraldine had taken Kate under her wing. Through all Kate's employment difficulties she'd offered advice and comfort. Several times Kate had been down to the Brasswell's homey rooms to dine with them and stayed on to chat a bit or even play a hand of gin rummy while they watched the evening news.

"Lord love that sportscaster, can't he do nothing but go on about a stupid horse," Kate remembered Mrs. Brasswell complaining to her husband, Eddie, only a few days earlier. "Why's he making such a fuss?"

"It's because Seasonwine's had such an interesting career, luv," Eddie had replied, scratching his bald head as he peered over the top of the newspaper. "He used to be a prime steeplechaser, won at Newbury and Sandown three years back. Then he lost his jockey in a big smashup and after that he couldn't seem to jump over a bale of hay. Word is that his owner sold him for peanuts last year and he was put out to pasture."

"But," Mrs. Brasswell had objected on the particular evening Kate was remembering, "they're saying that he's the sentimental favorite in the Grand National this year."

"That's because his old jockey got himself patched up and is coming out of retirement to ride him again," Eddie had explained.

"So the poor animal is being yanked out of his nice comfy pasture," Mrs. Brasswell commented with a disapproving cluck. "Poor old thing. Just when he'd thought he'd got it made."

Eddie had laughed. "Seasonwine's not so old, only nine it says here. Some horses go on racing long after that. And maybe he's bored with retirement. We old boys need a bit of excitement now and again, too, you know." He waved a restraining hand. "Now, quiet—I want to hear this."

They'd all refocused on the television set. A videotape of a steeplechase that had taken place two years earlier was being run. It showed a dozen tightly packed horses thundering toward an enormous hurdle.

I'd hate to be a rider in a scramble like that, Kate had thought as she'd followed the frenzied action. Years ago in high school she'd known a girl who'd been crippled for life in a riding accident. She'd fallen, and the horse had stepped on her back. The incident had made Kate decide that she never wanted anything to do with horses—not that she'd ever had much chance.

"Look how fast they're going, and they're so close to each other," Kate exclaimed.

"Oh it's always like that in a National. There's a field of forty," Eddie explained.

Kate shook her head. It was like a killer dash to a sales counter during a half-price markdown, only speeded up by a factor of ten and with hooved participants who weighed half a ton.

"Now watch closely," the announcer was saying. "Becher's Brook is one of the most dangerous jumps at Aintree. Horses must clear a fence five feet high and then a natural brook that is five and a half feet wide. This is where the accident that ruined Nick Conti's career and put him and Seasonwine into an early retirement happened."

All the horses seemed to be trying to leap the fence at once. Suddenly an animal went down, thrown off kilter by the pumping legs of the equine hedging him in. Several other horses stumbled over the hurdle in a chain reaction. Riders were catapulted into the melee of kicking legs and churning hooves.

"My God," the announcer's recorded voice had cried, "it looks as if Nick Conti is down under all that!"

As the train to Rome rattled through the night, the memory echoed in Kate's mind. *What a stupid way to make a living,* she thought. It was a wonder that the man hadn't been killed. She thought of Susie, the injured girl she remembered from high school. Frowning, she got to her feet and began threading her way out of the lounge. Yet, he must be quite a rider. Well, there had been an air about him, a kind of quiet confidence that only people who were really good at something exuded.

Kate flashed back to the horrifying image of him falling beneath that pile of crashing horses. She really didn't see how he could have escaped unscathed. Yet he'd looked healthy enough in the dining car. In fact he'd looked like a man in peak condition, everything about him fine-tuned and ready for reckless deeds. Why was that so darned intriguing? Kate frowned. "No more reckless men in my life," she muttered under her breath as an image of the wind man in her trio, daring, dashing, utterly undependable Billy Rockland, flashed across her mind. "I've had enough of that breed."

Kate unlocked her compartment and stepped in. *All quiet,* she thought with a small sigh of relief. Silently, she checked each boy. Rudy and Randy were sleeping like angels, lulled by the rhythmic clackety-clack of the train.

Kate undressed in the tiny bathroom and climbed up into her own bunk. But as she lay under the covers, her eyes remained wide open. She couldn't keep her mind off Nick Conti. If he was going to ride Seasonwine at Aintree in a few weeks, what was he doing on a train to Rome, she asked herself. Didn't jockeys spend time working out with their horses before a big race? It didn't make sense for him to be heading in the opposite direction.

That night, instead of sheep, Kate counted thorough-bred racehorses. In her dreams, sleek, long-legged animals leaped effortlessly over tall white fences. And aboard each was a slim, well-built man with dark, wavy hair. He had a wicked grin and a pair of challenging blue eyes that gazed directly into hers.

CHAPTER TWO

AFTER HIS VISIT with Owen Byrnside, Jake Caine stopped off the road for lunch at a nearby café. He felt relieved to escape the oppressive atmosphere in Taleman Hall. It wasn't just that Byrnside's heart condition had turned a dynamic man into an invalid and the process couldn't be pleasant to watch. It wasn't even that Taleman Hall resembled a stage set for a gothic tragedy. "More to it than that," Jake muttered under his breath.

Meditatively, he lifted his coffee cup. It had to do with the people around the old man, he reflected. There was his personal secretary who'd been a fixture for over thirty years, the distant relations hovering around the fringe, the flock of executives who held positions of power in his sprawling publishing empire. They all stood to gain—or lose—from his death.

Jake had seen enough of human nature to know that the vast supply of money and power involved in an empire like Byrnside's would inevitably bring out the worst in some people. Cynically, he pictured prehistoric vultures hovering over an expiring behemoth, only waiting to swoop down and tear each other to pieces for the best bits.

If this lost granddaughter existed and could be found, how would she fit into that rather ghoulish picture? he wondered.

THREE HOURS LATER Jake strode into the paneled offices of Foster, Brighton and Caine. It was a prestigious law firm with historic ties to many of the wealthiest families in New England.

The reception area had been carefully decorated to reflect that fact. In its hushed serenity the horses leaping fences in the hunting scenes framed on the walls seemed caught in timeless motion. Tastefully worn Oriental rugs glowed on polished parquet floors, and leather wing chairs in muted reds and greens added just the right, not-too-inviting, accent.

After a cursory glance at the new administrative assistant one of his partners had recently hired, Jake headed for his own office. "Miss Bonner, would you come in please," he said after he pressed a button on the intercom. Then he opened a manila file folder on his desk and sat down to study it.

A moment later a slim young woman with a pale oval face and wedge-cut blond hair knocked on the door and then walked in. Briefly, Jake glanced up at her, noting that she was reasonably attractive. He hoped that she was also reasonably efficient.

"Miss Bonner, I have a job for you."

"Yes, sir."

"You see this list?"

He held out a neatly typed sheet of paper, which she took and studied through her oversize horn-rimmed glasses. "It's a list of foundling homes in the Boston area."

"Yes. I'm looking for three female infants who were sent to one or more of those homes from Broadstreet after it burned down on the date you'll note printed at the top. See if you can find them."

"Certainly, sir." Miss Bonner nodded and then turned toward the door.

As he watched her exit, Jake clasped his hands and wove his fingers together. She had appeared quite unruffled by the assignment. Was she up to completing it? he wondered. Well, time would tell.

Two hours later there was another light tap on his door.

"Yes?" Distractedly Jake looked up from the brief in which he'd been immersed.

The door opened a crack and Miss Bonner's neat blond head appeared around it. "I'm sorry to disturb you, sir, but I thought you'd like to know that I have the first name you requested."

Jake's eyebrows lifted slightly. "Yes? What is it?"

"Kathryn Humphrey."

SOMETHING CLANGED in Kate's ear. "Help, Miss Humphrey, Miss Humphrey, fire! Help! We have to run for it!"

"What?" Kate's eyes flew open. She'd been having the most delicious dream about recording her own album and was still hopelessly disoriented.

"Fire, Miss Humphrey! Help! Help!" With their belt buckles Rudy and Randy beat against the metal frame of the bunk bed.

Kate winced, her befogged brain struggling out of the pleasant fantasy of her dream. Those were the twins' high-pitched voices shrieking at her. Oh, my God! There must have been an accident. She had to save them! Still not fully awake, Kate swung her feet over the side of the bunk and slithered down in a tangle of blankets. Too late she realized that something was wrong. Her legs didn't seem to be working right.

"Ouch!" she yelped as she crashed to the floor in an undignified heap.

"Ha, ha! We fooled her, we fooled her! Ha, ha!"

Like a pair of demented pygmy warriors, Randy and
Rudy, clad only in pajama bottoms, danced around her
prone body, emitting war whoops of malicious delight.

"Very funny!" Kate tried to scramble to her feet, but
once again she toppled over like an unbalanced punching
clown. It wasn't just her twisted blankets impeding her
movements, she realized. "What's this? You've tied my
ankles together!"

Shooting satisfied smirks at each other, the two dark-
eyed eight-year-olds burst into earsplitting gales of hilar-
ity. Then, while Kate labored to unknot the bathrobe sash
with which they'd hobbled her, they bolted out the compartment door and sped away.

An hour later, they sat opposite Kate in the dining car
hungrily wolfing down breakfast. When she'd caught up
with them at the far end of the train she'd dragged them
back to the compartment and given them a good tongue-
lashing, but somehow she doubted that it had had much
effect. Their expressions as they gobbled down toast and
juice were distinctly unchastened.

"Are we going to see our father today?" Randy demanded through a half-chewed piece of toast.

"Don't talk with your mouth full. Yes, that's the plan.
We're due to arrive in Rome a half hour from now. When
we get in he'll meet us himself or send someone."

"My mum says he's really mean," Rudy commented.
"She says if you look at him cross-eyed he'll plug you right
here," he added, pointing at a spot between his eyebrows.

"Your mother was just joking," Kate assured him.
Where in the world had the little boy gotten such an idea,
she wondered. She couldn't believe that Jillian LaFiore
would actually have said that to them about their father—
no matter what she thought of her ex-husband. "Stop that!
Serve you right if your face got stuck in that expression!"

Kate scowled across the table at Randy who'd puffed out
his cheeks and crossed his eyes violently.

When his features had fallen back into a more normal
configuration, she signaled for the check and took a last
glance around the crowded dining car. She'd half expected
to see Nick Conti this morning, but there was no sign of
him. Just as well, she told herself. Another meeting between them would only have been awkward.

Sighing, she paid the bill and then took Rudy and Randy's grubby little hands. Keeping a firm grip, she herded
the mischievous twosome back to their compartment
without major mishap.

Getting off the train in Rome, however, wasn't quite so
easy. In addition to the boys who seemed determined to
bolt off in opposite directions, there was quite a lot of
luggage to be managed. Kate kept checking her purse,
nervous of losing Mr. LaFiore's address in case they missed
each other in the train station. It wouldn't be easy to
manage if that happened, she worried. While she spoke
some schoolgirl French, her Italian was nonexistent.
What's more, she still had only the most rudimentary grasp
of the value of the lira.

Massive confusion reigned at the Rome station. Like
atoms whirled through a cyclotron, passengers rushed off
in a million different directions. Porters with terrifying
expressions shouted imperiously and grabbed up suitcases
without paying the slightest attention to their owner's
gabbled instructions.

It was all Kate could do to keep a determined porter
from disappearing with her own small mountain of luggage. "No," she insisted as she kept trying to explain.
"We're waiting to be met. No, please leave that alone."
Holding onto the boys for dear life, she looked around for
the short, thickset man Jillian LaFiore had described. Why

wasn't he here? And why did she have the disturbing feeling that she was being watched by someone, someone hidden who was observing her closely?

BEHIND THE NEWSPAPER STAND where he'd stationed himself, Nick kept an eye on the ill-assorted little trio across the way. Lou LaFiore wasn't likely to miss them. In her black jersey harem pants, long-sleeved purple T-shirt and vintage brocade vest and with her brilliant curls catching the early morning light, Kate Humphrey stood out from the dark-haired Italians swirling past her. The boys, romping about like hyperactive pups, were damn noticeable, too. Despite himself, Nick grinned as he observed the growing desperation of their redheaded nanny's efforts to control them.

The minutes crept past and Nick's grin turned into a frown. Where was LaFiore? He might not be the most devoted father on earth, but surely he wouldn't leave his only legitimate offspring standing around in a railroad station. Nick glanced down at his watch. Something here had a funny smell to it.

He'd been standing behind the newsstand watching Kate and the boys for close to half an hour, and he was beginning to feel conspicuous. To allay the stand operator's suspicions he'd bought two newspapers. When a uniformed railroad official passed his post for the third time and shot him a measuring glance, Nick unrolled one of them and pretended to read the headline. Suddenly, as the Italian words penetrated, he started to study them in earnest.

Mafia Casino Owner Held in Protective Custody, it read. "LaFiore to Testify."

My God, no wonder Lou wasn't here collecting his children, Nick thought and rolled the paper into a tight club.

To save his own skin he was about to spill the beans on some of the most organized and violent criminals on earth. That meant that anyone close to him was in grave danger, which certainly applied to LaFiore's children. At this moment, Nick realized, they were in much worse trouble than he.

"DO YOU SEE ANYONE who looks like your father?" Kate asked Randy. But both boys were too busy trying to snatch at the ears of a pair of white poodles passing on the end of a pink velvet leash to pay attention. Anyhow, she knew the answer was no. They weren't exactly an inconspicuous threesome, but so far no one hurrying about the cavernous station had shown the slightest interest in them.

Kate began to fret in earnest. From the outset she'd been more concerned about this end of the trip than any other part of it. What if for some reason Mr. LaFiore didn't show? After wiping a smudge of dirt off Randy's cheek, Kate straightened. That would just mean that she would have to get the boys to him on her own.

Once again Kate began to dig around in her purse for his address. At that moment a porter rushed up, mumbled something unintelligible and grabbed her suitcases.

"No—hey, no! Let go of that! I'm not ready!"

He merely snapped out a phrase in staccato Italian and marched toward the exit with the boys trailing him. Still fishing in her purse, Kate trotted behind.

"We need a taxi to Monteverde Vecchio," she cried at his heels, quoting the address on the bit of paper she'd unearthed.

He hitched a shoulder and veered off to the left. Seizing the boys' hands and all but dragging Rudy and Randy, who protested vigorously, Kate did her best to keep pace.

Outside, the street was chaotic. A sea of shouting porters flagged down taxis. Those taxis not screeching to a halt or belching out wild-eyed passengers wove about honking their horns furiously, their drivers bellowing what sounded like unforgivable insults.

Despite his high-handed behavior, Kate's porter did seem to know what he was doing. No sooner were they outside than a cab pulled right up to them. Indeed, it even ignored several other travelers who tried to signal it. It hadn't even quite slid to a stop when the porter yanked open its trunk and began slinging Kate's luggage inside.

"Oh, please be careful!" she gasped as she staggered up with the boys in tow. "Those are brand new. Can you tell the driver that we want to go to Monteverde Vecchio?"

The man leaned over the vehicle's window and hissed something into the driver's ear. Then he opened the passenger side and motioned peremptorily at Kate. Too flustered to protest, she handed him a bill she hoped was the right amount for a tip and moved forward to slide in. It was then that what had only been confusion became a scene straight out of a gangster movie.

Another cab darted in behind the first. The door was flung open and, to Kate's amazement, Nick Conti leaped out. Without a word to her, he seized Rudy and Randy and shoved them into his vehicle's backseat.

"What . . . what are you doing?" she gasped. Kate took several steps toward the boys. But at that instant the porter she'd followed bellowed something harsh, hooked an arm around her waist and started to drag her back.

"*Abbiamo la testa rossa!*"

"*Vuòi farne qualcosa?*"

His mouth grim and his eyes hard beneath his dark brows, Nick shoved the man backward and then roughly propelled Kate toward the taxi where the boys huddled, goggling. "Get in," he hissed.

"But—"

"Get in if you don't want to have your throat cut!"

To Kate's horror, she saw that the man Nick Conti had just disentangled her from was pulling a wicked-looking knife out of his sleeve. Behind him, the driver of the taxi where he'd stowed her suitcases got out. Crouching like a bear, he growled *"Ti rompo le gambe!"* in gutteral Italian and launched himself at Nick.

Whirling out of his reach, Nick aimed a sharp, chopping blow at the knife-wielder's wrist. As his weapon clattered to the pavement, Nick shoved his palm into the other man's face, knocking him backward into his vehicle. Then he snapped an impatient curse at Kate who still stood frozen in the middle of the melee. With a strength that belied his size, he lifted her bodily and all but hurled her in with the boys.

"Oh, my God! Oh!"

Ignoring her cries, he joined her and slammed the car door behind him. *"Sbrigati!"* he yelled at the driver, who then exploded away from the curb like a rocket to the moon.

While the boys squealed and yelped, Kate lay sprawled on top of them, fighting to right herself. It was nearly impossible in the ricocheting vehicle.

"They're chasing us, they're chasing us!" Randy squealed. He'd torn free of her and propped himself up on his knees so that he could look out the back.

After rattling off more Italian orders at their driver, Nick reached across Kate. "Keep him away from that window," he commanded as he yanked the boy down flat on the seat.

Randy started to howl and Rudy, whose arm had gotten mashed when Kate landed on top of him, joined in. But their cries were drowned out by screeching brakes and blaring horns as their taxi and its pursuer raced through the Roman traffic.

Kate's thoughts pinwheeled, and her gaze darted from side to side. Was there any means of stopping the hurtling automobile? What was happening? Were they being kidnapped? Should she try and signal to a policeman? With her heart in her mouth, she glanced back and saw that the cab pursuing them had been blocked by a bus discharging passengers.

Abruptly, their taxi swung into a narrow alley and then sped out the other side where it fishtailed into a U-turn and went hurtling down another narrow byway. After yet another rapid-fire exchange of Italian between Nick and its driver, it cruised through several more streets before pulling to a sudden stop in front of a large building that resembled a parking garage.

"I demand to know—" Kate began.

Nick cut her off. "I'll explain everything. Just let me pay off this man before he throws us out on the street." He handed the driver a wad of bills, spoke several more curt phrases to him and then yanked open the door.

The moment Kate and the boys had shakily climbed out, the cab zoomed away and disappeared around a corner as if a pack of demons were in hot pursuit.

"Quick, inside!" Nick seized Kate's arm.

"Just wait! You have no right—"

"No time for rights. We have to get off the street!" He hustled her and the boys into the shelter of the concrete building, which turned out to be a car rental agency. "Just sit down right there," he ordered, pointing at a row of wooden seats in the waiting room. "I need to sign a few papers, and then I'll explain everything."

"Really..."

"Trust me." His blue eyes swept from her face to the boys and back. "Just a few minutes more and then I'll try and make everything clear. Just trust me."

Under the force of the stare he bent on them, the boys plopped into the chairs. With a crafty show of docility, Kate joined them. But her shocked brain was beginning to work again. She had to get Rudy and Randy away from this madman, she told herself. The moment Nick had his back turned and seemed fully occupied with the girl at the business window, she leaned across the fidgeting twins and whispered, "Quick, let's get out of here!"

"But he said to stay. Won't he be mad?" Rudy hissed.

"It doesn't matter." She shot the back of their captor's well-shaped head an outraged glare. "Just follow me. We'll find another taxi to take us to your father's."

She rose and tiptoed out the glass door with the twins at her heels. They got as far as the street where, predictably, there were no taxis in sight.

"Come on," Kate said. She flung an apprehensive glance over her shoulder and then gathered up Rudy and Randy's hands. "We'll cross over to that café and wait there until we see a cab."

INSIDE THE RENTAL AGENCY Nick finished his business with the girl. "A driver will bring your car around in ten minutes," she promised.

"*Grazie*. The sooner the better." Stuffing his passport and other papers back into his pocket, he turned, expecting to see the trio he'd just rescued waiting where he could sit down and try and explain their dangerous predicament to them. But Kate's, Rudy's, and Randy's chairs were unoccupied. "Blast," Nick muttered between his teeth and hurried toward the exit.

Since he hadn't had his back to the twins and their red-headed nanny for more than five minutes, Nick expected to find them on the street. But they weren't there, either. While his gaze searched the avenue, Nick stood fuming. Could they have gotten another cab so quickly? It didn't seem likely. Now, where would I go if I were a woman in a foreign country saddled with two obstreperous little monsters, and I wanted to get out of sight in a hurry? he asked himself.

It wasn't tough to answer that one. Nick headed toward the dingy *gelateria* across the street.

"Bingo," he muttered when he peered through the little shop's dusty window. To one side the twins perched on round red stools. Nearby, Kate leaned over a counter gesticulating at a rotund man wearing a stained apron and an uncomprehending expression.

She must have felt the weight of Nick's stare because at that instant she turned. Her eyes opened wide when they fell on him, and her pink mouth rounded into an unwelcoming O. Immediately she shouted something at the store's proprietor who shrugged and then picked up a telephone.

In one stride Nick pushed open the door, and in another he was through it. Inside the dark little shop was warm, its heavy atmosphere laden with the fragrance of vanilla and melting chocolate. A display case showed a variety of elaborate baked goods that looked as if they had been been petrified on their paper doilies for at least three decades.

As Nick exploded into the shop, Kate straightened and positioned herself between him and the children. "Stay away from us. Mr. Ponza here is calling another taxi. I warn you, if I scream, he'll phone the police as well.''

That might be the answer to his prayers, Nick thought, if only he could be sure that the children would be safe under the protection of the police. But since he had no such naive confidence, he planted himself in front of her. ''Look, Miss Humphrey, I know what's just happened is hard for you to make sense out of. But believe me, I am only trying to help. You and those kids are in danger.''

''We're in danger from you.'' Her voice was firm, but her hands shook. To hide the fact, she balled them into fists. ''You were trying to kidnap us!''

Nick shook his head. ''Believe me, Miss Humphrey, if I were trying to kidnap you, I would have succeeded. Only that wasn't what I had in mind.''

''Then why did you yank us away from our cab at the train station? Why did that man pull a knife?''

''Because he was the one trying to kidnap you and LaFiore's children. Maybe I didn't rescue you in the most genteel fashion, but I didn't have much time to plan ahead.''

Briefly, Nick summarized what he'd read in the Roman newspaper. ''Don't you see? If the wrong people got their hands on those kids, they could threaten to kill them to keep their father's mouth shut.''

''Why should I believe anything so crazy?'' Kate's face was a study in incredulity. ''Where is this newspaper story? Show me.''

Nick's nostrils flared with impatience. ''I don't have it with me. I must have left it in the taxi. But I'm telling the truth. What possible motive could I have for making up something like this?''

"I can't begin to imagine. All I know is that these boys are my responsibility, and if you try to touch them I'll scream the place down."

He believed her. With that red hair practically standing on end and her green eyes glaring at him as fiercely as a defensive cat's, she looked capable of shattering glass with one screech. Nick glanced at the man behind the counter, who'd been listening to their exchange avidly. Then Nick took a cautious step backward. "Have it your way, all right? Stay where you are, and I'll go get a newspaper. I'll be back in just a minute with proof of what I'm telling you. Do you agree to that much?"

"I agree," she snapped.

"Remember, don't go anywhere until I get back. Stay right there." With great reluctance, he turned and hurried out the door. Unfortunately, there were no newspaper stands on the nearest corner. Cursing his hellish luck this day, Nick hurried down to the next. He had to cover three full blocks before he came to a newsstand, only to find it empty—all the papers sold out.

"Oh great, just what I needed!" Nick darted a worried glance at his watch and then jogged another block. It was twenty minutes before he was able to buy the newspaper he wanted and return to the *gelateria*.

When he pushed open the door and strode in, the place was empty. He turned to the fat proprietor, who gazed at him warily.

"Where is the woman who was here with two young boys?"

"La bella signorina?"

"Si, the beautiful redhead."

"Her taxi came and she left in it."

"Bloody hell!" Nick twisted the paper between his hands. *Now what?*

As the cab inched its way through traffic, Kate began to feel less and less sure of herself. Half an hour earlier she'd been convinced that what Nick Conti had told her was pure nonsense. But what if it hadn't been? He didn't look insane. But that was what made psychopaths such convincing criminals, wasn't it? They appeared perfectly normal and reasonable—even attractive.

"We're going to see our big bad daddy. We're going to see our big bad daddy," Rudy began to chant.

"Daddy, schmaddy, daddy, schmaddy," Randy added in a shrill descant.

Clapping her hand over both their mouths, Kate leaned forward and spoke to the back of the driver's head. "Would you let us off a block before the address I gave you, please?"

"Come?"

It took some doing, but she finally made the man understand, and ten minutes later he slowed in front of a row of attractively aged stone buildings. There were several awkward moments while she figured out how much to pay him. When he was gone and she looked at her seriously depleted supply of lire, she was certain he'd taken more than was his due.

"Is this our daddy's house? I gotta go, I gotta go," Randy complained.

"No, your daddy lives on the next block up. Surely you can wait that long."

"I hope he has two bathrooms," Rudy muttered ominously.

Kate looked from right to left and then snared their hands and began to walk with them toward the next corner. At least she didn't have suitcases to deal with, she thought ruefully. Those had disappeared with the cab Nick Conti had dragged them away from. Would their luggage ever be returned? And what were they going to do for a change of clothes in the meantime? she wondered.

As these thoughts ran through her head, Kate kept darting nervous glances around her. Something wasn't right here.

"Why isn't there anybody in this street?" Randy questioned.

"How come it's so quiet?" Rudy demanded. He looked up at the buildings with their shuttered windows and drawn curtains and whispered, "It's creepy around here."

"Maybe it's just siesta time," Kate said. That could be it, she told herself. She knew that Italians shut down their businesses during the middle part of the day. Yet, like those of an animal sensing danger, the tiny hairs on the back of her neck had lifted. Was it just that Nick Conti's story had kicked her imagination into overdrive? Or was something really seriously amiss here?

She walked Rudy and Randy into the shelter of an entry and then went down on one knee so that she could look directly into each of their faces. "Listen, boys, I want you to stay here and be very quiet and still while I go on up ahead and take a look round that corner."

"Why? Cuz you think Nick was right and our dad really is arrested?" Randy questioned. In his round face, his shoe-button eyes were suddenly shrewd beyond his years.

"You think maybe somebody wants to get us?" Rudy added. His eyebrows corkscrewed in a worried little frown.

"No, of course I don't think that. I'm sure everything's okay. But just in case, I want to have a look—just to check things out. Now, will you do as I ask?"

Silently, they nodded, and for the first time since she'd taken over their management, she felt confident that they meant to obey her.

She gave them each a searching look and then straightened and adjusted the twisted waistband of her slacks around her T-shirt. Assessingly, she peered into the empty street and then stepped out onto the sidewalk. Sensing that a hundred eyes watched from behind the blank faces of the shuttered windows, she proceeded to the corner. Yet, all was eerily silent. Even the traffic on the next avenue up sounded like the muted roar of distant waves.

All at once Kate became uncomfortably aware of the click of her own shoes against the pavement. Feeling distinctly foolish, she took them off and rounded the corner in her stocking feet. At the next corner she stopped to consider. Louis LaFiore's residence should be down the street to the right. And it seemed even more eerily deserted than the one where she'd left the boys. Her heart thudded heavily against her breast and her skin felt prickly.

Cautiously, she peered around a building. Just as she'd suspected, not a soul was in sight. Shadows lengthened against the opposite row of buildings while the ones on her side stood out in the glare of early spring sunlight like felons in an inquisitor's spotlight.

Then a sudden movement caught her eye. A man in a slouch hat stepped out of a doorway and signaled up the street. There was a brief movement a few doors away as someone signaled back. Then the first man stepped back into the shadows and once more became invisible.

Kate drew in her breath sharply and then checked the number on the address she still clutched. Judging from the numbers nearby, the building opposite the place where the man had stepped out should be the LaFiore residence. And it was being watched.

Quickly, Kate drew back and flattened herself against the sandstone building. Panic jetted through her. Maybe Nick Conti really had been telling the truth. She didn't know. She only knew she couldn't take the boys down that street—not until she could be sure that they'd be safe. As quickly and silently as possible, she headed back to the place where she'd left them. She heaved a sigh of relief when she saw that they were still there.

"Listen," she said, "we have to get out of here."

"We're not going to my dad's?" Randy asked.

"I don't think so. Not right away, anyhow. Not until I'm positive that everything's okay."

"But where will we go?" Rudy wanted to know.

Good question, Kate thought as she guided them out onto the pavement. Where would she take them? Since this was supposed to have been the end of her journey, she didn't have a great deal of money left. And she knew nothing whatever about Rome.

Suddenly a shout shattered the oppressive quiet. Kate stopped, her eyes widening in alarm. The man in the slouch hat had just rounded the corner. He was yelling at her and motioning to a cohort who was still out of sight.

Kate turned and started to run with the boys in the opposite direction. But at the top of the street a car appeared. As it rolled toward them, Kate slid to a halt, automatically placing her body between it and the boys. Desperately, she looked back and forth between the men chasing her and the approaching vehicle.

The car, a white Fiat, slowed and Nick Conti stuck his handsome head out. "Can I offer you a lift?"

CHAPTER THREE

"Do you have to keep driving so fast?" The white Fiat slammed around another corner and then shot down a rough stone street. Huddling in the passenger seat with the two boys piled on top of her, Kate clutched Rudy and Randy's hands.

Before answering, Nick Conti threaded the car through a circle with a bronze statue on an island in the middle and then out into a wide boulevard. "I believe we've left them behind, but that doesn't mean we're safe," he finally answered. "You're right, however. It does seem to be time to try and blend in."

After he'd settled the Fiat down to the normal breakneck speed of Roman traffic, he shot a glance at the passenger seat, where Rudy had dug a foot into Kate's side and Randy squirmed like an eel. Kate's jersey slacks were pushed up around her knees, revealing a pair of shapely calves. The sleeve of her T-shirt was torn.

"Maybe you boys should get off Miss Humphrey and climb into the back."

"Yes, please," Kate seconded, all the while trying to protect herself from flailing eight-year-old limbs. But it was hopeless. Competing with each other to grunt and complain, Rudy and Randy climbed over her body and rattled down over the hump of the backrest.

"Oof!"

"Yow!"

"You're kicking me!"

"You're the one who's bloody kicking me!"

By the time they finally tumbled onto the rear bench Kate's vest and T-shirt were both torn. At the swift assessing look Nick Conti spared her ruined outfit, Kate flushed and began struggling to set herself to rights.

"Those men wanted to get us!" Randy declared in an awestruck voice.

"One of those blighters had a gun. I saw it!" Rudy added with juicy enthusiasm.

As she straightened the corkscrewed waistband on her pants, Kate twisted sharply. "You saw a gun?"

Both boys nodded. Their dark eyes looked about the size of quarters. While Kate stared at them, she felt the blood drain from her head. She turned to their rescuer. "Is that right? Did one of those men really have a gun?"

Nick had returned his gaze to the road. "I shouldn't be surprised."

"Oh, my God," Kate moaned. Guns, kidnappers, what in the world had they gotten into?

It was several minutes before she recovered her composure enough to say what she needed to say to Nick Conti. "I guess you were right, back in the ice cream shop, I mean."

"So it would appear."

"Thanks for coming to our rescue. It was good of you after... after I didn't keep my promise to wait for you."

"Think nothing of it." The cool tone of his clipped baritone was distinctly unfriendly. "This seems to be my day for damsels in distress."

Kate frowned. "Look, I really am sorry for mistrusting you before. But you have to admit that what you said sounded crazy. I mean, I'm responsible for these children, and I still don't understand what's going on here.

Can you explain it again? What did those men want? Why were they watching Mr. LaFiore's house?''

"I don't know the whole story yet, Miss Humphrey. But from what I've been able to glean, LaFiore is testifying against some ruthless criminals. It doesn't take much logic to figure out that until he gives that testimony in a court of law and those men are put behind bars, anyone LaFiore might care about, including members of his family, is going to be at risk.''

"You're saying that the boys could be...could be..."

He shot her a warning look. "I think you know what I'm saying.''

"Our dad's enemies want to get us and shoot us in the back of our heads so that our eyes pop out," Rudy crowed to Randy. "We've got to hide out.''

Kate felt as if she'd just stepped off the edge of an elevator shaft. Hide—yes, but where? How? She shot a desperate look out the window. The Fiat had left the worst of Rome's congested traffic behind and now speeded through the outskirts of the city on a broad highway. Boxy high-rise apartment buildings sprouted on the sides of the road like angular concrete growths.

"Where are we going?''

"Out of the city.''

"That's obvious, but where?''

"Someplace where you'll be safe, or at least safer.''

Kate swiveled around so that she could stare at Nick Conti's handsome profile. Thinking hard, she took in the straight nose, aggressive chin and thin, cleanly modeled lips. He had the kind of looks that bowled women over. Because he was so attractive, Kate wanted to believe him— which, given her history of poor judgment when it came to the opposite sex, made her all the more distrustful.

How did she know he himself wasn't one of the ruffians he'd been telling her about? What if those two characters who'd chased her had been police? What if their shouts had been warnings about this man, who once again had them all trapped in his car and speeding on the way to a mysterious destination?

"Mr. Conti, I have to be sure..." she began.

"Look, Miss Humphrey, do you want me to help you or not?"

"How can I be sure..."

She never got to complete the sentence because Nick swerved off the road and onto the shoulder where he slammed his foot on the brake. As the Fiat shuddered to a stop, he looked at her hard. "Would you like to get out here?"

"What?" Her hand flew up to her throat.

"Before we go any farther, let's try and get this straight. All day I've been trying to play Good Samaritan. Granted, it's not a role that comes naturally, but I'm not a criminal, either. Believe me, I'm not interested in kidnapping you or the two little charmers in back. You're not my prisoners and never have been. If you want to step out here, go right ahead."

From the corner of her eye Kate registered the bleak landscape of apartment buildings, the cars whizzing past, the billboards printed with legends in a language she didn't understand. "In the middle of the road like this in a foreign country? You know we can't do that!"

"Then give me an address in Rome, and I'll take you to it. In fact, if you want I'll take you to the police station."

"You'd do that?"

"Yes, only I have to warn you that the Roman police may not be able to give you the kind of protection you'll need."

Kate paused to think that over and realized he might have a point. "The only address in Rome that I know is Mr. LaFiore's."

"Well, luv, I don't recommend you go back there, but if it's your wish . . ."

"It's not my wish." Resentfully, Kate stared at Nick, her green eyes glittering. "None of this is my wish. I don't know what the best thing is to do."

"Then, you're going to have to trust someone, aren't you?" he answered coolly. "Since I'm the only one around, it might as well be me, wouldn't you say?"

At a loss for words, Kate continued to stare into his long-lashed blue eyes. He was right; she really didn't have much choice. And surely if he meant them harm he wouldn't have stopped like this and offered her a chance to go back to the police in Rome. Would he?

Or maybe it was all just a ploy. Kate's brain whirled in weary confusion, and she glanced at the children, who goggled back like nestlings waiting to be fed a worm. The most important thing had to be their safety, and all her instincts warned that returning them to Rome was not the way to guarantee that.

"All right," she said.

"All right, what?"

"We'll stay in the car and let you take us to wherever you think best."

"Well, I do thank you for the vote of confidence. Now let's get out of here, shall we? For all I know we're being followed." Nick put the car in gear and pulled back into traffic.

Without further comment, he settled down to blending in with the other motorists. Meanwhile the boys turned to gawk out the rear window and speculate on which of the vehicles around them might contain mobsters in hot pursuit. A numbing wave of exhaustion washed over Kate, and she leaned into the passenger seat and closed her eyes.

But a second later they popped back open. It behooved her to study their route, she realized. For what if she were making a mistake about Nick Conti? What if it became necessary for her to find her way back from wherever he was taking them—and what if she had to do it in a hurry? Kate sat up straight and stared out the windshield and then up at the sun. They were headed north. She opened her purse and fished out her guidebook. "'Umbria and Tùscany with all their rich history lie to the north,'" she read.

By midday they had escaped the city entirely and were cruising down a narrow two-lane road through a pastoral countryside. Acres of vine-covered hills were just beginning to show signs of spring greens in the unusually warm March weather. Nestled below the hills were square houses capped by deeply eaved roofs.

Inside the tiny white car, Kate had organized a game to entertain the boys. The first one to see a sports car was to yell, "Ferrari!" It had worked well on the crowded highway where low-slung sports cars abounded. But now that traffic had dwindled to an occasional beat-up truck or farmer hauling a wagon load of manure, the boys were getting restless.

"I have to go to the loo," Rudy whined.

"Me, too," Randy chimed in. He began to squirm on the edge of the seat.

Nick Conti, who'd been fixedly silent since their confrontation at the side of the road an hour earlier, muttered through his teeth, "Someone once told me that traveling with kids compares unfavorably with Chinese water torture. I thought that was his idea of humor, but now I'm not so sure."

Kate shot him a harrassed look. "Could you please give me an idea how much longer?"

"Roughly, an hour and a half, I should think."

"If we don't get there pretty soon I'm going to have an accident," Rudy declared.

"Me, too," Randy seconded. He squirmed more vigorously and clutched his legs.

Again, Nick pulled off to the side. With his foot on the brake, he pointed at the field opposite where several sheep grazed peacefully. "Best I can do."

Frowning, Kate looked at the acre of tall grass surrounding a small island of trees and then back at Nick. "But isn't there somewhere we can stop that has a regular bathroom?"

"Viterbo isn't far," Nick admitted, "but I don't intend to take you there."

"Why not? As a matter of fact, I just finished reading about it." She found the reference in her guidebook and started to scan it. "Viterbo dates from the Middle Ages and had a fortress and a museum with a fine collection of Etruscan art. I'd love to see it."

Nick shot her an amused look. "You really are an inveterate tourist, aren't you?"

"This is my first trip to Europe. For months I've been dreaming about seeing it. All this may be old hat to you, but it's brand new to me." She gestured at the scenery around them. "Couldn't we stop in Viterbo for lunch and walk around for just a few minutes?"

But Nick shook his head. "A redhead with your looks shepherding a pair like Rudy and Randy through the streets will be too conspicuous. The idea is that the three of you are going to disappear for a few days, not call attention to yourselves."

"What do you mean, my looks? What's wrong with my looks?"

Nick's teeth flashed. "Nothing. That's the problem. Italians tend to notice tall, pretty young women." He reached out and flipped a tendril of her hair back over her ear. "Especially ones with hair of spun fire."

Flushing, Kate drew back. She wouldn't have been human if she hadn't felt gratified by the compliment. But Nick Conti was just giving her the standard line all men used for flirting, she told herself. Hadn't her onetime heartthrob Billy Rockland said something similar only a few weeks earlier? It didn't mean a thing, and she'd be a fool to take it seriously. Kate sighed. She supposed Nick was right about her red hair being too noticeable, but she hated to accept the fact. It was so frustrating to be driving through Italy cooped up in a tiny car when she was longing to get out and explore.

"I have to go," Randy began to chant. "I have to go."

Kate dared not argue with the urgency in his tone. She opened the car door and climbed out onto the road. "C'mon you two, it's this or nothing, I suppose."

Crowing like escaped young roosters, the boys scrambled off the bench seat, leaped a narrow ditch and raced off.

Nick leaned an elbow on the window ledge and shook his head. "If they suffered any trauma over what happened at their father's place, it doesn't seem to have affected them permanently," he commented dryly.

"Well, fortunately they're young and resilient."

Nick chuckled. "Resilient is the operative word. I'd say those two are made out of solid rubber." He watched her face as he spoke, expecting her to laugh or grin, or add a similar comment of her own. Instead, she stiffly tucked the back of her torn shirt into her rumpled pants and said in a remote tone, "I think I'll stretch my legs."

"Sure, good idea." Nick sat behind the wheel staring after her, a faint frown wrinkling his forehead. The more he saw of Miss Kate Humphrey, the less he had her figured out. For instance, he didn't know what to make of her reaction to his remark just now. He'd meant it innocently. During the drive they'd both been bugged by the kids' antics, so he'd thought to try and establish some sort of bridge with her by acknowledging their common plight. But instead of being amused, she'd pokered up like a disapproving old maid schoolteacher. He stuck his head out the open window. "Did I say something to upset you?"

"No, why?"

"Just the stiff-necked way you reacted to my joke about the boys."

Kate shrugged. "Maybe I know too much about what kids sometimes have to bounce back from to be amused by humor like that."

Nick cocked an eyebrow. "May I take it that you're speaking from personal experience?"

"That's none of your business, is it?"

"My, we do have a flair for drama today, don't we? Let me see if I can guess what you're being so mysterious about." Teasing her, he slapped his forehead. "I've got it! You were abandoned at birth. Then you were adopted by a heartless old witch. Undoubtedly, she abused you and then threw you out in the street when you didn't work hard enough in her coal mine."

Kate stared at him coldly. "Something like that."

Nick's brows lifted. "You mean you actually *were* abandoned at birth?"

"Yes, I actually was. Anyhow, I know from experience that if Rudy and Randy are made of solid rubber, they're lucky because that's exactly what they're going to need to be made of to survive their parents' neglect.''

Embarrassed by the admissions she'd blurted out and uncomfortably aware of Nick's curious gaze pinned on her, Kate turned and paced down the dusty road away from the car. Then she walked back a few steps, shaded her eyes and stared over at the clump of trees where the boys had disappeared.

''I suppose I'd better make sure they're not getting into trouble,'' she muttered. Throwing a hasty, ''We'll be back in just a few minutes,'' over her shoulder at Nick who once again sat behind the wheel regarding her in thoughtful silence, she set off into the field. ''Rudy? Randy? What's going on down there?''

All she got for an answer was a brief silence followed by a series of high-pitched giggles and then a muffled scream. The scream made her heart accelerate, and she remembered the cab driver with the knife at the train station, and the two men who'd chased them in Rome. It was ridiculous to imagine that those two men might be lurking in that stand of trees. Nevertheless, Kate started to run.

''Rudy, Randy?'' Her heels sank into the sandy earth and the tall grass tickled her ankles. When she was within a few paces of the grove, the twins emitted a war whoop and rocketed out the other side. Yelling like wild men, they began racing back and forth between the formerly peaceful sheep.

''Oh, no!'' Kate dodged some sheep droppings. ''Rudy and Randy, you stop that at once! At once, do you hear!''

FROM HIS VANTAGE POINT in the car, Nick Conti gazed out at the field. The crease that already lined his brow deepened. He was thinking about Kate, about her admission just now that she'd been an orphan. No wonder his attempt to tease her had fallen about as flat as a biscuit in a rainstorm.

A flurry of activity out in the field captured his attention. Nick saw the twins dash out of the trees, clearly up to some new devilment. Gamely, their redheaded nanny chased after her two bratty pint-size charges. But her heels slowed her and the twins, obviously charmed by the prospect of terrifying a flock of sheep, were managing to elude her.

"Chips off the old block," Nick muttered as he thought of his many unsatisfactory dealings with their father. "Give them a chance to stir up trouble and they'll make the most of it every time."

As if to underline his cynical observation, their gleeful shrieks punctured the languor of the hazy afternoon. As the boys dashed amongst the sheep, shouting and waving their arms, the animals milled uneasily. A moment later they looked about to stampede into a newly plowed field nearby. Nick cast an uneasy glance at the farmhouse sitting on a hill in the distance. How long before an irate farmer bolted out of it waving a pitchfork?

"That's all I need." Snapping a curse, Nick threw open the car and strode toward the activity in the field.

DESPERATELY Kate lunged. This time, thank heaven, her hand connected with Rudy LaFiore's collar. "Ouch!" the youngster yelped as she yanked him back and then manhandled the stick he'd been flourishing out of his grubby hand.

"Aw, let bloody go! I wasn't hurting anything!" he protested. Rudy stuck out his tongue. "Wait until I tell my dad how mean you were to us! He'll take care of you!" Tightening her grip on Rudy's collar, Kate glanced around for Randy, whom she expected to find still running amok amidst the sheep.

Instead, she was just in time to see the struggling eight-year-old scooped up into a pair of apparently very strong arms. Wedging him like an oversize watermelon into the crook of one elbow, Nick Conti stalked across the field toward her. His eyes in his dark, slightly hawk-nosed face were very blue.

Shooting her a wink, he wrapped his free arm around the other twin's middle and balanced between the two, began to stride back toward the car.

"Oh, thank you," Kate cried as she stumbled along behind. She paused to take off her high-heeled shoes, which kept sinking into the clods of dirt and sheep droppings in the field. Then, shading her eyes against the sun, she took a split second to study Nick's departing back. He wasn't tall, but under his leather jacket and snug-fitting slacks his wiry body looked extremely fit. And obviously he must be very strong. She knew the boys were no lightweights. Yet he carried them both with ease.

When she saw him set Rudy and Randy feet first on the road and then squat down with his face only inches from theirs, she began to hurry after them. What was he saying to them? she wondered. Whatever it was, for the first time since Rome, both boys looked truly alarmed.

When she came up to the road, Nick had just ushered the twins back into the rear seat of the Fiat. After he'd shut the door and locked it, he looked hard through the window at the young miscreants, who gazed back in guilty dismay.

"I don't want either of you two little monsters to make another wrong move until we get where we're going. If you do, you'll be sorry! Understand?" When they bobbed their heads in unison, he turned his attention to Kate. "Prepared to get back into the chariot of a thousand tortures?''

"I know they're not exactly angels, but do you have to call them monsters?''

"Someone needs to, and if it's not going to be you, then I guess I'm elected.''

"Consider what they've gone through in the last few days," Kate pointed out. "They've had to leave their home and their mother and travel through strange country—then to learn that their father is in jail and to almost be kidnapped and have their lives threatened. Of course they're feeling upset.''

Nick snorted. "You said it yourself, Miss Humphrey. Kids this age are resilient. Those two in there are just rambunctious and spoiled. And why not, with Lou LaFiore's wild and wooly genetic code for an inheritance and Jillian, who's always been too busy admiring herself to pay attention to anyone else, for a mother?'' With that, he opened the passenger side door and made a sweeping, mock-gallant gesture. Reluctantly, Kate slid into the Fiat's overheated interior.

As Nick resumed driving, Kate observed him with narrowed eyes. "You seem to know an awful lot about Rudy and Randy's family.''

"I used to ride for the LaFiore stable.''

"Yes, but you don't sound as if you're particularly fond of the family. Yet on the train you sought me out and made a point of sitting down with me. Why?''

"Why not chat you up? You're easy on the eyes, and I had nothing better to do to kill time.''

"How extremely flattering, but that wasn't it. You weren't interested in me as a woman. Sitting down with me was all just a ploy to get information, wasn't it? You were pumping me, finding out where I was getting off with the boys."

"You're imagining things," he shot back. "The terrible two back there aren't the ones traumatized by today's three-ring circus. You are."

But Kate knew that she wasn't imagining things. Some motive beyond pure Good Samaritanism had driven Nick Conti to entangle himself with her and Lou LaFiore's children.

"What's this all about?" she demanded. "What do you want with these boys?"

"Right now all I want is to keep them safe—and quiet," he added dryly. "Stop overworking that imagination of yours and turning this into a bad melodrama for the telly. Relax, Miss Humphrey. We haven't got so far to go, now. Sit back and enjoy the scenery."

Kate turned her head away and pretended to do just that. But the Italian countryside, which had charmed her earlier, had lost its appeal. Now she gazed out at the fields of vines with a worried little frown.

The boys, too, were subdued. At one point Randy turned and peered up over the edge of the seat at Kate. "I'm hungry. Are we going to stop for tea?"

She looked questioningly at Nick.

"We'll eat shortly."

As he spoke, Nick swung the car off the road and down a rutted lane. As the automobile bumped along, Kate's fingers clenched on the edge of her seat. "Where does this lead? Where are you taking us?"

"We're going to spend a little time at a farm. You like chickens, don't you? And I know the boys are fond of sheep." She saw him grin. "It'll be fun. Tweedledee and Tweedledum here have spent too much time in London. A brief period of rusticity will do them good."

"My name's not Tweedledee," Randy objected.

"Isn't it?" Nick reached over and ruffled the child's hair. "Could've fooled me."

They rattled up to the top of a hill. At its crest, a valley lay spread beneath them. Nestled in it was a square white house and outbuildings. Kate's racing heart slowed slightly. So, just as he'd said, Nick really was taking them to a farm.

When they pulled into the yard a few minutes later, she saw that he hadn't been kidding about the chickens, at least. A flock of them roamed loose on the hard-packed dirt surrounding the house, clucking and pecking at bugs and bits of grain. As they scattered before the car's wheels, a short, thickset man with a ruffle of salt-and-pepper curls came hurrying out of the barn and limped toward them. He wiped his hands on his baggy overalls. "Nico," he cried, *"Bentornato, bentornato!"*

"Salve, Zio Mario!" Nick answered and quickly got out of the car. As the two embraced and then continued gabbling at each other in staccato bursts, Kate observed them curiously. She'd noticed before that Nick seemed comfortable speaking Italian, but she hadn't realized until this minute how fluent he was. But of course his last name was Italian, and if it weren't for his light-colored eyes, his dark coloring would make it easy for him to blend right in with the native population in this beautiful but confusing land.

"This is my Uncle Mario," Nick said, turning back to Kate and the boys. "He welcomes you to his farm."

"Sì, welcome, welcome," Mario said gazing at his nephew's three passengers with a look of uncertainty on his blunt features. His expression shifted to astonishment when the boys bolted out and he saw Kate's torn clothing and ruined shoes.

"Che succede?" he asked, turning to Nick.

"E successo un piccolo incidente. Spiego più tardi."

While Uncle Mario waited down in the hall, Nick escorted Kate and the boys up to an airy, sparely furnished room under the eaves on the second floor. When he'd found a change of clothes for Kate and left them all to wash and make themselves more comfortable, he went back downstairs to explain things to his uncle.

"NICO, MY BOY, you continue to amaze me," Mario declared in Italian as Nick came into the kitchen. "You are more impetuous even than your father, and he was the scandal of our family."

"How much have I put you out by showing up this way?" Nick queried.

"Put me out?" Mario waved a hand in denial. "How can you ask it? After all, if it weren't for your money, I would have lost this farm that's been in our family since the time of the Medici. It's yours as much as mine, and you're welcome here any time you wish." In a characteristic burst of warm emotion, Mario rushed forward, threw his meaty arms around his nephew's shoulders and kissed him noisily on the cheek. "Nico, Nico, how could you think that I might be angry because you arrive unexpectedly? Don't you know your foolish old uncle better than that?"

Nick smiled affectionately. "Turning up at your doorstep with three uninvited guests is not something I'd normally do. Believe me, Uncle Mario, I would have warned you if I'd had the chance. But there wasn't any chance." Nick began to describe the complicated sequence of events that had brought him to the farm.

Midway through Nick's narrative, Mario shook his bald head gravely. "Now I see that I was right to worry when I read that you were going to race that devil horse, Seasonwine. When I think how he almost killed you, when I think how many months it took for you to heal your broken legs and shoulder bone . . . all that time in the hospital . . .''

"What happened at Aintree was an accident," Nick interrupted.

Mario gazed at him doubtfully. "But, truly, is it worth such a terrible risk?"

"Risk? I know what you're thinking." Nick began to pace. "You're thinking that what happened at Aintree was no accident, that Lou LaFiore arranged it because of Jillian." He paused long enough to shrug. "No one ever said that steeplechasing isn't chancy. My father knew that, and I know it. It's just part of the game."

"*Sì*, but Niccolino, now you say that LaFiore's *banditti* have been threatening you."

"It's become a little more complicated than that."

When Nick finished describing the day's events, including the newspaper headlines and the car chase from the train station, Mario's expression went from serious to shocked. "But this is terrible! You and the pretty *signorina* are in formidable danger. Those men are criminals. If they find you, they will stop at nothing!"

"I'd hoped that we could hide out here for a few days until some of this died down. But if you think we're putting you in any danger . . ."

Again, Mario rushed at his nephew and seized him by the shoulders. "You insult me! Have I not said it before? This is your house. I worshipped my poor, unfortunate brother, God give his restless soul tranquility. Now you are his only son, and the only flesh and blood remaining to me. Stay here and be safe as long as you like."

"But how long do you think we will be safe here?"

Mario gave his heavy head a troubled shake. "This I truly cannot say. Those men are powerful, and even in the villages they have spies. But you say you weren't followed. Surely for a little while it will be all right."

CHAPTER FOUR

"THAT SOUP WAS MADE fresh by Adelina only this morning," Mario informed Nick in Italian. Proudly, he pointed at a huge pot simmering on the stove.

"Mmm, *bella,*" the younger man murmured, lifting his head to catch a whiff. He put down the bread knife, crossed to the massive, old-fashioned stove and ladled up a spoonful of the tomato-rich broth. It was a mixture of freshly picked zucchini, chick-peas and lentils, pasta and fragrant herbs and spices.

After taking a sip, Nick closed his eyes in ecstasy. "*Deliziosa.* Adelina Patrini is an angel descended to the kitchen, a goddess of frying pans and mixing bowls. Uncle, how can you let a treasure like this roam free? You should marry her and tether her to your stove."

Mario chuckled. "I'm too *antiquato* for the rigors of marriage."

"Too old? You're in the prime of life," Nick teased. "You would make a handsome bridegroom."

"No, no, I've been a bachelor too long. I enjoy my *indipendenza.*"

Nick put the bread on a plate and then began to set places at the table. "How long do you think a widow like Adelina will be left in peace, Uncle? She's hoping for a proposal. If you don't snatch her up, some other hungry bachelor will, and then you'll be sorry."

Grinning and gesticulating, Mario retorted, "You're a fine one to talk, Niccolino. It is you who is in the prime of life and still unmarried. *Sì, sì,* it's true you're still young and handsome. The women probably still go on making fools of themselves over you. But you're thirty-two, my boy, *trentadue,*" he emphasized, waggling a forefinger, "no longer such a spring rooster. It's time you stopped getting into trouble with wild women like that Jillian LaFiore."

Mario shook his head and then screwed up his mouth as if there were a bad taste in it. "Listen to your uncle who loves you like a son. You should find yourself a wife and settle down with her to raise up some fine *bambini.*"

Mario shot his nephew a speculative look. "This Signorina Humphrey with the funny clothes and no suitcase—all that fiery red hair around her pretty little face means passion. And I notice she has fine breasts, a little on the small side perhaps, but still very well formed. There's something going on between you two, no?"

"No," Nick denied gruffly. He finished slicing the bread and started in on the salami.

Mario looked unconvinced. "I see the way you admire her bottom when she climbs the stairs. She appears to be made very fine in this part of the female anatomy. A thing of great importance in a wife."

"Spoken like a true Italian farmer, but I'm not looking for a wife, Mario, and my interest in Miss Humphrey is strictly practical and temporary. *Temporaneo,*" Nick added for emphasis. "If I was watching her closely, it's only because I don't trust the woman—not because I want her in my bed. Until I'm sure that she really is what she claims, and not one of Lou LaFiore's spies, I can't afford to let Kate Humphrey out of my sight. Take my word for it, the sooner she and those two scamps she's nursemaiding are combed from my hair, the better.''

Mario cocked a grizzled brow in the direction of the entry. Nick pivoted and saw the young woman in question standing on the threshold. She'd changed out of her ruined T-shirt and vest into a green cotton shirt of Mario's that would have fit three of her, and she'd slipped her feet into rubber thongs several sizes too big.

Against his will and despite what he'd just said to his uncle, Nick had to admit that on Kate Humphrey this outfit looked appealing. In fact, he thought that just about anything would look appealing on Kate Humphrey.

She'd washed, he noted. Her hair, which had been dusty and matted from the train trip and the boys' romp in the sheep pasture, stood out from her head in a fetching aureole of rapidly drying curls. Cleansed of all makeup, her pale, lightly freckled skin had the translucence of a child's. Water had clumped her dark eyelashes into spiky points that framed eyes the color of peridot.

The expression in those lovely green eyes, however, was suspicious. Obviously, she'd heard her name being used freely and wondered what they'd been saying about her. Nick was glad that his uncle's earthy remarks had been made in Italian.

''Sorry to interrupt,'' she said politely, ''but Rudy and Randy are getting awfully hungry. Can I help with anything?''

Nick swept a hand at the soup on the stove and the bread and salami waiting on the table. ''Lunch is ready. Call down the ravenous hordes.''

Barefoot and with their hands and faces cleaned, Rudy and Randy clattered down the stairs and crowded past Kate and into the kitchen. ''Jolly good,'' Rudy exclaimed when he caught sight of the salami. Both boys rushed to the table and hurled themselves into chairs.

"Bene, bene," Mario kept commenting, his calloused hands darting and fluttering as he lingered to make sure everyone had what they needed. Then, he excused himself to go into the village and Nick and his three guests were left alone with the food.

The children devoured thick slices of spicy meat, dipped their bread into their soup and questioned Nick about the farm.

"Do you have horses here?" Randy wanted to know.

"There are two out in the barn, a mare called Bella and a senior citizen named Cesare."

"Can we see them?"

"Maybe later you can have a ride on Cesare. Bella's a little frisky with strangers."

While Nick answered more questions about the horses, Kate chewed slowly and cast curious glances around the kitchen. She was still uneasy about her decision to trust Nick Conti, but the big old-fashioned room with its tile floor and ancient appliances reassured her, as had Uncle Mario who appeared to be the soul of benevolence.

Through the open windows she could see brilliant afternoon sunlight and hear a medley of barnyard noises. Upstairs she'd done a quick search of the farmhouse's spartan second floor. On the one hand, she hadn't known what she was looking for. On the other, she hadn't found anything to indicate that this place was other than what Nick claimed. Kate told herself to try and relax.

As soon as their bellies were full, Rudy and Randy's eyes began to droop and Kate took them upstairs for a nap. She felt exhausted herself. But there were too many questions troubling her to allow her to drop down on one of the beds in their big dormitory-like room. Before she could do that, she needed to reassure herself by getting some straight answers from Nick Conti.

Kate returned downstairs, but when she poked her head into the kitchen, Nick was gone. She went outside, and after a quick glance around, strolled to the barn.

After her eyes adjusted to the darkness inside, she spotted Nick at the far end. He'd opened up one of the only two occupied stalls and was standing with his back to her feeding pieces of apple to a light-colored horse.

Something about the tableau made Kate stop in her tracks. Such a strong sense of communion between man and beast pervaded the scene that as she watched Nick stroke the animal's bent neck and heard him murmur into its cocked ear, she felt as if she'd intruded on a private conversation. She was about to turn and quietly leave when Nick suddenly looked around and spied her.

He straightened slightly. "Something I can do for you?"

"Well, yes." Hesitantly, Kate approached him. "There are still some questions I want to ask, and I couldn't put them to you while the boys were there. But if you're busy—"

"I'm not busy. Just saying hello to an old friend here. What's on your mind?"

Instead of answering immediately, Kate said, "Is your friend the senior citizen you were mentioning?"

Nick gave the animal eating from his hand another pat. "Yes, this is Cesare."

Horses made Kate nervous, and she didn't know very much about them. But even to her untutored eyes, the one quietly munching on a last piece of apple looked old. His muzzle was grayer than the rest of his coat and his flesh had shrunk around his bones. "He certainly seems happy to see you."

Nick gazed affectionately at the animal and volunteered, "Cesare and I go way back. Twenty-five years ago my father won a *palio* on his back."

"Goodness, he *is* old. What's a *palio*?"

"A wild and crazy race around the city of Siena. It's a very big thing in these parts."

"I'll have to look it up in my guidebook."

"You can try, but a *palio* has to be seen to be properly appreciated, I'm afraid. Maybe someday you'll get the chance."

"Maybe." Doubtful that this would ever happen, Kate sighed and then cocked her head, observing curiously as Nick began circling Cesare. He ran a sensitive hand over his flanks and gazed critically at his coat.

"Was your father a jockey, too?"

"Yes, though he did most of his riding in England. There was a time when his name was well known on the steeplechase circuit."

"What happened to him?"

"A horse fell on him during a race at Sandown and he was killed," Nick said matter of factly.

Kate's hand flew to her throat. "I'm sorry."

"It happened when I was eight years old, a long time ago." He bent to examine one of Cesare's hooves. While his fingers probed gently, Cesare stood patiently.

As Kate stared down at the top of Nick's closely clipped dark head, she thought of her school friend who'd been crippled in a riding accident and remembered that horrible racing collision she'd seen on her English landlady's TV. Knowing that Nick Conti's father had been killed in a similar crack-up made the violent images seem much worse. What would motivate a man to risk his life at the same dangerous sport that had killed his father?

She cleared her throat. "Is there something wrong with Cesare's hoof?"

"Yes, actually. He's got a bit of gravel stuck under his shoe. If it's left there it might cause problems." From his squatting position, Nick looked up at her and pointed. "I left my knife on that post when I cut up Cesare's apple. Would you mind pitching it to me?"

"Of course." Kate found the Swiss army pocketknife at her elbow and tossed it. But pitching had never been her strong suit. The knife landed well beyond his reach.

"Sorry." Overcoming her reluctance to get any closer to the horse, she walked into the stall and picked up the knife. Nick put Cesare's leg down and stood to retrieve the knife himself. At that moment the horse snorted and sidestepped, crowding Nick and Kate together against the wall of the stall.

It happened so quickly that Kate was totally unprepared for the shock of finding her body wedged against Nick's. All at once his strong, hard legs were pressed to hers and the healthy scent of his skin filled her nostrils. His belt buckle dug into her belly and his arm steadied her. As she gave him a startled look, a little scream of alarm died in her throat and an electric shock seemed to skip through her.

She was so transfixed by it that she didn't notice until the next instant that he was amused. Wicked laughter glinted in his eyes—that, and something else, because she suddenly knew he, too, had felt that same little buzz of electricity that had jolted her.

He laid a finger against the pulse in her throat. "Your heart's beating like a jackhammer. What's wrong? Are you scared of horses?"

"Yes," she answered breathlessly.

"It's nothing," he told her, his voice a shade deeper than it had been an instant earlier. "Cesare's just teasing us."

"Teasing?"

"He's a matchmaker. Likes to pair unlikely couples."

"Oh, I see. Very funny. But I really would like to get out of here."

Nick's teeth flashed. Then, as if the animal were an overaffectionate dog rather than a half ton of elderly stallion, he pushed Cesare out of the way. "Take it easy, boy. It's all right," he soothed as Kate hurried from the stall.

When Nick had finished digging the gravel out of Cesare's shoe, he pocketed his knife and slapped the animal's rump.

Kate, her stomach still fluttering from their encounter a moment earlier, asked, "Is he all right?"

"Oh yes, for his age Cesare is in quite decent shape. Why do horses frighten you?"

"I don't know. Maybe because they're so big. I'm just a city girl, I guess." She pointed at Cesare. "He doesn't still steeplechase, does he?"

"Oh, no. Cesare was never a jumper. In his prime he was a good flat racer, but he was never trained to steeplechase."

"I guess my ignorance is showing. Just what exactly is steeplechasing? I know it involved jumping fences, but I don't believe I've ever seen anything quite like it in the States."

Nick walked out of the stall and latched it. "There is some steeplechasing in the U.S., mostly on the East Coast. But you're right, it's basically an English sport."

"Did it start in England?"

"No, in Ireland, actually." He leaned against a post. "I'm asked this question fairly often, so I've looked up the answer. The first recorded steeplechase happened in 1752 when a couple of crazy Irishmen matched their hunters for a cross-country scramble. They used a church steeple for direction guide and winning post."

"That's where it got the name?"

"Righto. English hunt clubs took up the sport and by the mid-1800s it was second to none on English hunt programs."

As Nick spoke, a shaft of light from a small opening overhead bathed one side of his face, highlighting its attractive planes and angles. It made his eyes look as clear as glass. Again, Kate caught that wicked gleam glinting out at her and knew he was thinking about how they'd been crowded together in the stall. Her body tingled, as if the contact were being made all over again.

"But you're not really all that interested in the history of steeplechasing, are you?" he said dryly. "You came out here to ask me some questions. Well, ask away."

Kate pursed her lips. "All right, you've explained why the boys need to hide out, and I guess it makes sense."

"You guess?" He shook his head. "You're not a woman given to blind trust, are you?"

Kate's mouth firmed. "No, I'm not. I've trusted blindly too often in the past to be happy about having to do it now."

Interest flickered in his expression. "Oh, really? Now you've got me curious again. Tell me about these unfortunate adventures in misplaced trust. Did they involve men?" His gaze shot to her hand. "I never thought to wonder if you're married. Are you?"

Kate flushed. "I'm not married. I'm strictly all on my own and have been that way most of my life."

"Then where does all this worldly cynicism come from? Did your lover leave you?"

It had been many months since Kate had imagined herself in love. But her recent parting with Billy Rockland was still a painful memory. "When it comes to betrayal, aren't men usually involved?"

"That's funny. I would have said that betrayal was something in which the female sex specialized. Maybe we should trade war stories."

"Maybe, Mr. Conti, but now is not the time."

"Why so formal? Call me Nick, and I'll call you Kate, if you don't mind."

Kate did mind. When it came to Nicholas Conti, she wanted as little intimacy as possible and all her defenses firmly in place. She didn't like the way he was affecting her, the way she couldn't seem to take her eyes off of him. "You asked me if I had questions about this situation, and I do."

"Very well, let's hear them."

"You rescued me and the children today, and I'm grateful for your help. But there's more to it, isn't there? You're involved in this situation."

"Of course I'm involved. I'd say I've spent my whole day being highly involved."

"But that's not what I mean, and you know it. I asked you before, and now I'll ask you again. Why did you sit down with me on that train? For that matter, why were you on the train to Rome in the first place? Aren't you going to be competing in the Grand National in just a few days? Shouldn't you be in England practicing or something?"

Nick pushed himself away from the post, straightened and thrust his hands deep into the pockets of his snug-fitting trousers. His hips were very narrow. Though Kate was quite slender herself, she doubted she'd be able to zip up a pair of Nick's pants.

"All right," he said, beginning to stroll toward the barn's exit with his lithe, rolling gait, "let's be straight with each other, shall we? You've told me what your connection with Lou LaFiore is. Or what you claim it is."

"Claim?" Kate walked alongside Nick, hurrying to keep up. "I'm his sons' temporary nanny, that's all."

"Okay, I accept that. Now I'll tell you about my connection. You're aware that I used to work for LaFiore when he owned Seasonwine, the horse I'll be racing at Aintree. Well LaFiore doesn't own Seasonwine anymore. After an accident on the track a few years back he sold him—a major error, in my estimation. LaFiore now races Bold Turns, a snappy jumper who stands a good chance of winning some big purses this year. Bold Turns is good but, in my opinion, not as good as Seasonwine was when I happened to be on his back. It's a hard thing to explain to a nonrider, but that horse and I always had a special relationship. He'll jump for me when he won't make the effort for anyone else."

Though Kate was no equestrian, she had seen Nick commune with Cesare and could believe that Nick might have a unique effect on the horses he rode.

"Anyhow," Nick continued, "when I cut a deal with Seasonwine's new owner to bring the horse out of retirement and ride him in the Grand National, LaFiore didn't like the idea of serious competition for Bold Turns and sent some of his goons around to threaten me. That's why I happened to be a passenger on that train to Rome. I was on my way to reason with the man."

As they walked back out into the bright sunshine, Kate blinked. Goons, threats, big purses—trying to make sense of the whole complicated and dangerous sounding mess made her head ache. She stopped and lowered her voice.

"Are you telling me that the children's father is a criminal?"

Nick turned and looked into her eyes. Since Kate was above-average height for a woman, his gaze was almost level with hers. "Let's just say that he runs in some ethically suspect crowds and that where money is involved he isn't always strictly scrupulous."

"In other words, he's a crook."

"In other words, under certain circumstances, he can play rough—like the company he keeps."

"And you sat down with me on the train because I had his children, and you wanted to know why?"

"Exactly." Nick's lips quirked and as their gazes continued to tangle Kate became warmly conscious of just how close his mouth was to hers. It was an attractive mouth, cut along ascetic rather than sensual lines, yet somehow very inviting. Since he was so near her height, it would take only a slight inclination of both their heads for their lips to meet. Again Kate became conscious that the same thing that was going through her mind was going through his.

"I wasn't lying about finding you attractive," Nick said huskily. "Chatting you up on that train was no chore. It's no chore talking to you now. But you know that, don't you? I think we've both known that for quite a while."

"I . . . yes . . . but it doesn't matter," she stammered.

"Doesn't it? We're adults who like each other, Kate, and I think we'd like to do something about it. I would, anyway. What about you?"

Before she could think of an answer that made any sense, a rusty old truck rattled into the yard and Mario climbed out of it. In one hand he carried a string bag abulge with soap, toothbrushes and other odds and ends that he'd apparently thought his guests might need. In his free arm he juggled a pile of newspapers. "As usual," he complained, "the newspapers from Roma arrive *tardi, tardi*. But I wait until the truck, she comes."

He dumped the papers on top of a wooden cart and held up a front page. It featured a blurry photo of a balding, thickset man in a dark suit. If Kate hadn't been able to guess from his resemblance to the twins that he was their father, she would have known from the splashy black headline. LaFiore Dice Tutto, it blared.

"This is the paper you were so anxious to see back in that sweetshop," Nick remarked as he took it out of his uncle's hand and passed it to her.

Still rattled by their conversation of only a moment earlier, Kate accepted the newsprint as if it were rigged to explode and said, "Thank you, but I don't read Italian. I can only guess at what this really says."

"I think the words 'dice' and 'tutto' ought to indicate something. But if you want, I'll find you a dictionary so you can translate every line."

"Since I'm not a linguist, maybe that's not such a bad idea," Kate agreed. Folding the newspaper and tucking it under her arm, she thanked Mario for it and for lunch and then excused herself to join the napping boys. But it wasn't so much a nap as escape from the warm challenge in Nick Conti's beautiful blue eyes that she wanted.

WHEN KATE AWOKE it was late afternoon and long shadows slanted across the floor. With a start, she looked around. Both the boys' cots were empty. Groggily, she pushed herself off the bed and into a standing position, took another quick survey of the room and then headed out into the hall. From the kitchen she could hear the clatter of cookware.

When she poked her head around the kitchen door, Kate beheld a tiny woman with a round, pretty face, snapping dark eyes and graying hair pulled atop her head in a tight bun. She was dressed in black with sleeves rolled up to her elbows, her breast and lower half swathed in a voluminous white apron. When she spotted Kate in the doorway, she was manhandling a pot that appeared to be about half her size.

"*Che bella!* You must be the Signorina Humphrey," she exclaimed. Dumping the pot on the table, she hurried forward wiping her hands on her apron. "You sleep good, yes?" she queried, beaming as she took Kate's fingers and gave them a hearty shake.

"I slept very well, yes."

"I am Adelina, Mario's friend. I come to cook for him, to fatten him up, you see. He is such a skinny stick bachelor, I feel sorry for him."

Mario hadn't struck Kate as looking in the least like a skinny stick, but she smiled and nodded. "Was that your soup we had for lunch?"

"*Sì, mia zuppa.* Good, yes?"

"Delicious. Really, it was wonderful. Uh, have you seen two little boys?"

"Rudy and Randy?" Adelina waggled a finger humorously. "Two little *briccones*, no? They go with Mario to work in his garden. See?"

She pointed through the door that led out back. When Kate peered through it she spied Mario in the distance. As he leaned on a hoe, he pointed down at the recently plowed dirt and discoursed. The twins, who each carried a spade and a watering can, listened to him with apparent fascination.

"Excuse me while I go check on them," Kate said. But when she walked out to the large vegetable garden she found that the boys really were as engrossed in planting seeds as they seemed and Mario appeared happy to have their company. "We make good team," he told her, putting his large hands on each of the youngsters' shoulders and grinning.

"That's wonderful. But where's Nick?" Kate asked.

"Nico go for a ride on Bella," Mario told her, pointing at a distant pasture.

Kate shaded her eyes and watched the graceful outline of a horse and rider disappearing into a line of trees on the horizon. A few minutes later, after assuring herself that Mario and the boys really were getting along, she returned to the kitchen and offered to help Adelina with dinner.

"Sì, sì," Adelina answered with a chuckle. "Together we fix our men something *delizioso*, no?"

"No, er, yes, certainly." Only Nick Conti wasn't her man, a fact that Kate wanted to make clear in as diplomatic a way as possible. "How long have you and Mario been friends?" she asked.

"Oh, almost since we are *bambini*," Adelina answered forthrightly. She handed Kate a cutting board, a sharp knife, and some vegetables to dice. "We go to school together, we see each other in church and in the village square. And when I am young girl, he and his best friend Adolfo court me. They court me very well, with gifts of flowers and candy. And even Mario serenade me beneath my window."

A tender smile lifted her mouth. "Mario, he was so *romantico*, and he had a beautiful tenor voice." Sighing reminiscently, she brought her fingers together and touched her lips with them. But then she sighed again and shook her head. "Adolfo had a bigger house, so it was he I marry with. Mario, he never marry with anyone. Oh, it was sad for him. But now my husband, God rest his poor soul, is dead." She wiped away an invisible tear.

"I'm so sorry," Kate told her sympathetically. "Have you been a widow long?"

"Two year," Adelina answered smartly. "Is long enough for a woman to be without a man."

"Are you and Mario engaged?" Kate chopped away at tomatoes, onion and celery while Adelina chattered and bustled about like a small culinary tornado.

"Not yet." As Adelina stirred and then tasted the fragrant mixture in her cookpot, a canny look came into her fine dark eyes. "But soon, soon." She rinsed her spoon and then turned to focus her attention on Kate. "And you? You and Nico are together, no?"

"Oh, no," Kate hastily replied. "We just barely know each other, really."

Adelina shot her a sparkling look. "A *bella signorina* like you, a handsome young *cavaliere* like Nick, you don't stay strangers long."

Upstairs Kate had thought about Nick's advance and decided, despite her errant inclinations, she must reject it. "You don't understand," she answered. "I'll only be here for a day or two."

Adelina glanced at Kate's bare hands. "You have another *innamorato* in your life now?"

"No, there's no one I care about." And no one who cares about me, she found herself thinking as she had so many times in the past. So what else was new? That was the way it always had been and, she was beginning to suspect, always would be.

Adelina gave her sharp little chuckle and ground fresh pepper into a skillet. "Then watch out for Nico! Always the women are crazy about that one. I hear stories..." She shook her head, rolled her eyes and giggled wickedly.

"Yes, I can imagine," Kate muttered under her breath. She was both amused and a little startled by Adelina's girlish frankness. "Have you known Nick long?"

"Since he was a little boy visiting his uncle in the summer because he had nowhere else to go. Poor little one! Oh, it was sad!"

"Why didn't he have anywhere else to go?" Kate forgot the large, strong-smelling onion she'd started to dice and stared at her informant.

"Nick is *orfano*."

"He is?" Now Kate really was surprised. She hadn't realized Nick had lost both his parents. So she and Nick had something in common.

"*Sì*, his English mama die when he is born."

"That *is* sad." Unconsciously, Kate ran her finger along the edge of the freshly sliced onion.

"*Sì*, and then when Nick is only eight, his papa fall off a racing horse and kill himself." Adelina shook her head mournfully. "I remember when Eduardo Conti win the *Palio di Siena*. This dangerous horse-riding is in Nico's blood. It is a curse."

"But what about when he was a child?" Kate asked, returning to the part of the story that interested her most. "Didn't his mother's family take him in?"

"Oh, *sì*," she answered scornfully, "they are rich so they don't let him starve in the street. But they don't want him, either. So they send him away to the boarding school and then ignore him."

"It is sad," Kate agreed. She pictured Nick as a child. Now he was a wiry, athletically built man. As a child he'd probably been small and slight. Those long-lashed blue eyes of his were striking now. When he was small they must have dominated his face. How could his grandparents have let him languish all alone in a boarding school?

Forgetting that her fingers were soaked with juice from the onion she'd been chopping, Kate lifted her hand and rubbed the bridge of her nose. It was a mistake. Her eyes, already stinging from the strong odor, began to gush tears. "Oh, dear," she said, looking around for something to wipe them with. And when she picked up a kitchen towel and brought it to her eyes, that only made the situation worse. Moisture literally streamed down her face.

"Something smells wonderful in there," a pleasant baritone called out. A second later Nick Conti followed his greeting through the door. "Adelina my love, whatever you're cooking, save me a double portion."

But Adelina was too busy staring at Kate to answer. Nick turned around and stared at Kate himself. "What's wrong with her? Why's she crying like that?"

Gravely, Adelina shook her head. "*Che sensibile!* Nico, she cry for you. I tell her you are the *orfano* and you see for yourself. She cry for you."

CHAPTER FIVE

AFTER THE BOYS were bedded down that night, Kate felt far too restless to sleep herself. She took Mario's newspaper and her guidebook to the parlor, found an English-Italian dictionary on one of the shelves and settled into an old horsehair sofa.

Mario had accompanied Adelina back to the village and Nick, after he'd played ball with the boys for a while, had turned Rudy and Randy over to Kate and disappeared into the barn. So the house was quiet—a perfect opportunity to take Nick up on his challenge about translating the newspaper article, Kate told herself.

Matching the Italian words to English was slow work, but finally after an hour ticked past on the square marble clock facing the sofa, she got most of the gist of Lou LaFiore's situation. As she had known in her gut all along, Nick had been telling the truth. Possibly he had his own agenda for coming to their aid, but quite likely he really had saved their lives back in Rome.

As this realization sank in, Kate glanced through the dark window. She considered going out to the barn to offer Nick an apology. But remembering how intimate the atmosphere of the place had been that afternoon and the caressing light that had come into his eyes when he'd forced her to acknowledge their mutual attraction, she decided against it.

Ruefully, Kate thought back to her crying episode in the kitchen. After she'd explained to Nick and Adelina that her tears had been brought on by an onion and not, as Adelina had declared, by sympathy for Nick's lonely childhood, they'd all laughed the incident off. But the laughter, at least between herself and Nick, had been uncomfortable. And she'd been very aware of the curious, assessing look he'd trained on her all through dinner.

The two of them were like a pair of cats circling each other warily, she thought. But were those cats considering pouncing on each other to scratch, or to make love?

With a troubled sigh, Kate put down the newspaper and opened her travel book. She had been reading for a half an hour when the kitchen door banged. A moment later Kate heard Nick in the hall. Already she'd learned to recognize the rhythm of his quick, light-footed stride. He walked like a gymnast—or a cat. There was a sureness about the way he fit into his body, as if every muscle and joint had been honed to a higher tolerance than other men's.

"Nose buried in that travel guide again, I see," he commented when he came around the corner and spotted her curled up in the yellow glow of the stained glass lamp.

"Yes." Self-consciously, Kate straightened her legs and put her feet on the floor. She pointed at the newspaper and then at the dictionary she'd used to translate it. "I owe you another apology."

His brows lifted. "Oh?"

"Yes, you really have been helping us in a dangerous situation, and until now I haven't properly appreciated the fact. I'm sorry I've been so mistrustful. Can we declare a truce?"

"Of course." His guarded expression softened and he took a step toward her. "Really, it's only natural you should have some doubts. Before yesterday you'd never laid eyes on me, had you? And this is an extremely odd situation. I would have felt the same in your shoes.'' He glanced at her feet and then grinned. ''Speaking of which, we must do something about your wardrobe, mustn't we?''

''I can get by for a while longer. The boys will need a change, though.''

''Adelina is going to see what she can pick up for them in the village. She has nephews around their age.'' For a moment he stood regarding her, a faint smile on his finely cut mouth. Then his gaze returned to the open book in her hands. ''Playing frustrated tourist again, I see. What were you finding so enthralling before I interrupted?''

''My book has a good section on this area. I was reading about Viterbo's papal history.''

''Oh?''

''The first of the conclaves to elect a pope was held in Viterbo, and there are some fascinating stories.'' Kate looked down at the open page and cleared her throat. ''It says here that in the thirteenth century when the cardinals were locked in their palace to choose a pope and couldn't come to a decision for months, the *capitano* had the roof taken off the meeting room. When that didn't work, they were deprived of food.''

Nick chuckled. ''That must have done the trick. Italians aren't given to fasting.'' He cocked his head. ''You're a funny little bird.''

''What's funny about me?''

''Oh, I don't know. You're just an odd mix. When I decide you're one thing, you start being something else. I haven't got you figured out yet.''

''Well the same goes for me. I haven't got you figured out, either. And I'm not a bird, by the way. I'm a woman and have been for some time.''

Nick continued to eye her, his mouth quirking. "I've noticed, but in that getup at the moment you look about thirteen."

"I can't help how I look in Mario's old shirt. My top was torn to pieces this afternoon."

"I know. I remember it well," Nick answered dryly. He paced to the heavy desk where the marble clock ticked and then turned to face her. "Would you like to see the Palazzo Papale?"

"What?" Kate gave him a startled look. "I thought you said we couldn't go into any of the towns because someone might notice and remember us."

"True, but that red hair of yours could be covered up. And I wasn't intending to invite the boys to accompany us. Besides, you do need some clothes. What do you say? Would you like to spend tomorrow shopping and having a look at the sights?"

Kate's expression went very still, considering. "What about Rudy and Randy?"

"They can stay here with Mario. He's already offered."

"He has? That's very nice of him."

"Heroic, I should say."

Kate laughed. It was ridiculous how excited she felt at the prospect of spending a day alone with Nick, though she told herself it was surely the opportunity to sightsee that tempted her. "I'd love it," she answered gratefully.

"Then that will be the plan. We'll set off first thing in the morning. Now," he said, glancing at the clock, "I think what we both need is a good night's sleep." He surprised her by leaning over and giving her a light peck on the cheek. "Sweet dreams."

THE NEXT DAY Nick was waiting at the breakfast table when Kate and the boys came down. Freshly showered and dressed in dark pants, a white knit sport shirt and a loose linen jacket, he looked handsome and virile. "All set to see the big city?"

"As much as I'll ever be." Feeling slightly absurd in the same getup she'd worn the previous day, Kate waved her guidebook jauntily.

"Why can't we go too?" Randy demanded.

"You *bambini* stay here with me," Mario insisted good-naturedly. He brought a basket of warm rolls to the table and placed it next to a plate of pale yellow fresh-churned butter, which had been scooped out of a vat in delectable little curls. "Together we do something useful. We plow a field."

Fascinated by this idea, the boys relented and fell to arguing over who was going to drive the tractor. After Kate had washed down Mario's crusty rolls with rich milky coffee, Nick winked and whispered in her ear, "Now's the time to make our getaway."

She shot him a conspiratorial smile, and a few minutes later they admonished the boys to be good, wished Mario well, climbed into the Fiat and set off.

"This is for you," Nick said, plucking a scarf out of the glove compartment. "It's on loan from Adelina."

It was a pretty scarf, but Kate had never liked wearing things on her head. She sighed. "Do I have to put it on now?"

Nick's gaze lingered on her bright curls. "It can wait until we get into town." Turning away, he rolled down the window, stuck his elbow out and began to hum "Finiculi, Finicula." Kate watched him for a moment, then, listening to the cheerful tune with one ear, she looked out the side window and admired the hills and valleys rolling past and the blue spine of mountains in the distance.

It was amazing how good she felt—totally different from the frightened and bewildered person she'd been the day before. Now with Nick at her side and the boys safely tucked away at the farm she felt like an adventuress anticipating a pleasurable excursion with an exciting—and very sexy—companion.

Half an hour later, they left the countryside and drove into Viterbo. As Nick threaded the car through the town Kate craned her neck, staring around her and exclaiming at the solemn charm of it. Viterbo was a city full of fountains and old walls graced with stone shields. In its center stood a pure and complete townlet of the Middle Ages. If it hadn't been for the chicly dressed women to be seen strolling in the cobbled piazza, Kate could have believed she'd slipped back in time a half dozen centuries.

After she'd reluctantly donned Adelina's scarf and tied it around her forehead so as to completely hide her hair, Nick took Kate to a small but stylish dress shop. There, she picked out a midnight-blue ankle-length swirl of a skirt with a matching fitted top, a pair of pleated pants with a flattering fit, a change of underwear and a comfortable but attractive pair of walking shoes. Nick threw a couple of knit T-shirts, a pair of sneakers and a light jacket onto the pile. "Who knows if you'll ever see that luggage of yours again. My guess is you won't, and it's warm out now, but this early in spring it could turn cold again."

"I can't pay for all this," Kate protested.

He reached for his wallet. "I'll take care of the bill."

"But that's not right."

"Don't worry, Lou LaFiore will foot the bill in the end. Soon I'll be having it out with him. I intend to pay him a visit tomorrow, as a matter of fact."

"Oh?" Questions hovered on the tip of Kate's tongue, but just then the salesgirl, who'd been shooting Nick admiring looks from the instant she'd set her big brown eyes on him, returned with their purchases tucked into bright plastic bags.

When the transaction was complete, Kate changed into her new slacks, blouse and jacket. "The salesgirl thinks I'm crazy to keep this scarf on," she whispered as they finally walked out of the store.

Nick stopped in the street and cocked his head, surveying Kate with that maddeningly appealing smile of his quirking his mouth. "You're charming in green-and-purple stripes. Not quite the stunner you are with red hair, but still—very passable."

It was absurd—and alarming—how much pleasure his meaningless flattery generated in her, Kate thought. "I bet you say that to all the girls."

"Not all, just a select ten dozen or so."

"Oh, thanks a lot."

The sunny late-March morning was turning into a fine spring day with little puffs of clouds riding in the blue sky. Leisurely, Nick and Kate crossed the piazza and walked through the Porta della Verità to the church of Santa Maria della Verità.

The museum that Kate had wanted to see occupied the cloisters of the church. It was a place of cool rooms and walks covered with slant-tiled roofs. At its heart, neat quartets of arches surrounded a sunlit square filled with birds.

"After lunch I'll take you to the Piazza del Plebiscito," Nick said as Kate examined one of the many Etruscan sarcophagi the museum housed. "There's a tomb there with quite a dramatic story attached to it."

"Oh?" Kate turned away from the angular painted lion that had caught her interest.

"According to legend it belongs to a twelfth-century heroine, *la bella Galiana*. At the time of her death she was supposed to have been the most beautiful girl in Viterbo."

"Is that why she has a special tomb?"

"No, it's because a neighboring baron coveted her, and when she refused him he laid siege to the city."

"My goodness, poor Galiana. What happened?"

Nick crossed his arms over his chest, and for the first time Kate noticed how strong and businesslike his hands looked with their calloused fingers and sinewy wrists. But, of course, a jockey would need strong hands and arms. Doubtless his life even depended on it.

"This part of the story you probably won't like," he said with a wicked twinkle in his sapphire eyes. "The baron promised that if Galiana showed herself on the city walls the siege would be lifted."

"And did she do it?"

"Yes, but when she appeared he killed her with an arrow."

Kate felt mildly shocked. "If he loved her, why did he do that?"

"You obviously don't understand the medieval male mentality. He didn't love her, he coveted her. And if he couldn't have her, no one else could, either."

Kate rolled her eyes, and turning away, pretended to examine a marble bust of some ancient Roman dignitary, which rested on a low pedestal. "Men!"

The story disturbed her in some elemental way, the injustice of it, the rawness of that ancient, ungovernable passion. She was even more disturbed when she felt Nick come up behind her and lay a hand on her shoulder. His touch was light, yet she felt the heat from his palm seep through the thin fabric of her new blouse.

"You know, almost from the moment we met you've been taking potshots at me in particular and men in general," he murmured in her ear. "Don't you think you owe me an explanation?"

"No more than you owe me one about your private life."

"All right, then let me try my luck at fortune telling. Remember, yesterday I guessed right about your being an orphan. Now I'll see what my crystal ball says about your love life." As he spoke, he slipped his hands around her waist and let them rest on the bald head of the marble carving she faced. "Ah yes, now I see it all," he murmured. His breath would have stirred the tendrils of her hair had it not been clamped beneath Adelina's scarf. "You've had a bad experience with a man."

Kate concentrated on the statue in front of her. "Make it men, plural, and you'll be right."

"Are you talking about your love life or your career?"

"Both. Neither one has been worth much. So far, the men in my life have been about as reliable as rainfall in the Sahara."

"Ah, then you're due for a change of luck." Playfully, Nick rubbed the marble pate, his elbows brushing Kate's waist in a way that sent exciting signals tripping up her spine. "I predict that today you're going to get to know a dark stranger."

Kate giggled and then brushed his hands away and walked on to the next display, a collection of apothecary jars and examples of church crafts. Archly, she glanced back at him. "Now, Mr. Fortune-teller, it's your turn. Tell me about *your* love life. How many hearts have you broken lately?"

"My record is clean. I had a rather nasty accident a couple of years back and broke a few legs and arms, not to mention my collarbone. Since getting out of hospital I've been too busy trying to put myself back together and make a go of my horse farm in Ireland to break hearts.''

Kate studied him. "I saw a film of your accident on the television. It looked perfectly hideous."

"Wasn't much fun from my point of view, either."

Kate wasn't amused. "After something like that I don't know how you could even think of climbing on a horse, much less of racing the Grand National and taking the risk of winding up in the hospital all over again. You've really rehabilitated yourself. Looking at you, I'd never guess what happened. But you might not be so lucky a second time. Aren't you frightened of going through the rest of your life crippled?"

Nick shrugged, his muscular shoulders rolling smoothly inside his loose jacket. "It's very simple. If I'm to make a go of horse breeding, I need a superior stud. Season-wine's new owner offered to let me use the horse for stud at my farm if I agreed to come out of retirement for this race. Now that I've signed my name to the deal, I'm not about to let myself be bullied out of it." His face hardened and his jaw set. "That's why I need to have it out with Lou LaFiore."

WHEN THEY LEFT the museum, Nick led Kate through a montage of stairways bordered by flowers, fountains and arches. They found a small café overlooking a fountain where children sailed boats and, since the day was unseasonably warm, sat down outside to eat lunch.

Urged on by Nick, Kate ordered a Tuscan dish called *la fettunta*. It consisted of a slab of coarse country bread toasted over a wood fire, topped with white beans and tomatoes and a drizzle of green olive oil. Nick had *ribollita*, a thick mush of bread stewed with white beans, carrots, zucchini and chards topped with olive oil and grated cheese.

As they lingered over this hearty repast, Kate looked down at the fountain and the ancient stone buildings ringing the square. "Italy is such a beautiful land," she murmured.

Nick nodded. "You haven't seen some of the most spectacular places, the Amalfi drive, the harbor at Portofino. With such voluptuous scenery surrounding them, it's no wonder that its people are sensualists." He took a bite of his *ribollita* savored it, and then pushed the dish away.

"Goodness," Kate exclaimed, "when it comes to food you're no sensualist. Is that all you're going to eat?" She'd noticed the day before at lunch that he hadn't touched the spicy, fatty salami the boys had gobbled and hadn't finished his soup, either.

Nick looked over at his plate which was still two-thirds full. "I'm on a diet."

"A diet?" He was already lean as a half-starved wolf, Kate thought. She couldn't see where he had an extra ounce of fat on him to lose.

He caught the incredulous note in her voice. "I'm a jockey, remember?"

"Oh, yes." Actually, it wasn't so easy to keep in mind. Nick was so much larger than the small-boned men who worked as jockeys in the States. When she said something to that effect, he shrugged.

"Unlike flat racing jockeys, steeplechase riders can be fairly normal-sized men. But that doesn't mean they don't have to keep their weight down. In racing, weight is always important."

"And I thought it was only women who dieted constantly."

"Well, now you know differently. Every morning I step on the scale. When I'm racing I don't even allow myself an occasional beer, desserts are verboten and red meat is out of the question."

"And when you're not racing?"

He shrugged. "I loosen up a little, but I'm still abstemious. Habit, I guess."

"You make yourself sound like a paragon of virtue."

Under his level dark brows, Nick's blue eyes gleamed at her. "Oh I shouldn't describe myself that way."

No, she thought and lowered her own gaze back to her soup. There were vices that didn't involve food and drink, and Nick Conti didn't look like the prudish type. Kate spooned up a white bean.

Just as he'd promised, after lunch Nick took her to the Piazza del Plebiscito and pointed out Galiana's tomb, a sarcophagus jammed with carvings of lions, horses and warriors.

As they walked around it, Kate shook her head and murmured, "It's very..."

"Very medieval and very Italian."

"Yes," Kate agreed with a laugh. In the warm afternoon sunshine she was beginning to feel rather sticky. Unthinkingly, she reached up and pushed her scarf off her head.

"Put that back on, please," Nick said sharply. Then, before she had a chance to comply, he pulled the scarf down around her forehead himself.

"Oh, sorry," she said, feeling slightly ruffled as she pushed his hand away and readjusted the scarf. Frowning she pivoted and stared at a knot of men lounging under a clock tower.

"What's wrong?" Nick queried.

"Oh, nothing. I just had the feeling someone was staring at me."

"With your figure, it's a pretty safe bet."

"Do you think any of those men noticed my hair?"

"Probably, but it's not likely that any of them would give us trouble. Forget it."

"All right." Nevertheless, Kate gave a little shiver.

Nick took her arm and started to lead her back across the piazza. "Maybe we'd better get back to the farm. As long as your hair is covered, I don't think there's much danger in our being seen together in public. But it's possible that I'm underestimating the men who are looking for us."

"Do you think of yourself as Italian?" Kate asked as they headed back to the car.

"I don't think of myself as anything, just a citizen of the world."

She stopped, struck by the matter-of-fact tone of his statement. "What do you mean? Everybody thinks of themselves as something."

He hustled her along. "I'm a chameleon. Chameleons don't think of themselves as anything in particular, they just learn to blend in." He unlocked the Fiat's door and saw her into the passenger seat.

When he came around to the driver's seat, Kate said carefully, "Adelina told me your mother died when you were just a baby. That must have been very hard."

"It was hard on my father. He must have really loved her because he more or less fell apart when she died."

"How do you mean?"

Nick shrugged. "Started drinking, started taking too many chances on the track. My mother's family have money. When my father met her, he was working for them as a horse trainer. They were none too pleased when he ran off with their daughter. In fact, they promptly disowned her.''

''That was awfully harsh of them.''

''Yes, but my parents were in love, so they weathered the storm. My father was a talented rider. He was able to support himself and my mother quite well steeplechasing. After he lost my mother, his drinking and his fundamentally reckless nature caught up with him, though. I was in the stands watching when he broke his neck at Sandown.''

''My God!'' Kate gasped. ''That must have been horrible for you!''

As they left the city, Nick shot her a brief glance. ''A lot of kids have had to weather terrible things, and they've survived. Speaking of which, what about you, Kate Humphrey? You mentioned that you're an orphan. How did you lose your parents?''

Kate turned her green gaze back to the window. ''I don't know. I was abandoned when I was an infant. And then the orphanage where I had been left burned down and all the records were destroyed. So if there was ever anything to indicate who I belonged to, it was lost. Not that it matters. Obviously, my mother didn't care anything about me or she wouldn't have just dumped me that way.''

''Tough,'' Nick murmured sympathetically. ''Were you adopted?''

''Yes, and by very nice people. Mother was a music teacher and Dad had a marginal little appliance store. But they were an older couple and by the time I was thirteen I had lost both of them.''

''That really is tough. What happened to you?''

''Foster homes. They weren't so bad. Yesterday when I characterized myself as Cinderella, I was dramatizing. But I was never really happy in any of my foster homes. Music was my big outlet.'' She shot Nick's profile a quick, intuitive glance. "Maybe the way horses and riding have been for you."

"Maybe," he agreed.

"Anyhow, I won a place at a high school for the arts where I was able to continue my piano studies. Actually it was a British woman who got me interested in jazz piano. Marian McPartland came to give a seminar at the school, and her kind of music is all I've ever wanted to play since. When I was seventeen things got bad at my last foster home and I had to quit school and go out on my own. I've been on my own ever since."

"How old are you now?"

"Twenty-six."

Frowning, Nick stared through the windshield. He was just beginning to realize how much he had in common with the woman next to him, except that Kate Humphrey had had things a lot tougher than he ever had.

From what she'd told him, she'd been eight years on her own supporting herself as a musician. He wasn't intimate with the world of jazz-nightclub performers, but he knew enough to guess that she'd spent those years living hand to mouth, scrabbling for jobs that paid pennies and swallowing a lot of disappointments. For a woman, a young and pretty woman, it had to be damned rough. And to stick as long as she had, Kate Humphrey had to be a tough little nut with a lot of guts and determination. Yet she didn't come across that way. To Nick she seemed vulnerable and sensitive and very much in need of a champion.

Nick turned into the track that led to Mario's farm, navigated the rutted little lane and then pulled into the area of hard-packed dirt in front of the house. When he'd shut down the engine, he turned to Kate. She'd long ago removed Adelina's scarf and fluffed out her bright hair. Now, with the late afternoon sun behind her head, the creamy oval of her face seemed wreathed in incandescence.

"Thank you for a very nice afternoon."

Nick watched the prim words fall from her lips. The gloss had long ago disappeared from her mouth, but she didn't need artificial color. Lipstick only blurred the clean, sweet line of her arched upper lip, the soft, full swell of the lower.

"I'm going to do it," Nick said.

"What?"

"This." He reached for her shoulders, drew her toward him and pressed his mouth firmly to hers.

Too startled to react, Kate spent several seconds receiving his kiss passively. Though he'd been in no rush, it had seemed to happen so quickly—his hands on her shoulders lifting her as if she were a lightweight, the blue glint of his eyes between those sooty black lashes, and then the pressure of masculine lips she'd been furtively admiring all afternoon.

Kate had kissed enough men to know when she was in the hands of an expert. Nick Conti's kiss was firm but sensitive, with a silken control that was every instant totally in command. Yet there was nothing rough or insulting in his kiss. It persuaded, cajoled, teased, seduced.

As Kate's mouth softened under Nick's and her lips began to part, she heaved an acquiescent little sigh. One of his hands slipped down to her waist and then around to her back so that he could support her while he deepened the kiss, took it to another stage. Stirred by the solid strength of him, his scent, the texture of his skin, Kate's own hands curled, quivered, lifted to his shoulders and then his neck.

"Nico, Nico!"

Mario came racing around the corner of the house, his piercing tenor cries shattering the cone of silence that a moment before had seemed to enfold Nick and Kate. Abruptly they pulled apart and sat up. Nick pushed open his door and stepped out. "What is it? What's wrong?"

Mario's halo of gray curls stood on end and his arms flailed like windmills. "Come quick, quick. Rudy and Randy, they have big fight with the pigs!"

CHAPTER SIX

"THANKS, MATE," the Cockney taxi driver crowed when he took in the size of Jake's tip. "That's the place, eh?" He pointed at a faded display sign that showed a gigantic stiletto heel crushing the life out of a cartoon drawing of a cockroach-sized man. Then, with a grin and a chipper salute, the driver shot away from the curb.

As the cab vanished into the noisy stream of Chelsea traffic, Jake turned to study the raffish collection of buildings before him. The Yellow Heel nightclub was wedged between a liquor shop and a display window of black leather punk fashions. At this early hour and with the watery sun casting an unflattering light, all three sagging storefronts wore the air of an aging roué whose better days have been left far in the past.

Normally a seedy jazz club like the Yellow Heel was not the sort of place Jake would have troubled to visit in London. His tastes ran more to theater and symphony concerts. Yet immediately after receiving the club's name and address from the detective employed to work with him on the Byrnside case, he'd hopped the on first available flight from Boston.

Inside the Yellow Heel, it took a minute for Jake's eyes to adjust to the gloom. He supposed that late at night with the right sort of audience and performers and with several drinks under one's belt, the place might have a certain bohemian charm. Right now, it had none.

"What can I do fer yer, mate?" a balding little man in a checked shirt asked from behind the bar. "'Fraid we're not yet open for business, but I can get you a pint if you like."

"No, thanks." Jake's gaze had settled on a poster. It reposed in an easel atop the tiny stage at the end of the club and featured a photograph of a busty brunette with a come hither smile and tired eyes. The legend printed in yellow glitter below it read, "The Yellow Heel presents Miss Dusty Durham, Songstress Divine."

Frowning, Jake turned to the man behind the bar. "Is Miss Dusty Durham performing tonight?"

"Indeed she is, indeed she is, and worth waiting for, let me assure you," he declared with a lascivious wink. "Want to make a reservation for dinner with some little bird of your own?"

"No, thanks. I came to see a Miss Kathryn Humphrey. I was told that she played here with a jazz trio called the Grace Notes."

The barman shook his head. "You're too late. That was last week."

"Last week? You mean she doesn't work here anymore?"

"'Fraid not."

While Jake suppressed a groan of frustration, his informant swiped the bar with a damp rag. "Too bad about that," he went on. "Nice kid, very pretty and quite good at ticklin' the ivories. Just not enough oomph, you know."

"Oomph?"

"Myself, I liked her fine. But when it comes to female entertainment the boss likes 'em a little brassier, if you know what I mean. Wanted her to wear a dress that showed more skin and to spend less time playin' the piano and more time smiling at the customers, if you catch my drift.''

"And you don't know where she's gone to?"

"Not an idea, mate."

As Jake shifted his briefcase from his right hand to his left, he contemplated the bone-jarring night he'd spent while his plane bumped its way across the Atlantic through turbulent weather. Disoriented by the time change and bleary-eyed from exhaustion, he'd arrived badly in need of a few hours' decent sleep. Nevertheless, after an interminable customs check at Heathrow he'd dumped his bags at a hotel and grabbed a cab into Soho. Now it was beginning to look as if all that had been in vain.

"Are you sure Miss Humphrey didn't leave some sort of address? It's very important that I contact her."

"Death in the family, something like that?"

"Not quite, but close. It is a family matter."

The barman looked doubtful and began to shake his head. Then suddenly his expression shifted to become a bit more hopeful. "Say, wait just a minute. I do believe I might be able to 'elp you out with that." He threw down his rag, came out into the open and slouched back toward the stage. "Seems to me she did leave a for'arding address. Just a matter of whether or not the boss kep' it aroun', if yer know what I mean."

Jake crossed his fingers and hoped for the best. If this lead were lost, it might take weeks before he could locate the elusive Miss Kate Humphrey. And, unfortunately, his supremely impatient client Owen Byrnside didn't have weeks to lose.

KATE EYED THE TWINS. "It'll be weeks before we get them completely clean."

"You underestimate the power of strong soap and a scrub brush." Nick's teeth flashed as he dumped a bucket of warm water over Rudy and Randy's heads.

While the muddy, bedraggled pair squealed and struggled, Mario held them down with a firm hand.

"Lucky for you two it's like summer out today," Nick declared unsympathetically and went to refill the bucket. As he returned with it, he paused, shading his eyes and staring up at the hills in the distance.

"Something wrong?" Mario called.

"Oh nothing—I just thought I saw a flash of light up there. It's gone now, though."

"Well, hurry up. These kids, they need to be washed."

Grinning, Nick broke into a gallop. "Ready or not, here I come!"

"Aw, can't we just take a shower?" Rudy exclaimed. His protests turned into splutters of consternation as Nick upended another bucket, sluicing away the worst of the loose muck coating his chubby form.

"I no let you in my clean house covered with pig slime," Mario declared stoutly. "*Mama mia,* they stink!" he complained as he began stripping away Randy's ruined clothes.

"It's not our fault your pigs are so mean," the youngster gurgled. As Mario pulled off his shirt, Randy tried to wipe water out of his streaming eyes. But his hands were so filthy that he only made matters worse and ringed his eye sockets with black so that he resembled a raccoon.

"What you think happen when you climb into pigpen and start pulling tails? You think the pigs gonna' like that? How you like I pull your tail?" Mario demanded, tweaking first Rudy's ear and than Randy's. "Maybe it's good my pigs they teach you a lesson!"

While the boys screeched more protests, Nick's merry gaze snagged Kate's. When he winked she choked on the giggle she'd been trying to suppress. The twins had been very naughty, teasing the pigs and then rolling around in the muck with them, and she knew she shouldn't laugh while Mario vented his spleen. But as Rudy and Randy stamped around like a matched set of misbehaving cupids in their birthday suits, they really were a hilarious sight.

"Now that we've rinsed away the loose stuff, it's time for a serious scrub-down," Nick announced. He pushed up the sleeves of his knit shirt and hoisted first one and then the other of the wriggling, protesting twins into the wooden vat Adelina had just filled.

"Ahh! Ooh!" the two young miscreants screeched as they sank into the hot, sudsy water. Instantly it turned a muddy brown from the stubborn dirt that still clung to them.

"Now we fix," Adelina declared and came forward with sponges and scrub brushes, which she distributed to Nick and Mario. Because of her new clothes, Kate had been instructed to stand clear and watch.

It was quite a show. While Mario stood guard, Nick tackled necks, arms and backs, and Adelina set to work on each boy's hair. With one hand Adelina held her nose while with the other she squeezed quantities of shampoo out of a plastic bottle. Then, muttering colorful imprecations, she worked the shampoo up into stiff peaks of foamy lather on Rudy's and Randy's heads.

"Now they look like the *angeli*," she said, standing back to admire the halo of foam she'd created to frame each chubby face.

"But we know they really *demoni*," Mario countered.

Playfully, Nick molded soapy horns out of each boy's hair. "There, that's more like it," he teased.

Taken with their new hairdos, Rudy and Randy started to giggle, too. As Kate chuckled along with them, her gaze was drawn back to Nick. With his muscular forearms bare, his short, dark hair attractively disarrayed and a streak of dirt emphasizing the line of his prominent cheekbone, he appeared younger, more carefree, and handsomer than she'd ever seen him—which was saying something.

Suddenly she remembered what he'd said about being a chameleon. Yet he seemed so at ease here at the farm with Mario and Adelina, so much at home. Kate had never felt that way anywhere in her life. In some sense she'd always been a displaced person.

Wistfully, Kate gazed at Nick, envying him his relaxed confidence, his air of having the situation, no matter what it might be, under control. He also seemed to know exactly how to handle Rudy and Randy, she observed. Yet he wasn't lenient with them—in fact, he was stern, even authoritarian. But he always tempered his authority with just the right touch of humor. It was obvious that they admired him. In fact, he would make a wonderful father, she suddenly thought—as well as a wonderful lover. Or was that just wishful thinking?

Kate's hand flew up to her mouth. All at once her lips seemed to burn, and she felt herself flush as she remembered Nick's kiss. As if he sensed what was going on in her mind, his gaze sought hers and held it for a beat. The instant she was able to gather her wits, Kate looked away. But each knew what the other had been thinking.

Dinner at Mario's farm that night was a festive affair. Adelina lived up to her culinary reputation. The big, old table in the kitchen groaned with steaming platterfuls of pasta laced with mushrooms and prosciutto. This "appetizer" was followed by salad and chicken beaten thin and cooked to melting tenderness in olive oil and spices. Finally, Adelina produced a huge, brightly painted bowl loaded with fresh fruit.

Undaunted by the result of their escapade with the pigs, the boys teased each other unmercifully. But Mario and Adelina seemed merely amused by their antics. "You leave your brother alone," Adelina scolded good-humoredly when Rudy flicked a grape at Randy and scored a bull's-eye on his nose. "What if he grow up to be stronger than you are and beat you black and blue?"

This was a new idea for Rudy. "We're twins. Why should Randy grow up to be stronger than I am?" he demanded.

Adelina shook her head. "You never know." She shot a teasing glance at Mario. "Remember when Eduardo and you have the big fight in the village and he knock you silly?"

Ruefully, Mario shook his grizzled head. "*Sì*, I remember. Such a foolish thing. Eduardo and I, we argue all the time when we were young. But I love him, anyway. The fight between us I remember, but what it was about..." Again, Mario shook his head. "That, I don't remember. Yet it was the reason why Eduardo went to England, and going to England change his life forever."

Kate shot a curious glance at Nick. She knew without asking that Eduardo must have been his father.

The boys left the table to chase around the grape vines. As they pursued each other through the maze of plants, their bat-squeak cries shattered the tranquility of the warm evening. Suddenly there was a yelp of fury. "I think I'd better see what those two are getting up to," Nick said, excusing himself from the table.

While he supervised the twins, Kate helped Adelina clean up. It was a major operation, for the older woman had dirtied every pot in the kitchen.

As Kate scrubbed a big cast-iron skillet, she watched through the window. Using a beat-up old soccer ball Mario had unearthed, Nick and the boys had started a casual game. Again, she observed that Nick handled Randy and Rudy very well. Though he reprimanded them occasionally, they didn't seem to resent him for it. How could she ever have worried that he might do them harm? Now that she knew him better, the notion of Nick as a kidnapper of children seemed utterly impossible. Yet other things about him were far less clear, Kate thought as her gaze followed his lithe figure.

It was unsettling how the more she learned about the man, the less she felt she really knew. There was something different about Nick, something mysterious and complicated—and dangerous. Kate sensed that enigma hidden just beneath his sleek, rather conventionally good-looking surface, and despite herself, she was intrigued and attracted by what she knew should have warned her away.

And then there was his kiss and her melting response to it. It was stupid, foolish, totally illogical to want it to happen again—but she did. God help her, she did.

The night after she'd bedded the boys down, Kate returned to the parlor with her travel book. But she was too restless to read, and after ten futile minutes of trying to concentrate on a description of Etruscan graves in Tarquinia, she threw it down. Outside she could hear Nick and Mario joking with each other as they emptied out the old wine vat in which the children had bathed. The close harmony of their male laughter, Mario's tenor, Nick's baritone, resonated on the evening air almost like music.

Kate went to the antique piano that occupied a far corner of the room and removed the dusty red-velvet cloth that covered its keyboard. Experimentally, she ran her fingers along the ivories. She had expected to find Mario's piano horribly out of tune. To her surprise, it was no worse than some of the nightclub instruments she'd encountered.

Smiling, Kate sat down on the padded leather stool, adjusted its height and then struck several light chords. Music had always been her solace. No matter how troubling, difficult and disappointing life was, she could always turn to music. Kate had a large repertoire. She could play almost any request and had worked out distinctive arrangements of all the classics. She also had tunes of her own that she'd composed and arranged. Lately she'd begun to do more and more of that.

Tonight she started with some of her favorite old standards from Duke Ellington and Johnny Mercer. Then she moved to show tunes of the thirties and forties. She'd just finished rather languorous versions of "Smoke Gets in Your Eyes" and "Our Love is Here to Stay" when a faint noise made her lift her hands and turn her head.

"Nick! How long have you been sitting there?"

"I don't know. Twenty minutes, possibly." His legs were stretched out before him; his cupped palms cradled the back of his head.

"Where's Mario?"

"Gone to take Adelina home. You're very good, you know."

"I..." Kate swiveled around on the bench and folded her hands in her lap. "Thank you."

"Do you sing like an angel as well as look and play like one?"

"I haven't got much of a voice. I'm strictly an instrumentalist. It's a handicap. Nightclub managers would like me better if I were more of a singer and less of a pianist."

Nick nodded. "Yes, I can see that." He looked at her thoughtfully, as if he were adjusting to the idea of seeing her differently. "I suppose I shouldn't admit it, but I didn't expect you'd be as good as you are."

"Why is that?"

"You're so young and pretty. I couldn't picture you playing jazz, which I think of as fairly tough and masculine. I expect that makes me sound an awful chauvinist."

"Yes, it does," Kate replied seriously, not acquitting him, "but it's nothing new. I ran into that attitude a lot." Her soft mouth took on a faintly bitter cast as she thought of the humiliations she'd endured in her chosen profession. There were times when she'd practically gone down on her knees for a job and been rejected anyway. So often the men who booked performers refused to believe she could be as good a jazz pianist as a man. And then there were her male colleagues, who'd sometimes resented her professionalism and wanted to undermine it by exploiting her femininity.

"If it's so tough, why do you stick with it?" Nick asked curiously.

"Why? Because music is what I want to do. It's my life."

He nodded and sat forward. "I should have known what your answer would be. I used to feel the same way about riding."

"Don't you anymore?"

"My life is still horses, but I don't have to be on their backs. Speaking of which," he glanced over at the marble clock, "I was intending to check on Cesare's hoof when your playing stopped me in my tracks. Care to walk out there with me now?"

"Oh, I don't know."

He cocked his head. "Afraid I might try to kiss you again?"

Kate swallowed. "Yes, actually. Things were getting very warm in that car before we were interrupted."

"Do you want me to apologize to you for that?"

"I..."

He held up a hand. "Kate, I have no intention of apologizing. I enjoyed that kiss far too much and so, I think, did you."

She couldn't deny it.

He grinned crookedly. "Listen, if you'll come with me, I'll promise to try to behave myself. I'd just like to talk to you, get to know you better. Wouldn't you like to know a little more about me? I'll bet you have some good stories to tell about your nightclub days."

"I do, but are you sure you really want to hear them?"

"Absolutely."

That smile of his was irresistible. Despite all her doubts, Kate dissolved under the charm of it. She replaced the red velvet on the keyboard. "Okay, but just for a little while."

As they strolled across the yard to the barn, Nick asked Kate about her first job.

"It was in a tiny little bar in Detroit's Greektown." Kate shook her head. "I lasted a week."

"Why? What went wrong?"

"Two customers got into a fight over me. They were the ones who were out of line, but I was the one fired."

"Has that been a consistent theme during your career?"

"It's happened more than once, but what's more likely is that jobs just fade away or someone I'm playing with has problems that mess the gig up and everyone gets stranded. That's partly what happened at the Yellow Heel."

"The place in London where you were working?"

"Yes." She thought of Billy and winced. "The trumpet player missed a couple of performances. Then when the manager wanted me to wear a dress with tacky cutouts on the front and I refused, he fired us. The wind man and bass player were furious at me for not wanting to sit in front of a nightclub audience with my breasts practically bared."

Nick was silent a moment, absorbing that. "You must have had some successes to have stuck with it this long."

"A few. I've had some good jobs in Florida. Last year I played for months at a little place in Chicago. If it hadn't folded when it lost its liquor license, I'd be there still. And several critics have written some nice pieces about me. But that's not what keeps me going."

"Then what keeps you going?" Nick asked. He switched on the electric lantern and let her into the darkened barn.

"The music," she answered simply. "It's what I want to do, that's all. I can't imagine getting through life without it."

"I understand, and I admire your dedication. But for a woman with a mission I'd say you've been seriously sidetracked," Nick commented. As they walked back through the warm dark barn to Cesare's stall, the straw littering the hard-packed earth crunched and whispered beneath their feet. Animals rustled in their enclosures, their earthy fragrances lacing the close atmosphere with a pungent tang.

"What do you mean?"

"I mean here you are baby-sitting the Misbehavior Twins, a long way from the nearest nightclub or music critic." Nick shone his torch on Cesare's stall. Then he set it down on top of a rail and, murmuring a litany of meaningless but comforting phrases, he opened the stall door and went in. After feeding Cesare a piece of apple, he ran his fingers lightly over the animal's haunches and then lowered himself to check the horse's feet.

With her hands in her pockets, Kate stood watching. As long as she didn't have to get too close to him, the old stallion was beautiful, she thought. In the shadowy light his gray coat shimmered like a ghost's. Kate's gaze played over the curved half-moon of his neck, the bunched muscles of his hindquarters, the strong yet slender legs. Then her gaze went to Nick, squatting there, his own leg muscles bunched beneath the fabric of his slacks.

"The same could be said of you," she commented. "Right now you're a long way from the horse-racing section in England."

"True, but I intend doing something about that tomorrow."

"Tomorrow?"

Nodding, Nick got to his feet and, after giving Cesare's rump one last friendly pat, exited the stall. "First thing in the morning I'm going to drive back to Rome."

"Yes, you mentioned that at lunch. You're going to see the boys' father."

"That's the idea."

Unconsciously, Kate began to twist her hands together. "Are you going alone?"

"Of course. You and the twins will stay here where you're safe."

"But what about you? Will you be safe?"

Nick shrugged and lay his arm along the top of the stall door. "There's no reason why LaFiore's enemies should want to harm me. It's his friends I need to worry about. They're the ones who've been making trouble because I've agreed to ride Seasonwine."

"Isn't it possible that you might run into them in Rome, that LaFiore might sic them on you?"

Nick looked unfazed. "It's possible, but I don't think it will happen."

"Why not?"

"Because I'm in a position to exert some leverage on LaFiore, myself. I've got something which I have to presume he values. I've got his sons."

Kate stared back at Nick in shock. A sick feeling began to spread through her. "You mean you'd use Rudy and Randy to blackmail their father?"

In the lantern's yellow glow, Nick's blue eyes held her green ones. "Do you think there's any possibility I would ever harm those two youngsters?"

Kate swallowed. Her throat ached and her breath came out in a rasp. "No," she said, and knew she would stake her life on it. Whatever else he might be, Nick Conti was simply not a villain. She was convinced of the fact.

"You're right, I wouldn't. But LaFiore can't know that for certain."

"So you're going to threaten to harm them?" Kate found that notion almost as distasteful as the real thing.

"No, because I don't happen to be a liar, either. But I have rescued the twins, and I am, to the best of my ability, keeping them safe. I think LaFiore may appreciate that fact enough to call off his dogs. At any rate, I intend to find out."

Kate sighed. But her relief was short-lived. Nick was going to put himself in danger, she realized. Suddenly, as she gazed at him, a rush of tender emotion swept over her. He looked so attractive standing there. The fine-boned, rather aristocratic features he must have inherited from his mother's side of the family were leavened by the curly abundance of his thick, dark hair, the squareness of his jaw, the muscled strength of his wiry frame.

She couldn't stop herself from touching the back of his hand where it lay along the top of the stall door. "I'm going to be worried sick about you."

"Whew, that's a change of pace, isn't it? Only yesterday you were wishing me to the devil."

"Yes," she admitted. She knew she should take her hand away. Instead, she ran her finger down the length of tendon mapped just below the surface of his tanned skin.

Beneath her hand, he went very still and his flesh seemed to grow warmer. Or perhaps it was she who was generating the sudden heat.

"You're not helping me to keep that promise I made about behaving myself," he said huskily.

"I know." Self-consciously, she lifted her hand. "Oh Nick, couldn't you wait another day? Do you really have to go tomorrow?"

"Yes, I must. But there's something else I have to do first." He reached out and drew her to him. As before in the car, it wasn't sudden, but slow and steady. Kate had plenty of time to pull back or shake her head or otherwise protest.

Instead, her skin quivered at his closeness, her bones seemed to liquefy beneath his touch and her mouth lifted to his.

"I'd like to finish what I started back in that car," Nick murmured.

"Men's ideas about finishing what they start are different from women's."

"Men have a lot of ideas which are vastly different from women's. That's part of what makes life interesting. Umm, if you only knew the ideas in my head right now." He brushed his lips against her forehead and then her eyebrows.

It was the simplest of caresses, yet it undid Kate. She felt strange, confused, almost as if she were awake inside a dream. Her hands stole up to his shoulders and clung. She tilted her head while his mouth moved to hers, kissing her ever so lightly. He pulled back just a fraction of an inch and murmured. "You smell of lemon soap and fresh air."

"And you smell of horse and straw and grass."

"Nature Girl and Nature Boy—we must be a well-matched pair."

She kept looking into his eyes as he pulled her to sit on a bale of hay to the left of the stallion's door. Intimately, the length of Nick's side pressed against hers. He put his arm around her and, slowly, almost as if she were floating, she turned toward him and closed her eyes.

They kissed again. This time it was long and slow and sweet. Drugged by the honeyed sweetness, Kate sagged against him and gave herself up to all the lovely sensations coursing through her. Then suddenly Nick's kiss stopped being merely sweet and became insistent, urgent, demanding. As his arms enveloped her body, pulling her close, his kiss deepened and he plundered her mouth with his tongue. Overwhelmed, Kate moaned, answered his intimate invasion, grasped the sides of his back and clung. But when Nick started to lower her back against the hay, she realized fully what he was doing and where this was leading. She opened her eyes and her arm stiffened, suddenly keeping him at bay.

"There's no one to see us here but the animals," he whispered.

"I know."

"Then what is it? Don't you want to make love with me?"

"I do, and I don't."

"Just at the moment I'm not up to anything that complicated. You'll have to explain your dos and don'ts."

"I'm sorry. Part of me wants to, but the other part knows this is stupid. I'm behaving stupidly."

"Which part is going to win the debate?"

Kate braced her free hand against the hay and pushed herself back up into a sitting position. "Nick, I don't know you. In a few days we'll be strangers again."

"Strangers can be lovers."

"But I don't want to love anybody. I don't want to fall in love. It hurts too much, and in the end it's always a mistake."

Through the shadows he gazed at her. Then he leaned away and straightened. "You're much more cynical than you look, but all right." In a fluid movement, he rose to his feet. "Time to go?"

"Yes." Sitting alone on the hay bale, Kate felt lost, abandoned. He put out a hand to help her up, and she took it. When she was on her feet beside him, he brushed some hay from her skirt. Then he picked up the lantern and walked with her back out of the barn and up to the house.

"Good night," he said when they parted at the kitchen door. "Thanks for the concert. I enjoyed it." He reached out and ruffled her hair. "And thanks for the company. I enjoyed that, too."

"No hard feelings?"

"Of course not." He gave her hand a friendly squeeze and then, still carrying the lantern, turned and walked off into the shadows.

GERALDINE BRASSWELL was a tiny woman who just at the moment resembled an angry robin. As she faced Jake Caine, she pressed her high-heel-clad, disproportionately thin legs together stiffly, and her puffed breasts, which were encased in a bright red sweater, quivered with distrust.

"I've no idea where Miss Humphrey might be. She didn't tell me what her plans were, I'm sure."

Jake tried to look harmless. "She didn't leave an address where you might forward her mail?"

"I said I'd no idea, didn't I?"

Jake studied Mrs. Brasswell's pursed mouth and round suspicious eyes. It was hopeless, he decided. She might know more than she was admitting, but she wasn't going to give away any information to the likes of him. Politely, he handed her his card with the address and phone number of his hotel written on the back and asked her to please let him know if she should hear from Miss Humphrey.

Mrs. Brasswell took it between her thumb and forefinger and held it at arm's length as if it might be contaminated. "Foster, Brighton and Caine—you're from an American law firm, are you? Katie, I mean Miss Humphrey, isn't in trouble, is she?"

"Oh no, nothing like that."

The little woman stuffed the card into her pocket. "Well, I'm afraid I can't help you, because I doubt I'll hear from Miss Humphrey again. She was just passing through, y'know."

"Well, if you do—"

"Yes, if I do—all right." And with that, Mrs. Brasswell shut the door in Jake's face.

If Jake Caine had been the kind of man who let his broad shoulders droop, they surely would have slumped. First the disappointment of not finding his quarry at the Yellow Heel, and now this. He'd had a long, difficult day, and so far it looked as if it was all going to be for nothing.

As Jake hailed a taxi, he considered his options. He'd already contacted the detective on the case and put him back out on the elusive Miss Humphrey's trail. The man knew his business, and Jake felt confident that eventually he'd track her down. But Jake wasn't the type who could twiddle his thumbs while someone else struggled to accomplish a job he wanted done.

"Byrnside Enterprises," Jake told the cab driver and gave him the address of the multistoried glass-and-steel building where the recording branch of the Byrnside empire had its London offices.

Twenty minutes later a glossy-looking receptionist announced him and he strolled into the plushly furnished inner sanctum of Winston Deeping.

"Jake, my dear fellow, good to see you in London again," Deeping exclaimed heartily as he came out from behind his acre of gleaming rosewood desk. "To what do I owe this honor?"

While Jake shook Deeping's hand, he ran an assessing eye over his slim, pinstripe-suited person. Attractive, affable, impeccably dressed and blessed with a winning smile and a British public school accent, Winston Deeping had worked his way up through the ranks of the Byrnside empire. Now he was in the very highest echelon and perfectly positioned to take over even more power when Byrnside himself finally let go of the reins.

"I've come on a private matter, actually," Jake said, "and what I'm going to reveal to you is privileged information, that should go no further than this room."

"My lips are sealed and my ears are open."

After Jake had sunk down into the chair Winston offered and accepted a much-needed cup of strong, black coffee, he succinctly outlined his problem with regard to Kate Humphrey.

When Jake finished, Deeping ran a hand through his silvery gray hair. "My word, what a tangle. So you're actually going to be chasing about the planet hunting for three girls who might or might not be Owen Byrnside's granddaughter. Sounds dotty to me, if you don't mind my saying so."

"Maybe it's dotty, as you say, but that's what Owen wants. He doesn't want to die without knowing whether he's leaving someone of his own behind. If this girl exists, he's determined to find her. And I'm the one he's commissioned to do it." Jake took a sip of his coffee. "I just hope I don't disappoint him."

Winston nodded. "Yes, it's annoying if you've done all this traveling for nothing. My heart goes out to you. But Jake, why have you come to me with this? Do you think I can help you?"

"Possibly." Jake put his cup down. "You're at the top of a very large and very successful recording company. Your talent scouts are running around all over the place. Kate Humphrey is a musician who's been performing at various clubs for years now. Surely it's possible you may have a file on her."

"I suppose it's possible," Deeping admitted. He stood for a moment tapping his high-bridged nose and thinking. Then he smiled. "Look, I'll put the word out and see what I can do. It may take some time, but if I come up with anything useful, you'll be the first to know." He leaned against the edge of his desk and smiled affably down at Jake. "Now, my friend, since this is your first night in London and you've had a hellish day, what about dinner at my club? The chef there does a delicious sorrel soup and a truly excellent trout Florentine."

CHAPTER SEVEN

"WHERE'S NICK?" Randy wanted to know when they came down to breakfast the next morning.

"Gone to *Roma*," Mario said with a faint frown.

"To Rome!" The boys stared at each other. "What's he want to do that for?"

"He have business in *Roma*, important business."

While Mario set a pitcher of fresh milk on the table, Kate busied herself slicing bread. Nick must have left very early, she reflected as she glanced out the window at the vacant spot where the Fiat had been parked.

After the scene between them in the barn and their awkward parting, Kate had spent a restless night. She felt tired and irritable. A million questions and worries seemed to pound just behind her temples.

"Can we feed the pigs this morning?" Randy asked as he slathered an inch of butter on a roll.

Mario's frown turned into a scowl. "You stay away from those pigs. I no want you make those pigs crazy again."

"I'll go out with the kids," Kate intervened. "I'll make sure they don't get into trouble."

"Not even *Santo Francesco* himself could guarantee such a thing," Mario muttered darkly. But he relented, and after breakfast Kate followed Rudy and Randy outdoors with some chicken feed and a bucket of scraps from breakfast and last night's dinner.

A chill wind from the north scudded through the trees. "Looks as if it might rain," Kate commented. She glanced up at the overcast sky and pulled the edges of the sweater Mario had lent her tight over her chest. The boys, who wore heavy clothes Adelina had found for them, seemed untroubled by the change in the weather. In fact, since coming to the farm they had been merrier than Boy Scouts on a spree.

"Oh, look at the way that fat black-and-white one goes for the pasta," Rudy cried after they dumped the pail into the pig trough. "Mario says she's going to have piglets in a week or two."

"She certainly looks as if she's going to have *something*," Kate agreed, eyeing the animal's drooping belly. "Aren't you ashamed of yourselves for teasing her?"

"She didn't mind," Randy maintained stoutly. "She liked a bit of fun!"

Despite herself, Kate chuckled. Then suddenly, her laughter died and she shivered.

"What's wrong?" Rudy asked, seeing the changed expression on her face.

"I don't know. I just had the feeling someone was watching us."

"The pigs are watching us."

"Yes, that's probably it." Kate draped a reassuring arm on each of the youngsters' shoulders. Nevertheless, she lifted her head and looked up beyond the pigsty to the hills in the distance. There was nothing to see there, only mist and the tufted contours of trees and vines. Yet she shivered again and tightened her grip on the twins. "I think we'd better get back to the house," she said. "I think it's going to rain."

A MILE AWAY a burly man with unshaven cheeks lowered a pair of high-powered binoculars and made a disgusted noise. "It's going to rain. I just felt a drop," he said in Italian.

"Franco, a little rain won't make you melt," his partner, a rat-thin fellow with a puckered scar on his cheek retorted. "What's she doing now?"

"Taking LaFiore's brats back to the house."

"They'd be easier to get if they stayed out in the open."

"They'll be easy to get inside the house. Now that the jockey's gone, there's only an old man with them. He won't put up much of a fight."

"He'd better not." Vincente, the man with the scarred cheek, screwed a silencer onto the end of his handgun and gave his partner an evil grin. "Ready to take shelter from the rain with a pretty little redhead?"

Franco laughed and winked. "Very ready."

MANY MILES AWAY in Rome, Nick had been cooling his heels in a waiting room of the police station for two hours, and he was losing his patience. Once again he strode up to the officer guarding the desk.

"It's almost noon. When am I going to be allowed to see Mr. LaFiore?"

"You'll have to wait until your request has been processed," the stern clerk informed him in clipped Italian.

"And when is that going to happen? In a week or two?" Meaningfully, Nick glanced at the clock on the wall. "I need to see Mr. LaFiore today, now. The matter concerns his children and is very urgent."

Despite Nick's protestations, it was another hour before a gimlet-eyed police officer escorted him to a room where he was then thoroughly searched. Finally, however, Nick was led into another barren little chamber where he found a pale and grim-faced Lou LaFiore waiting, seated at a table. Another guard stood directly behind him.

"What about my kids?" Lou said without preliminaries. "Where are they?"

"They're in Italy, and they're fine. Your boys had a little trouble when they arrived in Rome, but they're fine," Nick assured his former employer and the man who was now his declared enemy.

Lou eyed Nick suspiciously. "How do you fit into the picture, Conti?" LaFiore was a heavyset man with a thick neck, blunt features, a receding line of thin dark hair and wary eyes the color and hardness of anthracite. "How do you happen to know about my kids? And why aren't they with their mother in London?" His heavy lids drooped. "You and she still fooling around?"

"Jillian and I never fooled around, Lou." Nick pulled out a chair opposite and straddled it.

"Oh yeah? That wasn't her story."

"What Jillian told you about her and me was just that, a story. I'm not such a fool that I would help my employer's wife to cheat on him."

"You've got a reputation with the women, and Jilly can be very persuasive."

Nick dismissed that. "You neglected her and she was bored. She made up a little fantasy about me and her just to get your attention. And that's all there ever was to it."

Lou went on looking unconvinced. "You didn't answer my question, Conti. Why aren't my kids home safe in London?"

"You didn't know Jillian was sending them out to stay with you?" Nick was surprised.

Lou shook his head heavily. "If she ever sent word, I never got it. But then, you might say the last couple of weeks before I was taken into protective custody here were pretty confused."

Nick could imagine. To agree to testify against his mob connections, Lou must have been terrified for his life.

"Anything that looked like a letter bomb I didn't open," Lou said. "A lot of things went past me—a lot of things that otherwise I would have taken care of, all neat and tidy!"

From the grim look on his former boss's face, Nick knew that he referred to the—thus far unsuccessful—attempts to keep him from riding Seasonwine in the Grand National.

Nick's own tightly controlled expression became grimmer. "Let me fill you in on what's been happening, so we'll both know where we're coming from."

Tersely, he outlined his meeting with Kate on the train and their harrowing escape from Rome. Though he told Lou that his boys were now safely hidden away, he did not tell him where. Nor did he allow his expression to accurately mirror his attitude toward the situation. If there was one thing Nick had learned from experience, it was how to deal with bullies. Perhaps that was the most important lesson his expensive but lonely and humiliating boarding-school education had taught him.

"Now let me see if I've got this straight," Lou finally said. "Jillian hired this Humphrey bird to bring Rudy and Randy to Rome, and she's taking care of them still?"

"That's right."

Like Nick's, Lou's eyes gave nothing away and his blunt-featured face remained impassive. It was impossible to guess what was really going on behind that carefully controlled exterior. But Nick knew Lou to be a man of strong and violent passions. Perhaps gratitude was too much to expect from him. But surely he must be relieved to know that his offspring were, for the moment at least, safe.

"Well, I guess I owe you one, Conti," he finally muttered.

Nick leaned back in his chair and waited tensely.

"While all this was going on, I never thought to worry about my kids." Lou glanced around at the bleak little room and hooked an ironic thumb at the guard who still stood at the ready directly behind his chair. "Trust Jillian to shoot the twins off to me at just the wrong time. She always did know exactly when to do the wrong thing."

It was true enough, Nick reflected. Two years ago Jillian LaFiore's willful bad timing had been responsible for ruining his career. For a lark, she'd tried to seduce him. And when he'd rebuffed her, she'd vented her frustration and anger by lying to her husband about the episode. The result had been the devastating crack-up at Aintree. For Nick was certain that Lou, in a fit of jealousy, had engineered the accident that had put Seasonwine out of commission and had broken what seemed like half the bones in his body.

"But Rudy and Randy are still in Italy, you say."

"Yes, safely hidden."

"Conti, I don't care how well hidden you think they are, as long as they're in this country they're not safe. I know the men I'm testifying against. I may not make it out of this in one piece, but I'm cornered, so I don't have any choice. It's them or me. But I don't want my boys dragged into it."

For an instant, Lou's mask slipped and Nick saw how deeply he felt about his sons, how frantically worried he was for their safety.

"What can I do to help?" Nick said. There'd been a time early on when he'd thought to bargain with LaFiore.

But he'd long ago realized he'd do whatever he could to save Rudy and Randy, whether or not their father called off the vendetta against him.

"Is this Humphrey woman someone I can trust?"

An image of Kate came into Nick's mind. He could see the freckles lightly dusting her creamy skin, her eyes like semiprecious stones behind the fringe of her burnished lashes, her fiery hair backlit by the sun. "Yes. Take my word for it, the young lady's pure gold."

LaFiore's heavy jaw worked. "Can you get my kids back to their hoity-toity grandparents in England?"

"I can try."

"Do that and we'll be quits."

"Quits?"

"Don't play games. You know what I'm saying, Conti. I'll call off my men. You won't need to worry any more about being hassled when you climb aboard Seasonwine for the Grand National. Is it a deal?"

Nick had already decided to help Rudy and Randy to safety no matter what, but he would have been a fool to turn down LaFiore's offer. "Deal," he said and gave the man's hand a firm shake.

Lou leaned forward and whispered gruffly, "Be careful on your way out."

"What do you mean?"

"You were right not to bring Rudy and Randy here. The place crawls with spies. Just be careful."

As NICK LEFT the police station, he turned his collar up against the light rain weeping down from overcast skies and made a point of not looking around. He knew that he wouldn't see any familiar faces. He also knew that he was being watched. The hairs on the back of his neck tingled like radio antennae picking up enemy static. Somehow he had to get himself safely out of Rome without being followed. But how?

Nonchalantly, he sauntered along the broad avenue, stopping periodically under awnings to peer into shop windows featuring the latest Italian fashions. He even bought a paper and got out of the rain and into a restaurant for a dish of pasta lightly seasoned with a basil sauce. No wine—he'd need all his wits about him. After spending a leisurely hour sipping cappuccino and perusing his paper, he used a public phone to see if he could line up an ally.

Carlo Tipola was a distant cousin who'd made a killing in the export business. He also happened to be a race-car driver and loved, in reverse order, wine, women, adventure and fancy cars. Of the latter, he usually owned at least three, all of which were kept in immaculate shape.

"Nico!" Carlo exclaimed, his tone filling with pleasure as he recognized Nick's voice on the other end of the phone line. "So my *inglese* cousin finally takes time off from his racehorses for a little *dolce vita*. We go out on the town tonight, no?"

"No," Nick answered and, casting a sideways glance out of the corner of his eye, gave a no-frills explanation of his situation.

"That sounds serious," Carlo answered soberly when at last Nick had made him understand. "Now let me guess what you need. You want a fast car, yes?"

"Yes. The sooner the better. Can you help?"

"What a question! Of course I can help. I was having a boring day. Now you give me something interesting to do with the rest of the afternoon."

Nick grinned, picturing the boyish glee that was probably lighting up his cousin's handsome black eyes.

"Let me see," Carlo was going on. "You like a Ferrari or a Lamborghini? The Lamborghini is *una bella macchina*, but its transmission just a bit stiff. The Ferrari is bright red and not inconspicuous, but it go like the wind."

"The Ferrari sounds fine."

"*Bene.* In half an hour I pick you up and we lose your not-so-friendly companions. Then I fix you up with something a little less noticeable. *Ciao,* cowboy."

"*Ciao.*"

Carlo appeared exactly on the dot. As Nick pretended to loiter in front of a magazine stand, a gleaming red, low-slung racing machine suddenly roared out of traffic and screeched to a stop directly in front of him. Carlo pushed open the door, and Nick leaped in. Carlo didn't even wait for Nick to shut the door before hurtling back out into traffic.

"Howdy, cowboy," he chortled. Grinning merrily, he darted in and out of the Roman traffic like some large, exotic hummingbird. "We have ourselves some fun, yes?"

"That all depends on what you find amusing." Nick craned his neck to look around. They were being followed, all right. Behind them a black Lancia hurtled through traffic almost as heedlessly as Carlo was doing. Without slackening his breathtaking speed an iota, Nick's fearless cousin swerved around a corner, through a series of narrow alleys and out into a rain-slick roundabout. The Lancia stuck like glue.

"Now I show them some fancy driving," Carlo murmured through his teeth. He was grinning like a crazed ape, Nick thought, obviously enjoying himself tremendously. Nick was having a somewhat less amusing time. As their pursuer had rounded another corner an instant earlier, Nick had caught the dull flash of a gun barrel.

"Nice seeing you, Carlo," he muttered as the Ferrari screeched through a narrow alley.

"Good to see you, Nico."

"Sorry we have to meet under these circumstances. 'Fraid we're not going to have much of a chance for a get together. Listen, old chap, I think they mean to take a potshot at us," Nick warned his cousin.

"They wouldn't dare."

"Oh, yes, I think they would."

"Then I take them on a roller-coaster ride they never forget."

Suddenly the red Ferrari was whipping around corners and through narrow lanes like a demented falcon. When they lost sight of their pursuers long enough, Carlo pulled the Ferrari into a garage, braked to a shuddering stop and pointed at a sedate blue Cortina. "The keys are in the ignition. I'll take care of your Fiat. *Ciao,* cowboy."

"Ciao," Nick said with a grin and a salute as he settled into the inconspicuous little car. Then Carlo was gone and Nick was pulling out into traffic past the bewildered pair of thugs in the black Lancia who were looking around in vain for an erratic red Ferrari.

"I'M BORED," Randy declared.

"Me, too," Rudy echoed.

All morning a steady drizzle had kept the boys indoors. Kate had been trying everything she could think of to keep them amused. With a set of pencils Mario had tucked away in a drawer, she'd drawn pictures for them to color. She'd baked cookies and told stories. But none of these ploys held their attention for long. "What if I give you two a piano lesson?" she suggested.

The twins looked doubtful. "What do you know about pianos?" Randy queried.

Kate shot him an amused smile. "Oh, I know a thing or two. Come on into the parlor and let me show you." Though it was obvious when the boys followed her to Mario's old piano that they expected whatever she had in mind to be a failure, their bored expressions became animated when she started to play a popular rock tune, embellishing it with variations as she went along.

"Hello, that's bang on!" Rudy complimented her.

"See, what I tell you?" Mario commented as he came through the archway. "Your *bellissima* nanny, she's very talented. You should appreciate her more. Not try and drive her crazy all the time like you do."

"We do so appreciate her," Randy declared. "We like her fine. We like her almost as much as we do Nick."

Kate laughed. "Oh, thanks a million."

Mario shot her a sly wink. "I think Nick like you a whole much better than he do these *demoni*."

"Oh I don't know. For all his complaints about them, Nick seems to get along with the boys pretty well," Kate said.

Turning back to the piano, she bent over the keyboard so as not to let the blush creeping into her cheeks give her away. Nick had been on her mind all morning. What was he doing now, she wondered. Was he safe? She couldn't help but worry. The thought of anything bad happening to him horrified her. Images of that terrible crash she'd seen on television kept playing through her mind—even though the trouble Nick might run into in Rome was of an entirely different sort.

Half the night she'd lain awake, thinking about Nick, replaying the feel of his lips on hers. She'd thought herself in love before, but never had a man seemed more appealing to her than Nick Conti. It was worrisome.

"Someday Nick, he make a fine papa," Mario declared.

"You think so?"

"I know so. He just has to find the right girl."

"Oh? Somehow I don't get the impression that Nick is seriously looking for Miss Right."

Mario shrugged. "Is true, Nick no anxious to settle down and start his family. Miss Right, maybe she has to go looking for him. What do you think?"

Kate opened her mouth to reply when there was a sudden splintering crash. The front door burst open, rocked back on its hinges and two men rushed in. One was thickly built, with a mustache and shaggy eyebrows. The other was thin and shifty-eyed. They both carried guns.

As they hurtled into the room, Kate whirled around on the piano bench. Mario let out a hoarse exclamation and ran forward to strike out at one of the assailants. The thickset man hit him a vicious blow which sent him reeling against the horsehair sofa. Meanwhile, the thin intruder had seized the boys and wrapped an arm around their necks so that he could wave his gun at their heads.

As she gazed into the thickset man's glittering, snake-like eyes, Kate's scream died on her lips. "What . . . what do you want?"

"Get your coat on, *signorina*," he replied. His lips curled into a suggestive smile. "You gonna come with us and find out what we want."

NICK BEGAN TO HUM. All during his first hour of driving out of Rome, he'd been nervous about being followed. He'd glanced up at his rearview mirror so many times that his neck was beginning to develop a crick. But now that he was out on the less-traveled country roads he began to re-

lax. He was certain that, with Carlo's help, he'd given his
pursuers the slip and all was well.

Thinking about his crazy cousin, Nick grinned. He'd
have to tell Kate about Carlo, he thought. He'd bet she'd
like him. Most women did. And he knew that Carlo would
certainly like her. No, on second thought Nick decided,
maybe he'd not mention either of them to the other.

Nick was slightly startled by the hot streak of jealousy
that shot through him at the thought of Kate and his
cousin hitting it off. What was going on here? Unconsciously, he slowed the car slightly.

Last night in the barn he'd wanted to make love with
Kate—wanted it badly. She was exciting—exciting to hold
to touch, to look at, to talk to, even to argue with.

When she'd rejected him, he'd tried to let her think he
was taking her decision casually. But the truth of the matter was that he hadn't gotten much sleep last night.
Knowing that she was in the same house had made it
worse. He'd kept imagining her asleep, her breasts rising
and falling gently with each breath, her lashes brushing her
cheek, her lips soft and slightly parted. Even now he could
evoke the feel of her mouth against his, the weight of her
slim body in his arms.

As the lower part of Nick's body heated, his foot began
to press a touch more heavily on the accelerator. Suddenly
he was anxious to get back to the farm so that he could see
her, talk to her. They had to make plans to return the children to England, he told himself.

When he turned into the lane that led up to the farm,
however, he began to get a sense that something was
wrong. It was nothing specific, just an oppressive silence
that began to weigh on him.

"Mario!" he called, rolling down the window when he
came to a stop in front of the house. But there was no an-

swer, and no movement other than the chickens scratching for seeds in the damp earth.

Frowning, Nick got out of the car and walked around to the kitchen. "Mario!" He opened the door and stepped in. "Kate!"

The house remained eerily silent. Nick scratched his head. Could they be in the barn? he wondered. He was about to turn and go back out when some instinct made him head for the front parlor. Once again, the hairs on the back of his neck prickled. Even before he turned the corner he knew that something was very wrong.

Nevertheless, his stomach roiled when he saw the broken door, the overturned furniture. For a second he stood staring at it all, paralyzed. *Kate,* he thought. Oh, God! He'd been too complacent, bringing them here and imagining they'd be safe. What had happened? Where were they? Were they even still alive? And what about Mario?

Nick sprinted outside, took a quick look around at the deserted farmyard and then, with his heart thudding an alarm in his chest, began checking each of the outbuildings for some sign, some clue.

The chicken house yielded nothing, but when Nick opened the toolshed door he saw a crumpled figure huddled in the corner of the musty little building. "Mario!"

Mario was tied hand and foot and part of his shirt had been torn away and stuffed into his mouth. Blood stained his forehead and his eyes were closed.

"Mario!" Anxiously, Nick bent over him and checked his pulse. It still beat. Assured that his uncle was still alive, he used his pocket knife to cut away the older man's bonds and then sprinted to the pump to get water. A few minutes later, using a basin and a clean rag, he began to clean Mario's bloodied forehead.

"Ohh, *mama mia*," Mario groaned. "My head!" His eyes fluttered open and he raised a hand to the wound at his temple. "Ohh."

"Mario, are you all right? Tell me what happened. Where are Kate and the boys?"

"Nico?" For several seconds Mario's eyes were unfocused. Then light began to come into them. "Nico? Oh, Nico, such a terrible thing happen! Terrible! Terrible!"

CHAPTER EIGHT

"Ahh!" Kate stumbled over a tree root and pitched to her knees.

Roughly, Vincente, the smaller of her two captors, grabbed her arm and yanked her back to her feet. "Watch your step, *signorina*. I wouldn't want you to hurt yourself," he insinuated into her ear in a nasty parody of courtesy.

Ignoring Vincente's moist, onion-scented breath and evil grin, Kate pulled away and shot an agonized look at the boys. Like a matched set of miniature felons, Rudy and Randy trudged along in front of Franco, the larger of their jailers. After Franco and Vincente had disposed of Mario, they'd forced Kate and the twins to slog through the mud to a car hidden near some trees. Then they'd driven to the foothills, abandoned the car and compelled Kate and the boys to climb up a muddy trail.

Were they being taken to some deserted spot where Vincente and Franco planned to kill them? Kate wondered. Her blouse was wet and clammy from the drizzle, but a chill generated by pure fear flowed up her spine. Was there anything she could do to defend herself? she wondered. Her gaze darted around, seeking some weapon to wield or some avenue of escape.

She'd always been a good sprinter. But even if the opportunity arose for her to outrun the two ruffians shepherding them up the hill, the boys would still be at Vincente and Franco's mercy. By the time she brought help, it might be too late. No, she had to stay. She had to try and do what she could to protect Rudy and Randy and hope that somehow help would come. Surely Adelina would find Mario, Kate tried to reassure herself. And Nick would be getting back to the farm sometime before nightfall. He'd try and find them, wouldn't he?

The thought gave her a small ray of hope. But that was almost instantly extinguished. How would he ever guess that they'd been taken here?

Kate clenched her fists and then looked down at her hands. The silver ring on her middle finger had a distinctive green stone. It had been a tenth-birthday gift from her adoptive father who'd bought it on a trip to Mexico. She'd worn it ever since, and people often remarked on it, saying the stone matched her eyes. Nick hadn't said anything about it, but perhaps he'd noticed. Surreptitiously, Kate slipped the ring off and waited for an opportunity to drop it in the grass.

The chance came a few minutes later when Rudy suddenly veered away and made a run for it. Instantly, Randy followed his twin brother's lead. They didn't get very far. With a rough curse, Franco galloped after the two children. Kate would have followed, only Vincente wrapped a bony hand around her arm and patted the gun in his pocket.

"You stay put, *signorina!*"

"Oh, please!" Anxiously, Kate watched Franco seize a screaming, squirming Randy by the collar and shake him as a cat would a mouse. Simultaneously the burly thug's other hand reached for Rudy. "Little brat! You need to have a lesson."

When he cuffed the boy, knocking him flat on the ground, Kate strained against Vincente's strangling grip.

"There's no need to hit him like that! They're only children!"

But Vincente merely laughed at her, revealing yellowed teeth decorated with spectacular gold fillings. "Give the brat one for me," he shouted to his cohort.

Snarling, Franco aimed another blow at Randy. "You try and run away again and I knock your heads off," he hissed. Sniveling and clearly frightened, Rudy and Randy got to their feet and stumbled back to the trail.

With glittering eyes, Kate turned to Vincente. "What is it you want with us? What are you planning to do?"

"Wouldn't you like to know, *bella?*"

"Yes, I would." Stubbornly, Kate held back when he tried to force her on. If he were going to kill them, it would be better to die in the open, she thought. "Why have you kidnapped us? What are you planning to do with us?"

"Don't worry, *cara mia*. We just going for a picnic in the hills," Vincente taunted and then waved a gun at Randy. "You better come along. No polite to turn down an invitation."

Unwilling, Kate started back up the trail. Her hands clenched and suddenly she became aware of the ring she'd secretly been holding. When Vincente and Franco weren't looking, she dropped it in the grass. It was a forlorn hope that Nick or Mario or Adelina might spot it and realize that she'd passed this way, but it was all she could think of to do.

"Come along, *signorina,*" Vincente said, turning back to her with his jeering grin. "We go find someplace nice and dry where we get acquainted."

LIKE A SCIENTIST examining an archeological site, Nick squatted to study the layers of tire tracks imprinted in the rain-soaked earth. There were three sets. The first and least clear-cut were those of the Fiat he'd taken to Rome early that morning. The last were those of Carlo's Cortina, which he'd driven up to the house just a few minutes earlier.

Sandwiched between these two recognizable tracks was another, unfamiliar set. Nick had followed it out to the juncture between the private lane and the public road, where the Fiat's and the Cortina's tire prints angled to the right in the direction of Rome. The unknown vehicle's tires had angled left.

Grimly, Nick jogged back to the house. "Do you have a gun, Uncle?" he asked.

Mario was lying on the sofa in the parlor, an ice pack on his head. He blinked up at Nick. "What you want a gun for? You going to go after those men yourself?"

"That's exactly what I'm going to do."

"Nico, they rough customers."

"So am I."

Mario gazed up at his nephew, taking in the hard line of his jaw, the grim set of his mouth, the chilly glitter in his blue eyes. Slowly, he nodded. "Okay, I got a gun. But it's old, left over from the war."

"Does it shoot?"

"*Sì*, I take it out for target practice last year. It shoots."

"That's all that counts."

Fifteen minutes later, Nick loaded bullets into a dull black revolver, set it on the passenger seat in the Cortina and then started the automobile up and drove rapidly down the lane. As he swung left, he frowned through the windshield. Where had that car taken Kate and the boys? The possibilities seemed endless. They could be going to Terni or Spoleto or a hundred other points north.

But Nick had a hunch. He had remembered that flash of light he'd caught in the hills the day before while they'd all been bathing the twins. At the time he hadn't thought much of it, and it still might have been something perfectly innocent. But what if that reflection had come from the lens of a pair of binoculars? What if someone had been up there spying on them, waiting for the right time to swoop down on the farm?

There were caves in those hills. As a boy, Nick had even explored several of them. And he was familiar with quite a few of the trails off the road which led up to them. The caves were a long shot, but the situation was desperate, and they were all he had.

As Nick approached the first trail, he slowed the car to a crawl and looked for tire tracks in the soft mud at the side of the road. When he found none, he speeded up and drove on to the next spot. The process was slow and agonizing. Where were Kate and boys now, and what was happening to them? he kept asking himself. Suddenly an image of Kate lying face down on the ground, her bright hair dirtied by mud sprang into his mind. It sent a bolt of pure panic ripping through him. He had to find her, and he had to find her quickly!

Nick almost drove past the next turnoff without spotting the tire tracks, which were hidden in shadow. Fortunately, however, a stray shaft of sunlight breaking through a cloud picked them out and they caught his eye in time.

Braking to a fast stop, he rocketed out of the car and dropped down on his knees to study the blurry imprints closely. His heart began to pound. He'd swear they were the same ones he'd seen in the lane leading up to the farm. It seemed almost too good to be true. He glanced up through a tangle of vine at the foothills. Could Kate and the boys be up there somewhere? He'd soon know.

A moment later Nick located the mystery car behind a stand of pine. He looked inside for any sign of Kate and the boys, but found nothing. Still, he was convinced he was on the right track. They had to be up in those hills somewhere. Pray God nothing had happened to them yet. Grimly, Nick hefted the gun Mario had given him and then started to climb.

KATE FELT THE FLAT of Vincente's hand pressed familiarly to her backside. "This is it, signorina. Home sweet home." He gave her a shove that sent her lurching through a narrow crevice. It opened out into a small, dimly lit cave littered with camping gear. For a moment she stood blinking, trying to adjust to the gloom.

Two grimy sleeping bags lay crumpled against a rough rock wall. Scattered near where she stood at the mouth of the cave were the remains of a fire and a litter of cans and dirty cooking pots. Cans of beer and a half-drunk bottle of Chianti sat open near the sleeping bags.

"It smells in here," Randy complained when Franco pushed him and Rudy through the narrow aperture after Kate.

With a curse, Franco cuffed the youngster's ear and then forced him down to the stone floor where he rubbed Randy's nose in a grimy paper plate smeared with the remains of a canned spaghetti dinner. "You no like the way it smells, huh, kid? Well, that's too bad." Ignoring Randy's distressed yelps, Franco turned to his partner. "You want we tie them up now?"

"Sure, you do the kids. Then I get to do the pretty redhead." Vincente leered at Kate. "I make a good job on you, *bellina.*"

Shuddering at the implication of that, Kate turned to Franco and pleaded, "You don't have to tie them up."

"Oh, *sì*, they troublemakers," he replied stolidly as he picked Rudy up by the scruff of his neck and then forced him face down on the stone floor. "I fix."

Ten minutes later Rudy and Randy sat propped against one stone wall, their hands and feet securely bound and their mouths gagged.

"Now you," Vincente said to Kate. His insulting gaze played over her. "I start with your feet and work my way up. We have some fun, huh?"

As he came toward her caressing a length of rope as if it were living flesh, Kate's mind raced. "Please, I..."

He cocked his head.

"Please, I...have to go to the bathroom," she stammered.

Vincente raised his scruffy eyebrows. Then he chuckled and pointed to a dark corner. "Go ahead. I no peek."

"Not here!" Kate protested, shrinking away and looking shocked. "Outside somewhere."

He and Franco sniggered knowingly. Then Vincente shrugged. "Okay, but you better be a good girl. Hear me? You try anything, I make you sorry."

Kate believed him, but that didn't mean she intended to follow his orders. While he led her outside, her mind worked furiously. There had to be something she could do to save herself and the boys. There just had to be!

"You go behind there," Vincente said, pointing to a stand of cedar. "Remember, make it quick and don't try anything *stupido*. You be sorry if you do. I make sure of that."

"I won't," Kate fibbed meekly. She slipped in among the trees and then looked around, desperate for some weapon, a rock, a stick, anything! Her eyes fell on a length of fallen branch. When she picked it up and hefted it, it felt stout. With her hands clenched around its base, Kate peered out from behind the greenery. A dozen feet away, Vincente stood rocking on his heels. He'd taken a pack of cigarettes out of his pocket and was lighting one up. That meant she had a minute or two before he'd come looking for her, Kate told herself.

As silently as possible, she began to pick her way through the trees. Finally, she hid herself behind a particularly lush evergreen and, screened by its full branches, stood taking deep, quiet breaths and listening to her heart thud around in her rib cage like a berserk wrecking ball.

"Signorina, why you taking so long? You not playing games with me, are you? You be very foolish to do a thing like that."

From her hidden position Kate watched as Vincente glared at the grove of cedar, hurled his lit cigarette down into the weeds and then hawked and spat dramatically. Scowling, he began to stalk toward the spot where she'd entered the grove.

Kate tightened her grip on the club.

"Come on out of there, *signorina*. You naked? Vincente dress you himself." Sniggering at his own joke, the skinny thug pushed a branch aside and stepped into the green enclosure.

Kate had been lucky in her positioning. Though she was hidden from his view, she stood almost directly behind him.

When Vincente didn't find his quarry, he put his hands on his snakelike hips and spat out a string of Italian curses. He was in the middle of a particularly colorful imprecation when Kate brought her branch crashing down on his unprotected head. Vincente let out a squawk of rage and then sank to the ground as if all the starch had suddenly been knocked out of him.

Kate, whose heart banged so loud she could hardly hear herself think, stared down at him in horror. With the exception of a few childish schoolyard wrangles, she'd never struck a person in her life. Had she killed him? she wondered in horror. Tiptoeing up to his prone body, she bent and touched his wrist. No, he wasn't dead. His pulse still beat strongly. But that meant he'd likely be waking up soon. So she only had a few minutes to try to rescue the boys.

Straightening, Kate turned and peeped through the trees and out at the mouth of the cave some fifteen or twenty yards away. How was she going to lure Franco out? And once he was out, what could she do with him? She'd been able to put Vincente temporarily out of commission, but Franco was a mountain of a man and not likely to succumb to a blow from the likes of her—even if she were lucky enough to land one.

The problem solved itself when Franco emerged from the cave a few minutes later and stood in the sunlight with a scowl contorting his meaty face. "Vincente you lazy *buffone!*" he called. "Where are you? What you doing so long?"

Kate shrank back into the greenery.

"Vincente? What's going on? You playing around with that girl?" With a curse, Franco walked several yards out into the clearing and then veered left toward a clump of bushes. "Vincente!"

Using the trees for cover, Kate circled around closer to the mouth of the cave. Still calling after his partner, Franco disappeared into the shrubbery and she heard his heavy feet trampling down vines and undergrowth as he searched for Vincente.

Kate steeled herself, made a quiet dash for the cave entrance and slipped inside. "Shh, don't make a noise," she warned as she rushed over to the boys and pulled the gags from their mouths. "I'm going to untie you and then we'll try to run for it."

But untying them proved difficult. Kate had no knife to cut the rope and Franco's knots were tight and strong. Frantically she struggled with them.

"How'd you get free?" Rudy wanted to know. "Did you take Vincente's gun away from him and shoot him with it?"

"Did you stick a knife in his guts?" Randy queried. "Did he bleed all over the place?"

Kate winced and then muttered, "Never mind how I did it. Let's just get out of here." At last she managed to release the bonds from Rudy's hands. While he worked on those around his feet, she started in on Randy's. She'd just freed him when a bellow of rage thundered outside the cave. Obviously, Franco had discovered his fallen cohort.

"Let's get out of here, now!" Kate whispered urgently.

White-faced, the boys nodded. They leaped to their feet and crowded in front of Kate through the narrow entry. But just as they reached the out-of-doors, Franco burst through the trees, his thick features a mask of fury.

"Run!" Kate cried to the twins as she blocked the big man's path.

For an instant, Rudy and Randy lingered, uncertain what to do. "Run!" Kate insisted. Franco bore down on her with beefy arms outstretched. Shrieking, Rudy and Randy took to their heels.

As NICK HURRIED up the rough trail, his gaze searched the ground for signs. He'd already determined that someone had used the path not too long ago. In one muddy spot he'd even seen footprints that looked small enough to have belonged to one of the twins.

Suddenly he stopped dead and his heart seemed to quit and then painfully shudder back into action. A silver ring lay in the grass. Gingerly, he bent to retrieve it and then stared down where it rested in the palm of his hand. Several times he'd noticed this ring on Kate's small, slender fingers—noticed it and wondered if some man, some lover had given it to her.

As he remembered how jealous the thought had made him feel, an image of her hands moving with grace and assurance on the keyboard came to him and he felt something hard and sharp squeeze inside his chest. Pocketing the ring, he turned on his heel and redoubled his pace up the trail. Now he knew that Kate and the boys were somewhere at the end. Pray God he was in time.

Another five hundred yards up the rough path Nick heard the sound of pounding feet. He stopped, every one of his senses on alert. Rudy and Randy, their faces white with terror, burst around a turning. When they spotted him they began to scream. Disjointed phrases filled the air.

"Help! Help! Kate—he's killing her!"

As they slid into Nick, he grabbed Rudy's shoulder and held him still, his knuckles showing white. "What is it? Where's Kate?"

"Up there." Randy's chest heaved and his hand, as he lifted it to point up the trail, trembled.

"Hurry, hurry, hurry, that man is killing her," Rudy jabbered frantically. "He's killing her right now."

Nick dropped the boy and bolted up the path. Leaping rocks and fallen tree trunks, he dashed toward a cave he remembered from his boyhood.

Suddenly, a woman's gurgling scream pierced the taut woodland silence and his blood ran cold in his veins. Ignoring the path, he scrambled straight up a sheer rocky drop and hoisted himself over the edge in one surging movement. Leaping nimbly to his feet, he dashed around another outcropping of rock and then stopped short.

Two men were with Kate in a clearing. One, short, skinny and ferret-faced, stood rubbing his head at the edge of the trees. The other, a brutish-looking tough, held her in his thick arms. In their struggle he'd torn her blouse half off, and now he appeared to be trying to strangle her. Kate kicked, squirmed and fought for all she was worth.

"Franco, look out!" the skinny one shouted when he spotted Nick. Then he took a pistol out of his pocket, aimed it directly at Nick and fired.

KATE BATTLED for her life. So this was where she would die, she thought as Franco's dirty fingers closed around her throat. How strange. Well, one thing at least, she'd buy the boys as much time as possible. With all her strength, she scratched and punched, thrashed and flailed.

"Little wildcat," Franco growled, "You think you hurt me with those sharp claws? I fix you. I fix you good!"

His fingers squeezed and Kate's vision began to swim. Still, she refused to give up. Desperately, she aimed a kick at the big man's groin.

"Oof!" he cried. And then, bellowing with rage, he began to choke her in earnest.

Kate's ears thundered. The world went dark. Somewhere in the distance she heard a shout and a series of gunshots. But as she sank into the black tide roaring through her head, none of it seemed to matter. She was dying, she realized dimly. And she was still so young and hadn't yet recorded an album. What a shame.

"KATE, KATE!" Something cold and wet moistened Kate's mouth and then trickled down her neck.

"Uhh…" A terrible pain seared her throat and her head pounded as if a thousand devils were attacking it with sledgehammers.

"Kate, please, open your eyes and look at me!"

The deep male voice in her ear was so urgent, so compelling, that despite the pain beating at Kate, she forced her lids to open a crack. Blueness was the first thing on which she focused. Eyes the color of the Mediterranean at high noon stared down at her with an intensity that made her blink. It was almost as if they were willing her back to life. She felt a strong hand at the back of her head, another on her arm, and the eyes came closer, absorbing her entire field of vision.

A finger gently touched her throat. "Can you speak at all, or does it hurt too much?"

It did hurt too much, but Kate found her voice anyway. "Nick! The boys? What… what happened?" The broken words came out in a hoarse gasp that left her clutching her neck and moaning.

Nick looked down at her anxiously, seeing the bright curls, the clear green eyes, the ugly marks on her throat that were rapidly turning into even uglier bruises. Through her hopelessly torn blouse, he was aware of the the fine modeling of her shoulders, the full swell of her white breasts. It was impossible to describe his relief when, after he'd turned her over and laid his head against their soft cushion, he'd heard the faint but regular beat of her heart.

"Listen, Kate," he said urgently, "I know you feel bad, but we have to get out of here. Those two thugs who had you are gone for the moment, but they might come back. And we have to find the boys before they do."

As Kate absorbed this information, her eyes darkened and she struggled to push herself up. Nick helped her into a sitting position. She wanted desperately to get to her feet.

A thousand questions pounded in her brain. Where were the boys? What had happened? How had Nick found them? But the nausea that rose in her throat overpowered her and all she could do for several minutes was put her aching head between her knees and groan.

Gently Nick stroked her hair and murmured encouragement. Gradually she became aware that he was making the same soothing noises at her that she'd heard him make to Cesare. For some inexplicable reason, the realization angered her, and the anger gave her strength. Awkwardly, she pushed herself to her knees.

"Atta girl!" Nick put his hands under her arms and pulled her to her feet. But once she was upright, her bones seemed to liquefy and she would have fallen if it hadn't been for Nick's iron grip.

"It's okay, it's okay." Supporting her, he held her close so that through his light jacket and chambray shirt she could feel the heat of his body, the vibrant, wiry strength of him. "Just take a minute to pull yourself together. It's all right."

For a few crazy seconds it almost seemed as if some of that potent animal vigor he possessed in such abundance were flowing from his body directly into hers. Kate took a deep breath and then pushed herself away from him. "I'm okay now," she said.

"Are you sure?" He looked at her searchingly.

"Yes, yes." Her voice was a hoarse croak. "We have to find Rudy and Randy. My God, what happened? How did you get here?"

While they hurried back down the path Nick explained how he'd located the cave and some of what had occurred after Kate blacked out.

"You mean you actually shot Franco?" she asked incredulously.

"Winged him and took his gun away from him. But when he and his little pal took off, I was too worried about you to try to catch up with them." Ruefully, Nick shook his head. "Now they're loose somewhere around here, and I don't know what they're up to. They may have run back to their bosses, or they may have tried to round up the boys. I just hope Rudy and Randy were clever enough to have hidden from them," he said and quickly explained how he'd run into the boys on the path and they'd alerted him that Kate was being attacked.

At the thought of the twins being back in Franco's and Vincente's clutches, Kate moaned and frantically tried to quicken her pace. But her feet were at odds with her racing heart, and she slipped on a patch of loose rock. Once again, Nick's steadying hand kept her from a bad fall.

"Take it easy. We'll find them."

"I hope so. Oh, God, I hope so!"

With Nick grasping her arm to keep her from pitching forward again, Kate slipped and slid around the next turning, which was in heavy shadow from a thick stand of tallish trees. Suddenly a bloodcurdling yell split the air and two heavy bodies dropped down like living flyweights.

"What the—" Nick and Kate sprawled to the ground.

"Gotcha!" a high-pitched voice squealed.

"Hey, dummy," another scolded, "It's not them. It's Kate and Nick."

"You're right. It is!"

The two adults struggled to free themselves from a blanketing tangle of arms and legs. "Rudy! Randy!" Kate gasped, staring delightedly at two cherubic faces and four round and sparkling brown eyes. "Are you okay?"

"Yes, but we thought you were Vincente and Franco," Randy explained. "That's why we ambushed you."

"I'm glad you ambushed us and not them," Nick said with a chuckle as he once again helped Kate to her feet. "Somehow I don't think they'd be half so friendly about it." Suddenly Nick turned his head slightly. Then he held a warning finger to his lips. Everyone fell silent as they tried to hear what Nick's sharp ears had picked up.

In the distance a motor had sprung to life. Screeching tires echoed through the mountain stillness and then the vehicle roared rapidly away until a few seconds later its sound was no more than the whine of a dying insect.

CHAPTER NINE

"IT'S OBVIOUS we can't stay here any longer," Nick declared grittily, as he swung the car into the rutted lane that led back to the farm. "Those two thugs may be gone for the time being, but the men they work for don't give up so easily. Franco and Vincente or their clones will be back, and most likely with reinforcements."

Kate nervously fingered the silver ring that Nick had returned to her when they had reached the car. "What can we do?"

"We'll throw bombs at them," Rudy piped up from the backseat.

"Yeah, and grenades, too," Randy seconded.

Ignoring that, Nick said, "Just as soon as I've moved Mario to Adelina's, we're going to take off."

Kate half turned in her seat. "So much has happened so quickly, I haven't asked about Mario," she said anxiously. "Is your uncle all right?"

"He's got a head wound, and a few bruises, but so far as I can tell, it's nothing serious. He'll be fine. However, I do intend to insist that he stay with Adelina until this thing dies down. That way he'll be safe."

Mario, however, was not so easily persuaded. "I be fine right where I am," he declared when Nick urged him to leave his farm. Stubbornly, he added, "This my home, the home of my father and his father before him. I no let nobody scare me away."

Nothing Nick could say would change his uncle's mind. Mario refused to budge, and at last Nick resorted to the only means of persuasion left. Over Mario's loud and pungently phrased protests, he hoisted his uncle up into his arms and carried him out of the house to the car.

As Kate followed along behind with the boys in tow, she stared at Nick's back in amazement. Though no taller than his athletic nephew, Mario was at least half again as broad. Yet Nick seemed to carry him easily.

"Nick's got big muscles in his arms," Rudy commented.

"Yes," Kate agreed, allowing her gaze to dwell on the bunched thickness of his forearms which showed clearly beneath the rolled sleeves of his knit shirt. Her eye couldn't help but wander to the sculpted width of his back, which tapered dramatically to his lean hips with their tidy, masculine buttocks.

Suddenly she found herself remembering the tenderness with which Nick had comforted her on the mountain after he'd chased Franco and Vincente away. Until that moment she'd been in terror. But in his embrace, she'd felt safe. That was how it had been, almost from the moment of meeting him, she realized. When she was with Nick, despite the danger and confusion whirling around them, she felt safe—except perhaps from him and the emotions he evoked in her.

Adelina was delighted to welcome Mario into her large and comfortably appointed home. While Mario grumbled on the old-fashioned settee where he'd been carefully deposited, Adelina put together a light meal for everyone and cheerfully agreed to arrange for the care and feeding of his farm animals.

"Gisberto be happy to earn a few lire feeding the chickens and taking care of Cesare and Bella," she assured Nick.

"I don't want that old fool anywhere near my land," Mario protested furiously. His cheeks puffed out and his dark eyes snapped. "Gisberto doesn't know how to do anything but drink wine all day and gossip in the tavern."

But Adelina only chuckled at her *innamorato*'s overblown wrath. "I take good care of you," she assured him, walking over to pat his balding head. "You wait and see how fat and happy you get with Adelina for a nurse. When you get well, you no want to leave."

Mario grumbled a reply, pretending to be unconvinced. But when Nick and Kate left with the boys an hour later, Mario was munching on a slice of freshly baked bread Adelina had brought him and looking mollified.

"What about us?" Kate asked as she, Nick and the boys settled back into the Cortina. "You were being awfully mysterious back there. Why wouldn't you tell them where we're going?"

Nick turned the key in the ignition and adjusted his seat belt. "I wouldn't tell them because the less they know the better—for them *and* for us."

"Do *you* know where we're going?" Kate asked pointedly. "Have you got some sort of plan?"

"Yes, as a matter of fact." Nick put the car in gear, and it began to roll down the cobbled street of the village. "Right now we're heading back to Rome."

"Rome!" The boys' raised voices were added to that of Kate's.

"Are we going to stop and see my dad?" Rudy asked.

Over his shoulder, Nick shot a sympathetic glance at the youngster. "Not this time, I'm afraid. I don't intend to stop there, you see. I'm planning to drive on through

Rome and then head south." Diplomatically, he described his meeting with Lou LaFiore. "So, you see, your dad wants me to take you back to England where you'll be safe and where he plans to join you later on after all this trouble has been cleared up."

Listening to Nick speak, Kate appreciated the sensitivity with which he was handling this situation. While not lying to the children about their danger, Nick was managing not to frighten them anymore than was necessary. She knew he and Lou LaFiore were enemies, yet none of that was reflected in the way Nick talked to Rudy and Randy. He wasn't out to make them feel any worse than they already did about their father's predicament.

"You said we're heading south," Kate interjected, "but where? Why?"

Nick shot her a grin that gave her a warm feeling at the back of her throat. "I'm a much luckier orphan than you are," he said lightly. "Fortunately, I come from a big family and I have many talented and interesting cousins." With a chuckle, he described how Carlo, his race-car cousin, had helped him elude the mob in Rome earlier that day and then provided him with the fast, comfortable automobile in which they were now traveling.

Kate, who had just assumed that the Cortina was another rental vehicle, studied it appreciatively.

"Anyhow," Nick went on, "Carlo's brother Angelo happens to own a small private airfield outside Naples. On the drive back here this morning, I stopped and rang him up on a public telephone. If we can get down to his place without further trouble, Angelo has agreed to fly us over to another private airfield I know about near Monaco. From there we can easily make arrangements to get back to London."

Kate felt something that had been like a tight lump in her chest ever since Franco and Vincente had kidnapped them slowly uncoil. "That...why that sounds wonderful!" she exclaimed. She shot Nick's chiseled profile a grateful and admiring glance. "Thank you."

His finely cut lips twisted wryly. "We're not home free yet. Thank me when we're safely back on English soil and the boys are delivered to their grandparents." His expression lightened and he grinned at her again. "But I think if we're careful and we don't have any major patches of bad luck slipping us up, we ought to be okay."

The drive back through the country north of Rome was uneventful. But as they drew closer to the historic metropolis Kate sat up tensely and even Rudy and Randy began to look nervous. It was as if every luxury sedan they passed might house a squadron of mobsters patrolling the autostrada on the lookout for them.

Skirting the city seemed to take forever, but at last they were out the other side and headed south toward the Amalfi coast. When they reached the famous Amalfi Drive, Kate was dazzled by its beauty.

"Tuscany and Umbria were lovely," she exclaimed, "but this is unbelievable."

Nick nodded. "Dangerous to navigate, too. It's hard to keep your eye on the road when you've got this kind of scenery distracting you."

Kate sympathized. Edged by a road that was wound as tightly as a spring, the stretch of coast they were traversing was breathtakingly gorgeous. As the sun lowered in the sky, stunning views of sea and cliff pulled their eyes from the highway. Mountains shrouded by clouds plummeted into a sea of deep and lovely blues and aquamarines. Towns nestled in ravines between the surf-fringed cliffs or climbed the hillside in steep terraces.

Just at sunset they stopped in a small village. "Time for a break," Nick said as he pulled into the courtyard of a hotel that overlooked the tiled dome of a Byzantine church and below that a beach of slaty pebbles where fishing boats were drawn ashore and brown nets were spread to dry.

"I thought you wanted to drive straight through to your cousin's," Kate protested.

"Angelo's airstrip isn't far from here," Nick replied. "I'm going to go see what arrangements I can make with him. Meanwhile, you and the boys might as well get some shut-eye. It's been a long day."

That was certainly true. Rudy and Randy were pale with exhaustion and Kate felt ready to drop. Nick checked them into a comfortable room overlooking the sea and then set off for his cousin's. The moment Kate and the boys closed the door behind them, they all fell down on their separate beds and slid instantly into deep and dreamless slumber.

IT WASN'T UNTIL Kate felt a hand shake her arm gently that she awakened. "Uhh!" Her eyes flew open and she sat up, but for several seconds she could make out nothing in the dark.

"Kate," she heard Nick's whisper. "It's all right. There's nothing to worry about. But we have to go."

"Nick?" He was sitting next to her on the bed. His arms were still around her, his face so close that she could feel his breath on her cheek.

"My cousin's ready to fly us to the mainland, but we have to go now."

"So late at night?" There was a peculiar intimacy in their whispered conversation, a sense of excitement. Kate lay her hand on Nick's shoulder, absorbing the warmth and strength of him.

"Believe me, it's better this way. Safer. C'mon, let's wake up the boys."

It took some doing to get Rudy and Randy on their feet, but at last they all managed to leave the hotel and drive to the strip of land where Nick's cousin had a small plane gassed up and ready to go.

After an official checked their passports, things happened very quickly, but also with a dreamlike slowness. In the darkness and the midst of Kate's exhaustion, Nick's cousin was only a deep voice, a flashing smile in the blinding lights of a narrow dirt runway. His plane was so small that when they were all settled inside it there was only one seat to spare.

Kate had a lingering fear of air travel. Normally their takeoff into the darkness over the sea would have terrified her. But the whole experience had begun to take on an air of unreality for her. As they roared into the night and then lifted off into the velvety blackness, she held Rudy and Randy's hand and murmured words of encouragement. Yet all the while she felt distanced from the experience, as if she were watching it from the outside.

The only anchor was Nick, and his cousin's baritone voices as they exchanged jokes, remarked on the weather and flying conditions, caught up on family news. Nick had obviously already told Angelo the details of their situation, for that subject wasn't brought up at all.

"How's Uncle Mario? I haven't seen him in a year at least."

"Fine, though I think he's about to lose his bachelor status."

"Oh?"

"Adelina was widowed a couple of years back and she's zeroing in on him." Nick and his cousin laughed softly.

Just before dawn they landed somewhere in France and went through another passport check. But Kate never had more than a hazy impression of that brief stop. Another small airplane awaited them. And as Nick led them from one aircraft to the other he murmured comforting words to Randy and Rudy. "I know this is hard, but it's only a few hours more. Just hold on. That's it, take my hand and let me help you up these steps. You can sleep on the plane, and when we land we'll be safe."

For Kate the rest of the journey was a total blur. The skies were overcast when they landed and had their luggage and passports checked again. As Nick all but carried her and the boys out of the plane and into a beat-up old station wagon, rain soaked grass so green it had the intensity of crushed emeralds. Groggily, Kate wondered where they were. But she was too tired to really care. Wherever it was, Nick seemed to have the situation well in hand.

They arrived at another farm and Nick ushered them into a house with low ceilings and whitewashed walls. "Whose place is this?" Kate muttered.

"Mine. We're in Ireland."

"Ireland? But..."

"Shh. Everything's fine. There's nothing to worry about. But you need to lay yourself down and sleep for about twenty-four hours. Come, Shug will see to the boys. I'll show you your room."

"Who's Shug?"

"Just someone who helps me around the place. C'mon."

He took off her jacket, guided her up a pair of rough stairs and opened a door into a loftlike room. After that, Kate never had a memory of what happened. Somehow she'd undressed. Somehow she'd climbed into the wide bed and pulled its colorful patchwork quilt up around her shoulders and then let sweet oblivion fold her in its comforting cloak.

SHE WAS DREAMING of Nick when she heard his voice next to her ear.

"Time to wake up, my fine lady."

The rich aroma of fresh-brewed coffee penetrated Kate's dormant state. "W-what?" She opened her eyes and beheld Nick sitting on the edge of her bed, a breakfast tray balanced on his lap.

He wore jeans and a black turtleneck sweater and was freshly shaved and showered. Tiny beads of moisture still sparkled in his thick, dark hair, and his high cheekbones were covered by skin that was a smooth, creamy tan. Between his long black lashes, his blue eyes surveyed her with an indulgent light.

"You've almost slept the clock around."

Stiffly, Kate pushed herself up into a sitting position and then looked down at the oversize man's white T-shirt she had on. "What happened? How did I get into this?" she croaked.

"With a little help from yours truly."

Kate stared and then felt her neck begin to heat. "What's happened? Where are we?"

"You asked me that yesterday."

"I don't remember anything about yesterday. Was there a yesterday?"

"Most definitely." Nick began pouring them each a cup of the coffee that had been tantalizing Kate's nostrils. "We're in Ireland and this is my farm. The boys are fine. At the moment they're outside with Shug, my handyman, who is just about to drive them into town while he picks up some supplies. The sun is shining." Nick gestured at the window where golden light streamed in through the uneven panes of handblown glass and puddled like melted butter on the bare, wide-planked floor. "And, for the moment, all is well with the world." Nick held out her coffee cup. "Cream?"

"No, black, thank you." Kate rotated a tight shoulder. "Why are we in Ireland and not in England?"

"Because when I called here last night I found there was some business I had to attend to. One of my prize mares showed signs of going into labor. She foaled only a couple of hours after we got in, actually, and now I own a fine new colt. But don't worry. Tomorrow you and the twins will be on a plane bound for London."

Kate mulled that over and then nodded and took a sip of coffee. Her hand crept down beneath the covers to check on the status of her makeshift nightclothes. Yes, she discovered with relief, beneath the hem of the long T-shirt she had on panties. Her head turned toward the glowing morning window. On impulse she set her coffee cup down on the side table, pushed the covers aside and went to it.

Outside, green fields enclosed in white rail fences stretched into the distance. Off to the right she spotted Rudy and Randy dancing amiably around a short man in rough clothing and a wool cap who had to be Shug. He opened the door of a beat-up pickup truck and the boys climbed in. Then Shug got in the driver's side and started the engine. A moment later he drove off. As the truck disappeared down a lane, Kate turned back to Nick.

"Why is Shug taking the kids with him?"

Nick sat very still on the bed, his coffee cup balanced in his palm. "Because I asked him to."

"Oh?"

"I wanted a little peace and quiet, and…" His gaze ran over her, making her conscious of the picture she must present. The T-shirt was loose and fell midway to her thighs, so in theory she was decently covered. But that was only in theory. The shirt's knit fabric was thin and the light coming in directly behind her might be shining through it, revealing the outline of her breasts and hips.

Suddenly, from the darkness that had come into Nick's eyes and the way he very deliberately set down his cup and saucer on the floor, she knew the light must be doing exactly that.

"I wanted a little peace and quiet," he repeated as he rose to his feet and began crossing toward her, "and I wanted some time alone with you."

All at once Kate felt breathless. Her heart began to bang in her chest.

"Do you know how you look to me standing there with the sun turning your hair into flames?" Nick asked huskily.

"I . . . can guess."

"Adorable," Nick murmured, answering his own question as he put his hands around Kate's waist and drew her toward him. "You look adorable. That's how you've always looked to me—from the first minute I laid eyes on you. Even when I thought you might be some sort of unlikely Mata Hari."

He didn't wait for a reply, which was a good thing, because at that moment Kate was struck dumb. She gazed up at him and her lips, still slightly swollen from sleep, parted. His hands, very warm on her narrow waist, and his eyes, which looked into hers as if they could see much more than she felt ready to reveal, seemed to hold her in a network of electricity. The forces pulsing between them flowed and sang like living things. And then his head lowered to hers and her eager mouth lifted and parted.

Strangely, Kate's first sensation as they began to kiss was of how clean and velvety Nick's skin felt against hers. She had been right in guessing that he'd just shaved and showered. He smelled of freshness—fresh soap and water, fresh air, fresh spring grass. Yet there was an underlying masculine grit, too. Nick was like fine leather, she found herself thinking, supple and well-tanned, elegant yet strong, flexible yet stubbornly tough and enduring.

All of these qualities came through to her in his kiss. And, as her senses were first inundated then swamped, Kate raised her hands to his neck and kissed him back for all she was worth. He groaned and then gripped her more tightly yet. His mouth lost some of its gentleness, became harder, more demanding. Kate's lips opened and their tongues found each other, met, teased, dueled.

The world around them no longer mattered. Kate forgot that she was in Ireland and not Italy. Behind her tightly closed eyelids the light that streamed in across the emerald fields shattered into lemon-colored glass and then, with a silent explosion, bloomed into passionate gold and scarlet flowers.

With another groan they pulled apart and then stood staring at each other. Kate's legs felt weak and heavy. The area between them glowed with desire and her breasts ached. Nick's face was flushed and his eyes between his thick lashes looked a brilliant, almost feverish blue.

"Kate," he muttered thickly.

She swayed toward him. "Yes."

"Kate, my God I want to make love to you."

"Yes." She nodded. "Yes."

For a moment he stared at her as if he couldn't quite take in her meaning. Then, with quick decision, he swept her off her feet and carried her back to the bed. Her arms linked tightly around his neck, and as he laid her on the mattress, they kissed again. Heavily, Nick's body came down on hers. Their legs locked and they rolled together halfway across the mattress. Nick's lips on hers were so passionate and urgent that his kiss literally took Kate's breath away. After a moment she had to turn her face from his and gasp.

"Am I going too fast?" he whispered thickly. "I'm sorry. It's just that you've been driving me crazy. I've been lying awake thinking about you for days now."

Kate turned her head back and gazed up at him through her lashes. "I've been thinking about you, too."

"Like this?"

"Yes." Kate wanted Nick badly, and she could no longer pretend otherwise—to herself or to him.

He kissed her lips again and smiled. "Then it's time we did something about it, wouldn't you say?"

"Yes," she breathed.

He kissed her again, generating a flame between them that made Kate melt and cling. But then his body stilled and tensed. "I wouldn't hurt you for the world, so I have to ask this. Are you on the pill?"

"Yes, it's all right."

He nuzzled the tender side of her neck. "I don't have anything here to protect you with, so I don't know if I would have survived it if you'd said no."

"Me neither. But it's okay." Beneath the weight of his lean, masculine body, she moved sensuously. The heat of her bare thighs seeped through the fabric of Nick's jeans and their loins rubbed.

"Kate, Kate," Nick murmured, and then began to kiss her in earnest. While their lips melded, his hands pushed at the T-shirt until he found the bare, tingling flesh beneath it. At the feel of his fingers on her rib cage, Kate shuddered with pleasure.

"You're so lovely," he murmured and dropped kisses along the line of her jaw.

"I bet you say that to all the girls you rescue," Kate retorted huskily. She was busy pulling his shirt free of his waistband so that she could touch his back without hindrance.

He arched up, tugged the shirt over his head and flung it on the floor. "Kate," he said earnestly, "believe me. Since meeting you, I haven't given any other woman a thought."

At that moment it was a gratifying thing to hear, but Kate didn't stop to speculate on its true meaning. As her hands roamed up the taut, flexed arch of his back and then moved down to the waistband of his snug-fitting jeans, all she wanted was him, to get her hands on his beautiful body, to feel the living heat of him.

With a rough little chuckle, he gathered her up and flipped onto his back so that she lay balanced over him between his bent legs. "Unsnap my jeans," he whispered.

"May I?" she whispered back teasingly.

"Yes, but do it carefully. As you may have noticed, I'm having a little problem down there."

"I would say it's a big problem." As she spoke, her eyes admired what she could see of his torso. Except for a thin line of hair from his breastbone to his belly button, his elegantly sculpted chest was smooth. The muscles in his shoulders and forearms were clearly defined, explaining his easy strength.

After she undid his jeans and carefully slid the zipper down past the swelling manhood behind it, he kicked them off. Unlike his chest, his sinewy legs were furred with fine dark hairs. Beneath them a map of faint white lines was visible on his knees and calves. Kate suspected it was left from his riding accident and would have reached to touch one of the scars—only at that moment she felt Nick's hands go to the waistband of her panties and began to slide them down over her hips.

Quivering with anticipation, Kate arched so that he could strip them away more easily. When they were gone he stroked her flanks and then his exploring hand began to move more intimately, coaxing, fondling. Kate flung her head back. A new rush of liquid heat flooded the juncture between her legs and she gasped with excitement.

Nick, too, radiated contained frenzy. Abruptly, he rolled again so that she lay imprisoned beneath him. He pushed the wrinkled T-shirt up over her head and threw it down next to his own shirt. Then, with a gruff sound at the back of his throat, he kissed her breasts, stroking them with his hands and then sucking on each sensitive, stiffened nipple. "Beautiful," he murmured again and again. "God, Kate!"

Levering himself up, he slid sensuously down the length of her, caressing her rib cage, her belly, the sensitive flesh of her thighs. Kate squirmed and wriggled. "Nick!"

"I want to make love to you properly, Kate. Give me time." His voice deepened. "Oh what a beauty you are. Do you even realize how lovely?"

"Nick, please!"

Suddenly he was at her side, kissing her again. Their tongues entwined, fought another little duel. "Kate?"

She opened her eyes and looked into his. They were the color of deepest indigo. Like a swimmer adrift in a purple sea, she seemed to sink into them and then willingly drown.

"Has it been a long time for you, too?"

"Yes."

"I'll be careful."

"There's no need for that." She moved to enclose his hips with her open thighs. "There's no need."

Nick groaned. "Now," he murmured, "now?"

"Yes!"

He entered her quickly. Kate had no trouble receiving him. She was more than ready. As he began to drive for their mutual pleasure, building up slowly to a more and more urgent tempo, she locked her legs tightly around his waist and rode with him.

She had not expected to climax with such ease, but it happened very quickly. Nick's own release followed soon after and he collapsed on her, breathing raggedly as the sensations they'd just experienced together reverberated between them.

"Kate?" Nick whispered at last. He raised himself up on his elbows so that he could look into her flushed face. "Are you all right?"

She lay blinking up at him, still somewhat dazed. "I'm more than all right."

"It was good, wasn't it?"

"It was wonderful!"

He framed her cheeks with his hands and grinned. "I'd like to do it all over again."

Kate, still hardly believing what had just happened, lifted her eyebrows. "Could you?"

His grin widened. "Just give me a minute or two, lady, and then hold on to your hat."

"I'm not wearing a hat."

"So I notice." He fingered a tendril of her hair and then tucked it back behind her ear. He looked regretful. "I don't think we'd better try for an encore, though. I can't be absolutely sure when Shug might come back with the twins."

Rudy and Randy! Kate had forgotten about them, about the entire rest of the world, in fact. But now it all came back like a thunderclap. "Oh my God, they could walk right in on us at any minute."

He continued toying with her hair, a little smile playing at the corners of his mouth. "No. My guess is we've another hour at least." He moved off her and then took her into his arms, held her close and whispered, "But perhaps we ought to dress and have that breakfast we never got around to eating."

"Yes," Kate agreed. Then she giggled.

"What?"

"I didn't notice until you mentioned it. But I've just realized I'm starving."

CHAPTER TEN

AFTER NICK FINISHED dressing, he picked up the untouched breakfast tray. "I'd better reheat this coffee and make a fresh run on toast and butter," he said, casting a last warm glance in Kate's direction.

"Good idea." She sat in the middle of the bed, the sheet up around her breasts, her tousled curls a vibrant frame around her wide-eyed face.

When he was out the door, she pulled her knees up tight to her chest, wrapped her arms around them and hugged herself. She felt all aglow with wonder and excitement, half-frightened, half-amazed. At that moment she had no regrets. Making love with Nick had been glorious.

There had been other men in Kate's life. In her years as a wandering musician, she'd met sophisticated rascals who made a hobby of seduction. In her early days on the road, she'd naively fallen prey to a couple of these rogues. One in particular, Billy Rockland, still lingered in her mind—though he was no longer her lover. When Kate had first met Billy, she'd been young and lonely, hungry for the love and emotional security that had been lacking during her rootless adolescence in foster homes. But she'd only found disillusionment with such feckless lovers as Billy had been, and she'd soon become wary. Out of necessity, the shell she'd grown to protect her innermost feelings had hardened and she'd learned to exercise great caution when it came to her love life.

But where had that caution flown to just now with Nick? she asked herself with a little shake of her head. She didn't know, and just at that moment she didn't care. She felt too happy to be able to think of anything but jumping into her slacks and shirt and hurrying out the bedroom door to be with him again. Just looking at him and hearing his voice was a physical pleasure.

But first Kate had to dig out the little plastic container of pills in her handbag and take one. No matter how distracting life got, there were things a girl couldn't get careless about.

Downstairs, Nick had set a table and, when Kate came into the common room of his old stone farmhouse, he was just piling a plate with newly toasted slices of buttered bread.

"The coffee smells wonderful," Kate said, a trifle shyly. She felt herself flush as her eyes met Nick's, very conscious of the intimacy they'd just shared and not quite sure what the aftermath should be.

As she crossed toward him, she cast a quick glance around, noticing and appreciating the beamed ceiling and whitewashed plaster, the fireplace with its blackened bricks, the rough-and-ready furnishings.

But most of her attention was focused on Nick. Though he had always drawn her admiring eyes, she saw him with a new intensity. For now her fingertips knew the springy texture of his dark, wavy hair, the firm edge of his cleanly sculpted jaw. Now her lips had tasted his and she'd learned the strength and sensitivity of his touch. As he brought a tinware coffeepot to the table and filled a chipped white crockery cup, her gaze went to his hands and she shivered with remembered pleasure. He looked up at her, and they smiled into each other's eyes.

"Why don't you sit down? By now you must be faint from hunger."

"I could eat a piece of toast and some of that scrambled egg you're dishing out," she agreed, accepting the chair he'd pulled out for her. "It looks to me as if you're a pretty fair cook."

"There's not much of a trick to scrambling eggs. I'd have starved by now if I hadn't learned. There's no Adelina in my life to come around and whip up gourmet meals. Shug and I have been making do for ourselves on this place for going on two years now. And before that I did my own cooking as well." He sat down opposite and watched as she unfolded a paper napkin and then lifted a fork.

"Sounds as if you're a confirmed bachelor." Kate almost choked. Now why had she said *that?*

"Nothing's ever confirmed in this life, but I've gone my own way for quite a few years now—basically since my father died and I was sent off to boarding school in Switzerland."

"You were educated in Switzerland?"

When he nodded, she asked, "Why not in England?"

He shrugged. "I think my grandparents didn't want me around to embarrass their other grandchildren."

Kate looked at him thoughtfully. "You were born in England, educated in Switzerland, spent your summers growing up in Italy and live in Ireland. You really are a citizen of the world, aren't you?"

"You might say that," Nick agreed. "My home is where I decide to hang my hat—and I have to admit that I like it that way."

"Yes, well so do I—I mean, I've been on my own a long time, too, and that's the way I like it." Kate looked down at her plate and felt somewhat chilled by Nick's response to her unthinking remark about his being a confirmed bachelor. Was that a warning he'd just issued?

The romantic cloud on which Kate had floated downstairs dissipated. It shouldn't have come as a shock that Nick was like other men, out for what he could get and worried that a woman might want something more than a weekend fling. Well, he'd never pretended otherwise. There'd been no talk of love between them—just desire. What had she expected? So he was a wonderful lover. A lot of other women had probably thought so, too. Still, the fact wasn't something Kate cared to contemplate just at the moment.

The eggs she had just forked up felt cold in her throat. Nevertheless, she swallowed them and then picked up her coffee cup. Over its rim, she studied Nick. A stranger would never have guessed that he'd just made passionate love to her. He looked as calm and relaxed as always. Only the faintly stern cast of his mouth suggested that he might have something new on his mind. What was it, she wondered cynically. How to get rid of her, now that he'd had his way with her? But why was she thinking in this stupid fashion, she asked herself. She'd had her way with him, too. She'd wanted him every bit as much as he'd wanted her and their pleasure had been mutual.

"Does your farm have a name?" she asked to change the subject.

"Yes, it's called Newride. I think you can guess why."

"Something to do with a fresh start for yourself?"

He nodded. "After my accident, when I invested all my winnings in this place, I was still nursing broken bones. I never expected to race again. I hoped to make it as a horse trainer and breeder, which is a very different thing from being a professional jockey."

"Do you like training horses?"

He drained his coffee cup and sat back in his chair. "Very much. It's a demanding life, but it can be very rewarding. It's hard to explain in words to a nonrider. Maybe when you're finished with your plate there, you'd like to walk out to the barn with me and see one of those rewards."

"Of course. I'd love to."

A few minutes later Kate washed down the last of her breakfast, helped Nick rinse and stack the dishes in the sink. Then, after putting on a nubby gray wool jacket he handed her from a hook near the door, she strolled outside with him.

It was a cool, cloudy day with patches of sun and shadow. From the little rise where the house stood, they paused to survey the fields of lush green where clusters of horses grazed picturesquely behind white rail fences.

"I can see where keeping this place up must take a lot of work," Kate commented.

"Yes," Nick answered emphatically, and began to describe what went into running a horse farm. The operation was far more complicated—and risky and expensive—then she'd realized. But it was obvious as Nick talked that he loved it and was in his element.

As she listened, Kate found herself remembering what he'd said about being a chameleon. In Italy Nick had fitted right in. With his dark good looks and command of the language, he might easily have been taken for a native.

Yet here in Ireland he appeared equally at home. If she'd met him here on his farm for the first time, she would have thought that with his blue eyes, dark hair and wiry build he must be black Irish. What was he like when he traveled in England or America? she wondered. Did he change his spots there, too? Did she know this man she'd just made such sweet and stirring love with at all? Or was the picture she'd built up of him in her mind just an illusion?

Ignoring the queasy sensation swimming up her spine, Kate shaded her eyes and then smiled and murmured, "Of course, it's spring."

"What?"

"Those are mother horses with their babies out in those pastures."

Nick chuckled. "Yes, I'm beginning to have a hopeful crop of youngsters. Come on and see the newest addition to my nursery."

They walked on out to the barn and Nick opened the door and let her in. The interior of the recently refurbished building was very different from Mario's barn. It had been a rambling old structure that had housed only two elderly horses. Nick's barn smelled of new wood, and almost all its stalls were filled. He led her to an enclosure two-thirds of the way down the row and they looked over the gate.

"Oh," Kate exclaimed, "oh, a newborn colt. Isn't he beautiful!"

"It's a she, actually."

"A she?"

"Yes, she was born last night while you were asleep. I named her Kate's Flight. I hope you don't mind."

"Mind?" Kate gave a little gasp and then stared at Nick. "I'm touched, and very flattered. What made you think of doing that?"

"Isn't it obvious?" He smiled crookedly. "Just look at the color of her coat."

Kate gazed at the tiny colt busily nursing at her mother's side. Except for white stockings beneath its knobby knees, the baby horse was solid red.

While Kate took in this scene, Nick unlatched the stall door and walked inside. Softly, he approached the nursing mare. "That's a girl, Rosy. You've done very well for yourself, and I can see that you're a proud mama. And well you should be. She's a beauty. Yes she is, a real little beauty." He stroked the mare's neck and then ran a sensitive, exploring hand across her belly. When he was satisfied, he turned his attention to the wobbly colt.

Kate observed all this, listening to the comforting croon of Nick's voice, watching the expert way he used his hands, seeing the absorbed expression that had come into his eyes.

"You mean after we got in so late, you were up the rest of the night delivering this colt?"

"Yes, the timing couldn't have been more perfect. Kate's Flight and I saw the sunrise together."

The human Kate cocked her head. She had realized before that Nick had a special relationship with horses. But now the fact hit her with fresh impact. Horses were this man's life. Perhaps they were even really all that mattered to him.

The fact was drilled home even more forcefully after they walked outside the barn to find that Shug had just come back from town with the boys.

Shug turned out to be a freckled, fresh-faced middle-aged man with twinkling eyes and a thick Irish brogue. He appeared to have survived the last couple of hours with the twins, though every now and then he looked down at them as they danced and jigged in front of Nick and Kate and shook his head as if in wonder. Shrill and energetic as always, the boys certainly showed no ill effects from their harrowing last day in Italy, Kate noted with relief.

"Can we ride a horse? Can we? Can we?" Rudy demanded.

"Yes, can we?" Randy echoed.

Nick smiled and, after introducing Shug to Kate, told the boys, "Maybe later, but right now there's some work I need to do." He turned back to his handyman. "How's Misalliance?"

"Crazy and mean as ever," Shug answered. "He needs to be exercised, but you won't catch me on that devil's back."

Nick clicked his tongue against the roof of his mouth. "He just needs a good gallop." He shaded his eyes with his hand and gazed out toward the pastures. Kate followed the direction of his glance and noticed for the first time that one of the horses, a magnificent big black one, had been separated from the others in his own fenced enclosure. He was racing back and forth along the barrier, whinnying at the mares in the distance and stamping his feet.

"That's my bad boy," Nick explained to Kate with an indulgent chuckle. "He gets up to a lot of mischief, but beneath his rough exterior, he has a heart of gold—or at least, that's what I tell myself. Excuse me, I think it's time I went over and said hello to him."

Nick went back into the barn and reappeared a few minutes later with a bridle in one hand. While he strode toward the pasture, Kate turned to Shug. "That's certainly a beautiful horse out there. I gather there's something special about him?"

Shug chewed on a piece of grass. "Beauty is as beauty does. Misalliance is good-looking, all right. But that doesn't make up for his bad temper. There's a devil in that one." Shug threw down his chewed grass and plucked a fresh blade. "Unless Misalliance has a strong hand to control him, he'll bite and lash out at anyone. In fact, last year he kicked a stall to pieces and nearly brained his owner who was going to have him put down for sheer uncontrollable meanness."

"You mean he was going to be killed?" Randy questioned with a shocked expression.

"Yes, but don't worry your head, me lad. Nick took a fancy to the horse. He talked the man out of destroying him and bought the animal for a song instead." With Kate and the boys, Shug began to stroll toward the pasture. Nick had already opened a gate to let himself in with the restive black horse.

"I'll admit it was a good bargain," the handyman continued, "that devil is fast and he's certainly done well by our mares. Only Misalliance won't be such a good bargain if he manages to kill one of us, which if I know anything about horses, he's still got it in his mind to do. Just look at the expression in those wild eyes of his!" Shug shook his head.

"What makes him so mean?" Kate asked.

The handyman lifted his shoulders. "It you ask me, he was just born that way. But Nick thinks it's because he was abused. Up close you can see the scars on his hide where some blitherin' fool whipped the life out of him trying to tame him. So it's a case of the chicken and the egg, I guess."

They stopped a little way from the fence and watched as Nick fearlessly approached the huge stallion. Misalliance had quit prancing along the fence. He stood very still, eyeing Nick. His nostrils flared and he whinnied a nervous challenge.

As if it were the most natural thing in the world, Nick continued walking toward the big animal. Kate couldn't hear what he was saying to Misalliance, but on the grass-scented spring breeze she picked up that same comforting murmur he'd used to mesmerize Cesare and—this morning—her.

"If that horse kicked Nick, would it kill him?" Rudy whispered.

"You bet it would," Shug answered. "But a little thing like chancing getting his brains bashed out or his ribs staved in by a half ton of crazy stallion isn't going to stop the boss. Just watch."

Unconsciously, Kate held her breath. Her hands tightened on the boys' shoulders. Suddenly the horse, which had seemed beautiful a few minutes earlier, looked evil, threatening. As Nick drew closer to Misalliance, a tense silence hung over the scene. She wanted to scream at Nick to get out of that field and not take such a foolish risk. But the realization that any loud noise would only make matters worse froze her tongue to the roof of her mouth. Taking risks like this was Nick's life. He did it all the time.

At Misalliance's head, Nick slipped the bridle over his ears, secured it and then vaulted lightly up onto his back. For a moment Misalliance looked surprised by this quick move. Then the horse leaped straight up into the air. After coming down on its forelegs, it lashed out with its hind.

Nick's seat remained rock-solid. Smoothly, he drew the reins in tight against the beast's resistance until its neck was bowed. It reared several more times, but with less and less energy. All the while Nick kept the reins drawn tight and maintained a steady seat.

As she watched, bits of frightened thoughts flew disjointedly through Kate's head. How strong Nick's legs must be! Their pressure against the horse's sides must be what was holding him on in the midst of all that equine turmoil. She couldn't help remembering the feel of Nick's muscular thighs against hers as they'd striven together for ecstasy. Yes, they'd been strong. But a man's legs could so easily be crushed. One miscalculation, one unbalanced moment aboard an animal like this and Nick could be crippled for life.

Finally, Misalliance came down, danced around a bit, lashed out with his hind legs and settled. "Good boy." Nick reached down and gave the horse's satin neck a pat.

"Nick doesn't look mad at him for kicking and jumping like that," Randy commented.

Shug chuckled. "Mad? Listen to me, boy, Nick enjoyed that little tussle as much as Misalliance did. Those two are soul mates."

"Soul mates?" The term made Kate shoot Shug's back a curious look. He'd crossed to open the gate so that Nick could take the horse out onto what looked like a practice track. Soon Misalliance was pounding down it with his black mane flying and Nick so solidly astride his powerful back that it seemed almost as if Nick might have been born there. Yet Kate felt disturbed and unsettled by what she'd seen.

THAT EVENING, as Kate and Nick sat alone together on an ancient glider on his front porch, she commented to him, "You know, you always seem in command of the situation no matter what you're doing."

"Why, thank you, ma'am."

"It's the truth. I was impressed with the way you handled everything in Italy. But seeing you ride that big black horse really awed me. You looked so completely at home."

"I *am* at home on a horse's back. That's my profession."

"Yes, well it's a dangerous profession."

"A lot of things are dangerous if you don't know what you're doing. I like to think I know what I'm doing."

Kate disagreed with his logic, but suddenly she lost heart for arguing the subject. The boys had been tucked away in bed and Shug had retired to the little cottage where he lived with his seventy-year-old mother. Kate wanted to enjoy the starry solitude surrounding her and Nick. After all, they would be parting soon.

"Well, anyhow, seeing you handle Misalliance impressed the heck out of me. And the boys now think you're God."

"Believe me, if I were in charge of the world a lot of things would be different."

"What would you change?"

"There's such a long list, I don't know where to begin. Hunger for one, I suppose. Pain for another. I'd take those things away. How about you?"

"My list is long, too. I'd take away loneliness."

"Then you'd be making a great mistake. It's loneliness that has produced the best poetry, and some of the best music, too."

"Yes, I suppose you're right." She shot his profile a quick glance. He was looking up at the sky, a certain remoteness in his attitude. What difference did it make that they'd become lovers that morning? Kate found herself wondering again. So far as she could tell, it hadn't changed a thing. Nick behaved no differently, and she'd done her best to take her cues from him.

Yet all day she'd been feeling unsteady, as if the ground might fall away from her at any instant. And when she looked at Nick strange, unsettling things happened inside her. She wanted to say crazy things to him. She felt torn between resentment and gratitude at his unfazed attitude. She didn't know what she wanted, except to go someplace quiet and try and forget this maddening man as soon as possible.

"It was awfully nice of you to take Rudy and Randy for rides," she said.

"That was nothing. I'm just sorry I couldn't convince you to get up on a horse and take a little gallop."

"I'm afraid of horses."

Nick shot her a look that was half amused, half annoyed. "You've said that before, but it doesn't make any sense."

"It makes perfect sense. I told you about what happened to my school friend. Isn't that reason enough?"

"Just the opposite. Today was the perfectly opportunity to conquer your fear. I wasn't going to let anything happen to that precious bod of yours." For the first time since that morning, his gaze traveled over her in a way that wasn't merely friendly, and Kate realized, with an exciting little shock, that she'd miscalculated. Things were really not the same between them, after all.

It occurred to Kate that Nick had been treating her impersonally for the benefit of the children. But now that they were alone together, looking out at his softly moonlit fields, his gaze was suddenly warm, intimate. His hand which had been draped along the back of the glider, came lightly down on her shoulder and he began to massage the sensitive hollow at the back of her neck.

"You don't understand," Kate said a bit unsteadily. "I grew up in a city. The backyards where I played in my foster homes were the size of postage stamps. Horses seem like such huge, alien, dangerous creatures—" She shook her head. "Well, I can admire them from a distance, but that's really all I can manage. I'm a city girl, Nick. Always have been, always will be."

"You're just saying that because you've never given anything different a try. Maybe it's time you did some experimenting, tried another life-style." He turned her toward him and kissed her lips. At his touch, all the feelings that had overtaken Kate that morning began to stir anew. Yet she forced herself to remain passive.

Nick realized she wasn't responding to his caress and pulled back. In the moonlight, he looked at her searchingly. "Something bothering you?"

"I . . . I'm just worried, I guess."

"About what?"

"Well, an awful lot has been going on, hasn't it?"

His mouth quirked. "True. It has all been a bit overwhelming. But now you can relax, you know. You're safe here. There isn't a mafioso in sight."

"But the boys are still my responsibility. I still have to get them back to England. Shouldn't we be making some plans about that?"

"The plans are already made. I have a friend who'll fly you across the Irish Sea any time you wish. Tomorrow if that's your pleasure."

Ignoring Nick's hand, which still toyed with the curls at the back of her neck, Kate stared out into the darkness and swallowed. "Maybe that's what should happen, then. The sooner Rudy and Randy are safe in their grandparents' care, the better."

"All right, I'll get things set up first thing tomorrow." Nick's hand stilled. "What will you do once you're on your own again in London?"

"I don't know. Look for work so I can earn enough to get back to the States, I guess."

"Would you work as a nanny?"

"Oh, no!" Kate gave a sharp laugh. "I don't think I'll try that profession ever again as long as I live. I'll find myself a job playing the piano. If I can't get something in a jazz club, I'll do anything—weddings, bar mitzvahs. It doesn't matter. Somehow I'll land on my feet."

"Kate, I don't like the sound of that. There's no one you can turn to if you need help, is there?"

"No. But there never really has been. Almost from the beginning, I've been totally alone in this world."

Nick was gazing at her with a troubled expression. A little frown knit his dark brows. "We're both orphans, you know," he pointed out.

"Yes." *But that's where the similarity ends,* Kate thought. How could she have ever imagined that she and Nick had anything in common? So okay, when he was very young he'd lost his parents tragically. Yet, for all that, he was still firmly imbedded in a network of close and loving family. She'd seen some of his Italian relatives, and he had a whole English set that she hadn't yet encountered. No, Nick wasn't alone, utterly unconnected like her—not at all. If Nick ever failed to land on his feet, there'd be someone to help pick up the pieces.

"You could come back here if you wanted," Nick said.

Kate widened her eyes. "Thanks for the invitation. That's very kind."

"I'm not being kind. I'd like it if you came back. I don't know how you feel about our lovemaking this morning, but it was pretty remarkable for me."

"For me, too," she admitted in a low voice. "But you surprise me. I thought—the way you acted afterward and for the rest of the day, so casual—I thought . . ."

In the moonlight Kate couldn't tell for sure, but it seemed to her that Nick's skin darkened, as if he were flushing.

He looked away and said, "I was knocked off my pins and didn't really know how to act. I didn't want to sound like an utter fool and talk a lot of rot about love when we don't know each other well enough for anything like that. I thought we just needed a little time and space to sort of think things over and get used to the idea of our having become lovers.''

"And now you've done that?" Kate asked curiously.

"Now I've done that, and I've realized that I don't want you to go. I'll worry about you, for one thing. A nice girl like you all alone in the big city," he said in a lame attempt at a joke.

His expression sobered. "I understand why you have to take the boys to England as soon as possible. I'm going to be following you in a few days, actually so that Seasonwine and I can get in a bit of training together before the Grand National. But after that's over, I'd like it if you came back with me, Kate. I'd like you to give us a chance to get to know each other better."

It wasn't exactly a declaration of undying love. Nevertheless, Kate was flattered, moved, and felt horribly like crying. "Oh, Nick, it means a lot to me that you've asked. But I can't. What would I do in a place like this? There's everything for you here, and nothing for me."

He looked genuinely surprised. "Are you saying there's nothing to do? But I'm busy from morning until night. Believe me, there are millions of things to do."

"For you, yes. But for me?" She shook her head. "I could cook and clean, and maybe I could get used to the horses enough to help feed them or muck out their stalls. But that's not what I want for my life. Nick, music is my life. It always has been and always will be. You don't even have a piano here."

"Why should I? I don't play. But it would be easy enough to pick one up. There's an auction the first Saturday of every month down at Clancy's. You can never tell what's going to be on the block. I'm sure I could get you a piano—if not there, then somewhere else."

Kate would have laughed if there weren't so many tears at the backs of her eyes. He didn't understand. After all the talking they'd done at Mario's about how important her music was to her, he just didn't understand.

Once again she shook her head. "I have to be making music, Nick, and I have to be in a place where I can see and hear other people who are doing the same thing. Isolated on a place like this—" She continued, shaking her head, "I've worked too long and too hard trying to build a career for myself. Since I was a child music has been my mother, my father, my solace and my refuge. I couldn't just give it up to live buried in the country on a farm. It would be like throwing a part of myself away, maybe the most important part. Do you understand now?" she asked earnestly.

"I understand that you're turning me down. I understand that we probably won't see each other after tomorrow." Nick's voice was suddenly harsh. "I understand that it's not likely we'll ever make love again the way we did this morning. And I understand that's not an idea I like much." He reached for her and hauled her roughly into his arms. "Kate," he said as his mouth came down on hers, "we're wasting precious time."

At first Kate didn't want to kiss him, not when he was so clearly angered by her rejection. But that was only at first. After a moment she stopped struggling. And after another moment, she clung and returned his kiss as if it had been her idea from the beginning.

The night had turned chilly, and their noses and cheeks felt cool against each other. But their mouths generated more than enough heat to compensate. Beneath their jackets, their bodies strained together. Kate could feel her breasts swelling against Nick's hard chest. Her hands circled his neck tightly and his arms held her like a vise.

When they pulled apart, they stared at each other, their hot breaths making a little cloud of vapor between them. "Where?" he asked starkly.

"Not in the house, not with the boys there."

He nodded and pulled her to her feet. "Come with me."

After the first few steps, Kate realized he was heading for the barn. It seemed appropriate, somehow. Hadn't that been where she'd first refused him, in Mario's barn?

Inside, the place was dark, warm, close with the healthy, ripe scent of animals. Nick found a soft place in a pile of fresh straw next to Rosy and her newborn's stall and brought Kate down on it with him. Then, once again they were kissing. Nick's hands slid under Kate's shirt and jacket and onto her breasts. At his touch she felt them come up into hard points.

"Nick!" she breathed and opened her eyes. But there was nothing to see. The barn was so dark that it was like being in a black box, which seemed only to heighten all her other senses. Hearing, taste, touch, smell—they were all electrically alive.

As Nick's hands went to the closure on Kate's slacks, hers did the same for him. She was shaking with desire. Nothing else seemed to matter, and she could tell it was the same for Nick. Both of them could think of only one thing. Suddenly, as he pushed her down into the fragrant straw with the length of his taut body, Kate realized that he wasn't worried about pleasing her the way he had been before. He only wanted to have her, to possess her this one last time before they said a final goodbye. She didn't care, because she felt exactly the same.

As they came together, Kate's cheek rubbed against his collarbone. The healthy smell of sweat and the musk of horse clung to his half-open shirt and to his skin. It excited Kate even more and she arched up against him, alive with a sense of bittersweet inevitability and, strangely, of power.

She could feel how much he wanted her, how determined he was to have her. She had never felt anything quite like this in a man before, and something deep within her woman's body responded in a liquid rush. All sense of control and conscious thought dissolved. In that moment, as she clasped his body deep into hers, they were one.

When it was over, they lay next to each other, gasping, breathing hard. Finally, they struggled back up onto their feet and, hardly speaking, dressed. Silently, they returned to the house. Nick put his hand on the door, just before he opened it he said, "I'm sorry about jumping on you like that."

"Why?"

"I wasn't very considerate back there. I don't usually drag a woman into my barn and all but rape her."

"You weren't raping me. As you must have noticed, I was more than willing."

"You..." He stopped dead, and Kate wondered what he had changed his mind about saying. "This is really where we tell each other goodbye," he said instead. "Tomorrow the kids will be up and we'll have to put on our public faces."

That was true, but there really wasn't much to say now, and they both realized it. Solemnly, Nick leaned forward and kissed Kate on the lips. Then he opened the door for her and they walked inside and, without any more words, parted ways at the staircase.

THE NEXT MORNING it was as Nick had predicted. The kids were up and about and took up everyone's time and energy. That afternoon Nick drove them to a small airstrip and introduced the pilot who'd be flying them to England. Nick had made all the arrangements and even seen to it that a car would be waiting at their destination to drive Kate and the boys to their grandfather's estate.

After Kate had settled herself and the twins into the airplane, she looked wistfully out its small, scarred window. Nick stood at the edge of the runway with his feet planted wide apart and his hands in his pockets. Wearing his leather jacket and with his dark hair whipped by a sudden wind that had sprung up, he looked so handsome that a knife seemed to twist in her chest. For a crazy minute she wanted to run back out of the plane and throw her arms around him.

But at that instant the pilot closed the door and revved the engine. A few seconds later they were taxiing down the short runway and Nick was no longer in sight.

CHAPTER ELEVEN

"IF YOU'RE QUITE, quite sure you don't care to continue in the position, we'll just have to engage another nanny as soon as possible," said Sir Cedric Morton, Jillian La-Fiore's father.

As he spoke, he eyed Rudy and Randy warily. "We really haven't spent much time with our grandchildren. They're virtually strangers to us, I'm sorry to say."

"Oh? Why is that?" Kate couldn't resist asking.

"Jillian has always been such a headstrong girl. Perhaps we spoiled her." Ruefully, he shook his fine, silver-haired head. "When our daughter married, there was an estrangement, I'm afraid. Actually, we don't even know where she is at the moment. Jaunting about the world with some itinerant thespians, I daresay. She never bothered to inform us of her plans, so this all comes as quite a surprise."

"I see. Well, I'm sorry, but your grandchildren do need your protection now."

"Of course, of course," Sir Cedric huffed. "Of course we'll take them under our wing." Once again, he shot a doubtful look at the twins. Rudy and Randy, energized, if anything, by their flight across the Irish Sea and their limousine ride from the airport, were gamboling about in the acre or so of elegantly appointed east parlor in the Morton's family mansion.

Their grandmother, a fluttery little woman in an expensive powder-blue silk dress, followed after them, giving out little squeaks of alarm as she sought to protect the breakables from their grubby grasps. Chinese vases trembled on their stands. A cut-glass decanter narrowly avoided extinction.

From Kate's spot on a carved Victorian sofa, she glanced appreciatively around at the glowing linenfold paneling and the delicate antique tables and chairs, which sat atop oriental carpets. Clearly, Jillian LaFiore had not married into her own class—a fact of which her parents, sealed away from the real world in their stately little palace, were obviously too painfully aware. Perhaps a few weeks with Rudy and Randy were just the breath of fresh air they needed.

"Well, Lady Lavinia and I are a bit elderly to take on the management of two such energetic youngsters, but we'll simply have to do the best we can," Sir Cedric said resolutely. He shot Kate another look of appeal. "You're quite sure you don't want to continue looking after them? We'd pay you well. You'd live here on the grounds, of course. We could provide you with very pleasant quarters."

Kate was surprised at how tempted she was to accept the offer. She'd thought she'd be relieved to say farewell to her charges. But now that the moment had come, she felt distinctly misty-eyed. Despite everything, she'd grown fond of them and would even, she realized with some amazement, miss the two little devils. Nevertheless, she shook her head. "No, thank you. You've already been most generous in paying me for the two weeks I did spend caring for them and I have my own life to get on with."

"Ah, yes, you did mention that you were a jazz musician." If she'd told him she was a Martian, Sir Cedric couldn't have looked any more dubious.

Kate rose, kissed each of the boys and, without much hope of it actually happening, told them to be good.

"Are you going away forever?" Randy asked. Obviously, the possibility had just dawned on him and he looked distressed.

"Won't we be seeing you again?" Rudy's face began to pucker.

Kate sank to her knees and stroked each of their dark heads. "If it's all right with your grandparents, I may come out to visit you while I'm still in England."

"Oh, please! We had loads of fun together, didn't we?"

"Yes," Kate agreed. "We really did have fun. But we had some scary times, too."

"They weren't so scary as long as you were with us," Rudy volunteered.

"That's because you were very brave." She took their hands. "Both of you were very, very brave, and I'm proud to know you. But life isn't usually so exciting, and now it's time to settle down to less dangerous things like school-work and getting to know your grandparents better." As she gazed into their faces her eyes grew watery and she had to blink hard. Impulsively, she drew the boys to her and kissed each of their cheeks. To her surprise, they kissed her back and then gave her embarrassed little hugs.

"You be sure to come see us," Randy insisted.

"Just try and stop me," Kate said with a watery chuckle and then pressed her cheeks to each of theirs again. A few minutes later she was waving goodbye to them from the back of Sir Cedric's chauffeur-driven Rolls Royce limousine.

AS THE BIG SILVER-GRAY CAR glided toward the city, Kate dabbed at her eyes with her handkerchief and then clasped her hands in her lap and took stock of her situation. The twins' grandfather had paid her more than enough to buy a plane ticket to the States. Perhaps she should be heading for Heathrow rather than London. But Kate didn't feel ready to go back home yet. There was too much unfinished business.

Yet that didn't really make much sense. Frowning, Kate glanced out the window. It wasn't as if she had a job playing piano, or even the prospect of one. At least in the States she had friends she could go to for references or advice. Nick was the real reason she wanted to stay on, she acknowledged.

At the thought of him, her heart seemed to burn and she twisted her fingers. Soon he would be in England, preparing for the Grand National. It was better for both their equanimities that they didn't meet each other—oh yes, much better. Yet she wanted to see him again, if only from a distance and in a crowd. Kate couldn't fly across the Atlantic until she'd seen Nick get through that dangerous race in one piece.

"Here we are, miss," the chauffeur said as he pulled to a stop in front of a town house in Kensington. "This is the address you gave me."

"Thank you." Kate peered out at the familiar narrow brick residence. She'd called Mrs. Brasswell from the Morton estate and been assured that her old room was available.

"The hubby and me will be delighted to have you back, I'm sure," Mrs. Brasswell had told Kate with genuine warmth. "Oh, and while you were gone something funny happened. I'll tell you about it when you arrive."

Kate had been puzzled by that. But she'd had so many other things to think of that by the time she stepped out on the curb and watched the Rolls float away, she'd forgotten.

"Oh, my, look at you!" Mrs. Brasswell cried after she'd thrown open her door and literally dragged Kate inside. "Didn't those Eyetalians treat you right? You're thin as a rail! You must have dropped half a stone."

Kate smiled weakly. "It's a long story."

"Well, I've nothing but time, dearie. After you've gone upstairs and made yourself comfy, you must come back down and let me give you a cup of tea so you can tell me all about it."

Wistfully, Kate smiled down into her landlady's motherly face. Suddenly, she felt like throwing her arms around the little woman's plump shoulders and dissolving into tears. So many troubling things had happened and it was so hard to bear up under the confusion of it all with no one to lean on or offer solace.

A little later Kate sat in Mrs. Brasswell's cozy little parlor.

"You don't like sugar in your tea, do you, dearie?"

"Just plain, thank you," Kate said, accepting a rose-covered china teacup and saucer from her hostess. "Oh, it's delicious. Just what I need."

"A nice cup of tea always does the trick, I say. Now, tell me all about this trip to Italy. Was it nice? Did you enjoy yourself? Did those Eyetalian men behave themselves? Or did they give you a pinch the way I hear they like to do with a pretty girl?" Mrs. Brasswell's eyes sparkled with interest.

Kate cleared her throat. "Most of the Italian men I met were very polite, and I don't know if I'd call my trip nice, but it was certainly exciting." Briefly, she outlined a highly edited version of her adventures in the historic land of song and sunshine.

When Kate finished, Mrs. Brasswell's russet eyebrows had flown up to her hairline. "Goodness, if I'd have known all this I'd have been worried sick! Are you sure those boys will be safe with their hoity-toity grandparents?"

"Oh, yes. The Morton estate is well guarded, and Lou LaFiore is scheduled to testify today. Once that's over, we can all relax—except maybe for Lou himself." Kate frowned. "I suppose his former partners in crime might still want to avenge themselves on him. But there won't be any reason to harm any of the rest of us."

"Still..." Mrs. Brasswell *tsk-tsked* and shook her head. Then her eyes widened. "I wonder if that man who came around asking after you was one of those criminals."

"What man?" Kate sat up straighter. "Someone came asking after me?" Immediately she thought of Nick. But, of course, that was impossible. She'd left him only a few hours earlier. "When was this?"

"It was just a couple of days ago," Mrs. Brasswell was saying. "He came to the door asking for you. Nice-looking bloke, even though he did wear glasses. Here, he left his card with me. Now where did I put that thing? In the kitchen, p'raps. I've gotten so absentminded lately."

While the landlady bustled out, Kate took a sip of her tea and fretted about who her mystery caller might have been. A few minutes later Mrs. Brasswell returned and handed her an expensive looking embossed card. "There, I knew I hadn't lost it. It wasn't where I thought, though."

"Foster, Brighton and Caine," Kate read aloud. "Jacob Caine, Attorney at Law." She shook her head, more mystified than ever. "I can't imagine who this might be or what he would want with me."

"He was a Yank and it's an American firm, you see. I thought p'raps he might have come to tell you you'd just inherited a big pot of money."

Kate laughed at that. "Not likely. I've no one to inherit money from. What did you say when he asked about me?"

"Why nothing, nothing at all. And now that I've heard that hair-raising story from your lips, I'm very glad I didn't give away that you were traveling in Italy. He might have been up to no good." Mrs. Brasswell tapped the card, which Kate still held between her fingers. "It's easy enough to have one of these things printed up. How do we know he wasn't just pretending to be a lawyer so he could wheedle me into telling him where he could get hold of you?"

How indeed? The thought gave Kate a chill. She even wondered if it had been a wise thing to come back to Mrs. Brasswell's at all. Perhaps she should look for lodgings elsewhere. But the thought was so unpleasant that she quickly pushed it away. For just a few days she needed the comfort of familiar surroundings. But she certainly wasn't going to contact Jacob Caine, whoever he might be. Kate tore his card in half and then dismissed him from her mind.

THE NEXT MORNING, after a restless night, Kate dressed in the good clothes Nick had bought her and set out to make the rounds of the clubs. In her heart she knew she was remaining in England because she wanted to see Nick ride the Grand National. But that didn't take away the necessity of making a living. And then there was her pride to consider. She'd come to Europe to try and make good on the international jazz scene. Kate wasn't ready to give up on that goal quite yet.

By the end of the day, however, she was feeling pretty discouraged. Though she'd trudged all over London looking for work, nothing had turned up. Kate had no hope of that changing when she walked into the Red Candle on the King's Road.

"Sorry," Tony Diger, its hard-jawed manager told her. "We're booked for the next month with a guitarist who's been very popular with the after-theater crowd. Maybe you saw his name on the marquee outside?"

Kate nodded. She'd expected as much, but it had seemed worth a try.

"We might be in the market for your sort of thing next month."

"By that time I may not still be in England." By that time she would have run out of money and starved if her luck didn't improve.

"Well, you never know, do you? Why don't you give me your address and phone number? If something turns up I'll ring you."

Convinced that it was a wasted effort, Kate wrote the information out and then departed. When she was gone, Tony sat for a moment tapping the bit of notepaper she'd left with him. Then, after checking a card in his desk file, he picked up his phone and punched out a number. "I'd like to speak to Winston Deeping," he told the receptionist who answered. "I've got some information he wanted."

"MUCH AS I'VE ENJOYED your company these past couple of days," Winston was saying to Jake Caine, "I have to admit that I think you should give up on this wild-goose chase and leave it to the detectives. I'm sure you must have pressing business to attend to back in Boston."

"Yes," Jake admitted, crossing his legs as he shifted for a more comfortable position in one of Winston's cushy leather chairs.

He'd come to Winston's office to meet him for drinks and to relay some instructions he'd received from Owen Byrnside in a transatlantic call that morning. Jake was feeling distinctly discouraged. Not only had he made no progress in the search for Kate Humphrey, who appeared to have vanished off the face of the earth, but his employer had become so obsessed by the subject that in his impatience to find his mystery granddaughter he was beginning to sound a little paranoid.

"When I talked to Byrnside this morning, he was concerned about this new campaign you're mounting for the Garbage Boys," Jake told Winston.

A wary look crept over the other man's well-bred face. "Oh? I'm waiting with bated breath. Let's have it."

"Says he thinks holding press parties for them in landfills and garbage dumps is tasteless."

Winston grimaced. "Owen Byrnside is a dinosaur, a relic of the past who's been confined to his bed with a weak heart for almost a decade. What does he know about what's tasteless in the nineties? I must say, Jake, I'd appreciate it if the man would just leave me alone to do my job, which thus far, I might point out, has consisted of making tons of money for his company."

"Well it *is* his company," Jake reminded Winston gently. He couldn't say whether the garbage-dump campaign was a good idea or not. To Jake, who preferred classical music, the whole pop recording business seemed monumentally tacky and tasteless. But it was lucrative—no question about that.

Winston had just opened his mouth to retort when his private secretary buzzed from the outer office. "Call for you on line one—a Mr. Diger from a club called the Red Candle."

"Now what could a fellow like that possibly want with me?" Winston muttered irritably. Instead of bothering to pick up the receiver, he left the speaker engaged on his complicated phone and depressed the correct button.

"Deeping here."

"Mr. Deeping, sorry to bother you, but I got a message to let you know if I ever heard anything about a piano player named Kate Humphrey. Well, she just came in here a couple of minutes ago looking for work."

Jake, who'd been glancing idly around the office trying to decide whether or not to fly back to the States tomorrow sat up with a jerk. "Hooray!" he exclaimed.

Winston looked less pleased. His sandy eyebrows had crocheted themselves together into a ragged frown. "Are you quite sure it's the young woman I inquired about?"

"All I know is that she's a good-looking Yank redhead who plays jazz piano and is looking for a job. She says her name is Kate Humphrey and she gave me her address and telephone number."

"Tell Diger to give her that job," Jake whispered harshly. "Tell him if he goes along with us on this we'll pay her salary and slip him a fat bonus."

"WHOA BOY, whoa, that's a good boy, very good." Nick trotted Seasonwine around to the head of the course for another run at the jumps. Three days after Kate had left Ireland with the LaFiore twins, Nick had finished making sure that everything was shipshape at Newride and then flown across the Irish Sea himself. For the past week he'd lived on the manicured private estate of Arthur Marchmant, Seasonwine's new owner.

Marchmant had made his vast fortune in the grocery business. He owned a chain of American-style supermarkets called March-M's that extended all the way to Australia. Lately he'd taken up horseracing with the same drive and enthusiasm that had made him into a food mogul, and he had conveyed to Nick that he was determined to win the prestigious Grand National.

"You and Seasonwine make an unbeatable combination," he'd told Nick.

"In a mad scramble like the one at Aintree there's no such thing as an unbeatable combination," Nick had retorted.

"Oh, but . . ."

Determined that his sponsor take a realistic view of their likelihood of coming down the final stretch first, Nick had shaken his head. "It's partly because of the crowd. They always allow twice as many horses as the course will safely take. When you've got that many animals pounding down a track at the same jump it's anybody's guess what may happen."

"That's what makes it exciting."

"It can get a little too exciting if you're on my side of the rail," Nick responded dryly. "Not long ago in an American steeplechase a horse had a heart attack while going over timber. He died straddling the fence. You can imagine the pileup something like that might cause."

But Marchmant had remained cheerfully optimistic. "I've got the winning team. I'm sure of it."

Nick hoped his employer wouldn't be disappointed. Actually, Seasonwine was coming along nicely. The big chestnut appeared to have lost none of his strength and endurance. He'd always been a fleet, tidy jumper and that hadn't changed. It was his nerve that worried Nick.

Since Seasonwine had been out of retirement and in training for such a short time, there'd been no opportunity to try him out in a real race. The horse seemed fine now on this private course and in the couple of small events he'd participated in recently. But conditions during a hell-bent-for-leather race with screaming crowds and too many desperate competitors would be a lot different. Under those conditions Seasonwine had taken a devastating spill. It was sheer luck that he'd survived at all. In the thick of competition would he remember and start baulking at the jumps that he sailed over so easily now?

For that matter, Nick wondered how he himself would react. It had been a long time since he'd cracked up so badly in a race that he'd been forced to start a new career. After all these months, when it came to the heat of the real thing again, how would his own nerve hold up?

Nick urged Seasonwine on, and once again they made the round of jumps. After the chestnut took them all smooth as silk, Nick slid down and rewarded him with an affectionate pat and a lump of sugar. "I think you know what's coming up," Nick said as he led the animal back toward the whitewashed stables. "Big guy, I think you've been bored with nothing to do all day but eat grass and rendezvous with foxy ladies."

The horse whinnied and butted Nick's back.

Nick chuckled. "Oh, so it wasn't the stud service you minded, it was just that you missed racing. Well, I have to admit that I've missed it, too."

As they neared the stable an exercise boy brought out a roan mare. She whickered when she saw Seasonwine and, in answer, he pulled on his lead and did a prancing little dance.

"Well, well, quite the ladies' man, aren't you?" Nick commented after the mare was led away. "Can't say I blame you putting on a bit of a show for one like her. Between you and me, redheads are a weakness of mine, too."

As he said the words, Nick's amused expression sobered. It was alarming how Kate Humphrey kept turning up in his thoughts. The oddest things reminded him of her. Sunsets brought her image to his mind because it made him think of how her hair had looked like living flame when the sun was at her back. The sea beneath the plane in which he'd flown to England had reminded him of her eyes because it had been the same pale, clear, lively green. Grass made him think of her, too, because she smelled so fresh, like a meadow in spring.

But barns were the worst. As Nick stepped into the shade of the stable he was struck by a pang so strong that it was like a physical blow. The rustle of straw beneath his booted feet, the musky fragrance of the other horses, it all brought back that night at Newride when he'd made such harsh, single-minded love to Kate and she'd responded with a female complement to his passion so electrifying and elemental that it had taken his breath away.

How could they be so as one physically and so at odds in every other way? he wondered. Intellectually, Nick understood why Kate had turned her back on his invitation to stay in Ireland. Her arguments made sense. It was just that on every other level—in his heart, in his gut, in his very bones—he didn't understand at all and nothing made sense.

Nick ushered Seasonwine into his stall and then began uncinching the animal's girth. As he worked he wondered what Kate was doing now. Was she all right? Had she found a job playing the music that was so important to her? Was she still in London? Or had she decided to go back home to the States?

His fingers froze on the leather strap. Suddenly in his mind's eye he could see miles and miles of ocean stretching endlessly over the horizon and Kate lost to him forever somewhere far beyond.

That was ridiculous, he told himself. He brought breeding stock to the States fairly often. He could always look her up. But where? Short of hiring a detective, he had no idea how he'd go about finding a gypsy like Kate. For that matter, he didn't know how he'd go about locating her if she were still in London.

Thoughtfully, Nick finished putting away Seasonwine's tack and, after leaving instructions with the stableboy, strolled out into the afternoon sunshine. After a moment's hesitation, he turned and headed in the direction of the big house. Marchmant always kept a stack of London newspapers in the library. It wouldn't hurt to take a look through the theater and entertainment listings.

"AND TONIGHT, ladies and gentlemen, an extra-special treat. Direct from a rave review tour in the U.S.A., the beautiful and talented Miss Kate Humphrey."

Kate took a deep breath, smoothed the skirt of the forest-green velvet gown she'd bought for her opening night, and stepped from behind the curtain onto the small stage. Out on the dimly lit floor, desultory hand-clapping mingled with conversation, guffaws and high-pitched bursts of laughter, and the clink of glass and china. Cigarette smoke wafted toward the ceiling in sinuous blue trails.

Nightclubs were the same all over the world, Kate thought as she took a bow and then slid onto the piano bench. For her first selection she started with a complicated and upbeat arrangement of "Satin Doll." When that seemed to get their attention, she smiled and, using her smokiest tones, whispered into the microphone that had been set up for her on the side, "Ladies and gentlemen, that was one of my favorite tunes. But I'd love to play some of yours. If there's anything you'd like to hear, just send your request up with a waiter. In the meantime, here's a romantic little number we all know and love."

When the applause died down, Kate turned back to the keyboard and began a languorous rendition of "Deep Purple."

Tony Diger's miraculous offer of a one-month run at the Red Candle at a very attractive salary had come only the day before. Kate, after pausing five seconds to recover from her astonishment, had snapped it up.

"I'd love to take the job, but what happened to that guitarist you were telling me about?" she'd queried.

"Byrnside Enterprises offered him a recording contract and a tour in the States—which leaves us high and dry."

"Not any more you aren't," Kate had assured the man. After she'd replaced the receiver, Kate had paced the Brasswells' hallway, bubbling with excitement and worried at the same time that she might ruin the deal by bombing on her first number. Now, however, with her initial jitters gone just the way they always disappeared when she sat down at a piano, Kate was in her element.

She was on her second set when the waiter brought up Jake Caine's card. Kate's heart skipped a beat, and she remembered Mrs. Brasswell's suggestion that Jake Caine might be connected with the gang who'd been out to get Lou LaFiore. It was a terrifying idea, and for a brief instant she considered slipping out the back door at the end of her set.

But that was ridiculous, she told herself sternly. This job was too good to be frightened away from because of a nebulous threat. Thinking that she wasn't going to let herself get pushed around, she turned the card over. "Table number twelve," it read. "Please meet me. I have something important to discuss with you."

Kate gazed out over the audience. But the café was too smoky and dark to make out anything at the spot in the far corner but the shadowy figure of a man. Shrugging, she turned back to her instrument. "I've got a request for 'Autumn Leaves,'" she murmured into the microphone. "Now that's got to be on everyone's hit parade."

Twenty minutes later, when the second set was over, Kate took her bows and then began to thread her way through the crowded tables toward the one in the corner.

"Great playing." "What a beauty!" "Enjoyed your performance," people told her as she passed by. Kate smiled and thanked them, but all the while her attention was on the gray-suited man who, through the haze of smoke, was gradually coming into clearer focus.

Though he appeared to be tall, with a broad-shouldered, muscular build, he certainly didn't resemble a thug. In fact, with his short hair, clean-cut features and shrewd gray eyes watching her every move from behind silver aviator-style glasses, he looked exactly like what he claimed to be—a partner in a high-priced law firm. If it weren't that she was still suffering from the loss of Nick, Kate might even have been attracted. But Nick had left no room in her emotional life for another man, so she was merely intensely curious.

Kate stopped a foot away from the table and cocked her head. "Mr. Jake Caine?"

"Yes, Miss Humphrey. I enjoyed your performance very much. You're very good. Won't you sit down and let me buy you a drink?"

Kate hesitated a moment longer and then pulled out a chair. "I don't drink alcohol when I'm working, so a cup of tea will be fine."

He nodded and then called a waiter over to give the order. When that was done, he looked at her thoughtfully. "I suppose you're wondering what this is all about."

"Well, yes I am—naturally."

"It's a long, complicated story. But let me just begin by saying that there's a chance, a rather good chance, that you might be about to come into a very large fortune."

CHAPTER TWELVE

"You're joking, of course," Kate said.

"Not at all. Believe me, Miss Humphrey, this is dead serious."

Jake Caine regarded the slim redhead across from him with interest. What would Owen Byrnside think of Kate Humphrey? he wondered. Jake continued to study her, looking for some family resemblance—the steady gaze, the hint of stubbornness around the jaw, perhaps? And then there was the musical ability. Though Gloria Dean's life had been too short for her to make any kind of lasting success out of her talent, she had been musically gifted.

Well, if Kate Humphrey did indeed turn out to be the old man's granddaughter, Owen Byrnside would have nothing to be ashamed of. She was an extremely attractive young woman, and a talented one besides. Not only that, she had a cool dignity about her, a composure that suggested strength of character.

Jake cleared his throat. "Miss Humphrey, I'm going to tell you a story—one that may strike you as bizarre, even farfetched, but that is, I assure you, quite true. Have you ever run across the name Owen Byrnside?"

"Yes," Kate admitted, not bothering to keep the skepticism out of her voice. Who was this man, and what in the world was he up to? "Owen Byrnside is a multimillionaire. Among other things, he owns the Byrnside Recording Company."

Jake nodded. "Mr. Byrnside is an old man now, and not a well one, I'm afraid. In fact, for the past ten years or so, since he lost his wife and suffered a massive heart attack, he's been an invalid and something of a recluse. Before that, however, he was a man of rather overwhelming vigor. Singlehandedly he built a multinational recording and publishing empire that's literally worth billions."

"So I've heard, but I don't see what it's got to do with me," Kate replied somewhat impatiently. Breaks between sets were her treasured rest periods. She hated to waste one talking to this stranger about something that didn't really interest her.

"It may have a great deal to do with you, Miss Humphrey. If you'll just listen." Jake took a sip of his sparkling water. "Worldly success and wealth doesn't always bring great happiness. Though Owen Byrnside married a woman he deeply loved, their only son, Christopher, was a grave disappointment to them both."

"In what way?"

"He was a weakling, I'm afraid. Growing up in the sixties, he became involved with the drug culture. Since he had money to burn, he also became involved with a number of women on the fringes of the entertainment business—singers, starlets. At one point he had an affair with a beautiful young rock star named Gloria Dean. Have you ever heard of her?"

"I...the name is vaguely familiar. But I still don't see..."

"Christopher Byrnside was killed in an automobile accident. For Owen Byrnside and his wife their's son's death was a terrible loss. For one thing, Owen had to accept that there would never be anyone of his own blood to whom he could leave his empire. There would be no Byrnside dynasty. If you knew the man, you would understand what a bitter pill that was for him to swallow."

"Yes, I'm sure, but..."

Jake Caine held up a hand. "I'm getting to the point, Miss Humphrey. Just be patient a moment longer. A few months ago Mr. Byrnside received an anonymous letter that contained a startling piece of information. According to the writer, Christopher Byrnside didn't die without issue, after all. When he had his fatal accident, Gloria Dean was carrying his child."

Kate went very still. "Oh?"

"Again, according to the letter writer, Gloria Dean carried that child to term and then bore it."

"What happened to her baby?"

"That's where we have the mystery. If our letter-writer is telling the truth, on the night of April first, 1964 she put a gold locket around its neck and left it at the Broadstreet Foundling Home in Boston, Massachusetts."

Kate stared. "But that was where I..."

"I know, Miss Humphrey. That was where you and two other female infants were left on that same night. Unfortunately, as you surely know, the orphanage was destroyed in a fire only a month later and all its records were lost in the flames."

Kate put her hands flat on the table. "Mr. Caine, exactly what is it that you've come here to tell me?"

"Only that you were one of those three abandoned baby girls, and that the possibility seems to exist that one of them might be Owen Byrnside's lost granddaughter."

Kate sat staring at the man across from her. She felt as if she'd been poleaxed. Her ears buzzed and a dizzy sensation was spreading through her solar plexus. "You can't be serious."

His gray eyes were steady. "I'm dead serious."

"Then why have you come? What is it that you want from me? I've no way of proving that I'm anybody at all."

Jake Caine rotated his half-empty glass between his palms. "First of all, I'm here because I needed to find you." He shook his head. "It wasn't an easy task. You're quite a rolling stone."

"I get around," Kate acknowledged. Her thoughts flashed to her days in Italy. Life certainly had become even more harrowing than usual.

"Yes," Jake agreed dryly. "Now that I've found you, I'm here to ask a question and make a request."

"Yes?" A wary look came back into Kate's green eyes.

"Mr. Byrnside is most anxious to discover this lost granddaughter, if she really exists. To that end he has charged me with the task of tracking down all three of the girls who were abandoned. You are the first that I've located."

"Hmm. And what's he going to do when he's got all three?"

For the first time, Jake Caine smiled. It was a charming smile, Kate noted.

"It's rather complicated," he said. "Before I try to explain, let me ask my question."

"Ask away."

"As I mentioned before, there was a gold locket around the true Byrnside baby's neck, a locket that happens to have been a family heirloom. Do you have any knowledge of such a piece of jewelry?"

"You mean, do I have it tucked way in a vault somewhere?" Kate shook her head. "As far as I know, I came into this world wearing nothing but my skin."

Jake nodded. "That's as I expected, but it was worth a try. It would be a miracle if that locket were still in existence. Most likely it was lost in the fire." He took another sip of his drink. "Anyhow, on to the next item of business. You asked what Owen Byrnside intends to do with the three of you. First off, he'd like to meet you all."

Kate stiffened slightly, but said nothing. Again she felt a twinge of suspicion. Could this be some sort of elaborate ruse on the part of Lou LaFiore's enemies? But it was all so bizarre. Surely they wouldn't make up anything so farfetched just to lure her into their clutches! And why should they even be interested in her now?

"Secondly," Jake Caine continued, "once we've located all three girls, he'd like to gather you together on his estate in Massachusetts and have a painless procedure called DNA fingerprinting done on each of you."

Kate's eyebrows shot up. "DNA fingerprinting?"

"Paternity testing used to be pretty primitive and unreliable," Jake Caine began to explain. "But these days what can be done in a genetic lab is truly wondrous. Something as minute as a sample of dried blood, for instance, can be coaxed by technicians to reveal the chemical blueprint of a person, the very essence that makes you, you. Genetic patterns are as unique as fingerprints, hence the name."

"And this genetic fingerprinting could establish beyond a doubt whether or not I'm related to Owen Byrnside?"

"Yes, it could."

"Then, if it's really as easy as you say, why make it any more complicated than it needs to be? Why not just prick my finger here and now, take a sample of my blood away with you and let me know how it all comes out?"

Jake Caine cleared his throat. "I know that sounds like the logical way to proceed. But Owen Byrnside is calling the shots, and that's not the manner in which he wants things done. There's a very large fortune and a great deal of power at issue here, Miss Humphrey."

"You can call me Kate if you want."

"All right, Kate. And I'm Jake. Anyhow, a lot is at risk and Mr. Byrnside doesn't intend there to be any possibility of a mistake, or of fraud. He wants to meet all three of you. He wants all three of you to sit down together in front of witnesses when the blood samples are drawn. He wants all the technicians to be in his pay at a private lab he'll have established on his estate and he wants the witnesses to follow those blood samples into that laboratory where they can watch over every step of the procedure under the strictest security and confirm that no substitutions were made anywhere along the line and that the results are absolutely accurate beyond a doubt."

Kate let out a low whistle. "I see. Your Owen Byrnside may be old and sick, but he's nobody's fool, is he?"

"Mr. Byrnside's mind is still sharp as a tack. You'll see that when you meet him."

"And when will that be? My engagement here runs until the end of the month. I can't afford to jeopardize it, so I couldn't possibly go anywhere until it's over."

Jake Caine nodded. Should he tell her that she owed this job to Byrnside Enterprises? he wondered. But that would hurt her pride, and somehow he could see beneath her composed surface that pride was most of what this pretty young woman had and all she couldn't do without. Besides, he still had two other orphans to find.

"You have nothing to worry about," he told her. "I'll be in touch." And with that, he rose and put several pound notes on the table to pay the bill. After he gave her another copy of his card, he shook her hand and walked out.

Kate remained at the table a few minutes longer. Blinking like a dazed owl, she stared down at Jake Caine's card. If it hadn't been for the evidence in her hand, she'd have thought that she'd imagined the whole preposterous conversation. Then, shaking her head to clear it, she checked the thin watch on her wrist. Time to get back to reality—time for the final set of the evening.

OUTSIDE ON THE STREET a few nights later Nick studied the picture in front of the Red Candle's marquee. The Red Candle Café Proudly Presents, it read, and showed Kate looking like a glamorous stranger in an off-the-shoulder gown made of some dark, glittery material. Well, he needn't have worried about her, Nick thought. She certainly appeared to have landed on her feet.

Tearing his gaze away from the billboard, he began to pace back in forth in front of the building. After her very clear rejection, was he crazy to be here? he asked himself. Should he go inside, or should he just be sensible and walk away? It wasn't as if there weren't other good-looking women in the world. Only yesterday at one of Marchmant's cocktail parties a real stunner had practicality tried to carry Nick off to bed.

But he knew he wasn't going to walk away from the Red Candle. After spotting the notice about Kate in the entertainment pages, Nick had been able to think of almost nothing else. Other women, no matter how beautiful and aggressive, held no interest for him. He'd tried telling himself to forget her, but it hadn't done any good. He had to see her one more time.

Inside the crowded club Nick was lucky to get a table. With the Grand National only forty-eight hours away, he dared not drink anything alcoholic that might put an extra ounce of weight on him. But to please the waitress he ordered a club soda and waited for Kate to appear on the stage.

To pass the time he glanced around at the other tables. They were filled with a motley assortment—balding businessmen showing clients the town, punk couples in outrageous getups, lawyer-types out to impress trendy young women, and, of course, the inevitable seedy-looking derelict. Nick resented them all because he didn't like this nightclub and because its patrons now had the same access to Kate that he did.

When she walked out from behind the curtains and into a rose-colored spotlight, he felt something twist deep inside him. In his memory, images of Kate formed a kind of winsome collage: Kate in a torn T-shirt pacifying the twins, Kate in baggy harem pants and Mario's oversize shirt trapped against the boards with him in Cesare's stall, Kate as she'd been lying beneath him in the sweet-smelling Irish hay.

But now he saw her in a setting that was entirely and disturbingly new. The starkly cut, black silk gown she wore clung to her slender, curvy figure and then brushed the floor in a burst of fullness. Her makeup was dramatic and her hair had been brushed up in a way that lent her face a new sophistication. She looked like a young Rita Hayworth—warm, glamorous, too lovely to be quite real, and very, very sexy.

When the whistles and applause died down and she seated herself at the piano, the illusion was strengthened. In Italy, with the rambunctious twins and the everpresent threat of disaster, there had been times when she'd seemed out of her depth. In front of a keyboard she was fully in command, and Nick could feel the ripple of attention and interest in the audience as she started to play.

Up on the stage Kate could feel it, too. But tonight she sensed something different. And as her gaze swept the audience, she knew what it was. Nick was out there. A jolt of excitement quivered through her. He was sitting at a table by himself watching intently, and it was no coincidence. He'd obviously come just to see her.

Somehow Kate managed to get through all three of her sets that night. After each, she left quickly and retired to her cramped dressing room in the back. She knew that if she approached Nick before the end of the evening, she'd be too emotionally drained to complete her performance. Still, every time she returned to the stage her stomach tightened with the fear that Nick would be gone.

That never happened. He was always there, in the same place, nursing a different untasted drink and staring at her with an expression she found impossible to read yet that made her head swim.

When the applause died down for Kate's last performance, she threaded her way to his table and pulled out a chair. For a long moment they regarded each other in silence. Kate had never seen him in anything but casual dress. In his formal, dark suit he looked wonderful, she thought. She had forgotten how devastatingly handsome he was.

"Long time no see," he murmured with gentle mockery.

"Actually, I saw you only last night," she corrected.

"Oh?" He cocked his head.

"It was on television. With the Grand National so close, the sports-news people keep running footage of past races. They keep playing that one of you and Seasonwine cracking up."

"Yes, that. I've seen it a few too many times myself," Nick admitted with a grimace. "Not a pleasant home movie."

"It gives me the shivers."

"Does it?" A gleam came into Nick's eyes. "Does that mean you've missed me, Kate?"

Kate looked down at her hands. How could she lie? Since leaving Ireland she'd thought of him almost constantly. Even with her blessed job at the Red Candle and now this Byrnside thing to distract her, she'd lain awake each night thinking solely of Nick. Seeing him like this, within touching distance and so real and vital, made her shake with longing for him. "Yes, I've missed you. I've missed you a lot," she admitted huskily.

"It's the same with me, Kate. I wouldn't be here otherwise." He glanced around. "Why don't we go someplace where we can talk about it?"

Her legs felt weak. "All right. Just let me change and get my coat."

Outside the club they caught a taxi easily. Nick gave the driver directions and then, as their vehicle sped into traffic, sat back and looked long at Kate. "I'm sorry you changed out of that black thing you had on. You're really something else in it."

"Oh, that!" Kate laughed. "Thank you, I think, but it's strictly a costume for performance and not something I would wear out on the street."

"Not if you didn't want to cause a traffic jam," Nick joked as his eyes drank her in. Without her stage makeup and in an elongated corduroy jacket and matching ankle-length skirt she looked more like herself, he thought. The fact didn't diminish her attractiveness any. Right at this moment he wanted her so badly that it was physical torture not to simply reach out and pounce.

"How have things been going for you?" he asked, amazed at how cool and controlled his voice sounded when inside his pulses were pounding.

"Well enough." Kate considered telling Nick about the Byrnside thing, but decided against it. The story was so complicated and peculiar and might turn out to be just some sort of hoax. Why bother to mention it?

"You didn't have any trouble dropping off the boys?"

"None at all. Your arrangements at the airport all went very smoothly. Thank you."

"You're very welcome. I rang up their grandparents' place the night after you left, just to check. They said everything was fine."

"Oh, yes. In fact, I went out to see them a couple of days ago. They're all getting along together very well."

Nick smiled, partly at the mundane nature of their conversation when there were so many strong feelings churning between them, partly because he really was surprised by what she'd just said. "You amaze me. Somehow I expected that you'd be glad to see the last of Rudy and Randy."

She giggled and nodded. "I thought that, too. But I guess they grew on me."

"Did I grow on you, Kate?"

Her green eyes widened, and she opened her mouth to answer. But at that moment the taxi pulled to a stop.

After paying, Nick helped Kate out and guided her up to an apartment on the third floor of an old brick house. Inside, it was charmingly furnished with antiques and a view of sunsets across Chelsea Reach.

"Oh, how lovely," Kate said. She crossed over to the window and stood looking out at glints of moonlight on the fast-flowing river.

"This place belongs to Arthur Marchmant, Seasonwine's owner," Nick explained as he came up behind her. "He's letting me use it whenever I need to be in London."

"It's very nice. You're lucky."

Nick rested his hands on her shoulders, and as the warmth of his flesh seeped into hers Kate went very still.

"I debated a long time before I came out to that night-club tonight," he said. His breath stirred the fine hairs on the back of her neck.

"Why did you?"

"Because I couldn't keep away."

"Oh, Nick..." Kate reached up and covered his right hand with hers.

"I should be offering you a drink right now," he said. "Do you want something?"

"Not really."

He lifted her hair and dropped a light kiss on the back of her neck. "Bad strategy, Kate. You should have accepted. Then instead of torturing myself by standing so close and touching you like this, I would have had to go off to the kitchen. Drinks would have given us an excuse to sit down with glasses in our hands and a safe distance between us so that we can talk about this situation in a civilized fashion."

Kate's voice was husky, her throat tight. "We already talked, Nick. Talking more wouldn't do any good."

"No, I suppose it wouldn't. And the way I feel about you isn't civilized in the least. Oh God, Kate!" He slid his hands down her arms and then encircled her waist and pulled her close so that she could feel the length of his taut body pressed intimately to her back and buttocks. Then, firmly, he turned her around and took her mouth.

As Nick's lips captured hers, Kate leaned into him and flung her arms around his shoulders. She was hungry for him, ravenous. Everything about him, his outdoorsy scent, the clean, smooth texture of his skin, the fine-tuned strength in his greyhound-lean body, the urgency she felt flowing out of him toward her like an unstoppable current, seemed to ignite her senses and send her body flaming up with desire.

"How have I gone so long without you," he murmured raggedly.

"Oh Nick, I don't know. It hasn't been easy." She pressed her lips against the spare, angular line of his jaw. "When I saw you out there in the audience, it took all my willpower to stay put on that piano bench and keep playing."

Possessively, his hand ran down the elegant length of her back. "I never would have known. You were the consummate professional, as remote and beautiful as the moon up there."

She lifted her mouth back to his. "I'm the consummate fool and there's nothing remote or moonlike about me now. A furnace would be more like it."

They kissed again, the passion between them like a lightning flash searing through dry tinder. Then, decisively, Nick took Kate's arm and led her out of the living room and down a short corridor. Together, they walked into a shadowy bedroom dominated by a large four-poster.

Without preliminaries, they began stripping off each other's clothing, murmuring words of endearment, laughing sometimes, dropping kisses on bared shoulders, lips and breasts. "You're so lovely, Kate. Every time I see you—"

"I know what you're going to say. It's the same with me. You're such a beautiful man, Nick. Those blue eyes and black eyelashes. The way you move. It isn't right for a man to have such beauty."

He pulled her to him. "Everything is right about this, everything!"

A moment later they were on the bed, their bodies writhing together in ardent need and longing. Sighs and groans and muffled cries of excitement punctuated the stillness around them.

Their mutual desire had been under intolerable pressure from the long, agonizing days they'd stayed apart. It seemed to explode and they took their release together with quick, sharp pleasure. They rested briefly, holding on to each other with arms like tight bands of need. But then, with the edge of that fierce appetite satisfied, they made love again. This time it was languorous and tantalizing, filled with the delicious ache and wonder of healthy bodies demanding each other.

"How I kept away from you this long I'll never know," Nick whispered as he took the point of Kate's stiff nipple into his mouth and teased it with his tongue.

She moaned in ecstasy and then pushed a lock of his dark hair away so that she could kiss his forehead. "We have to stop this," she murmured regretfully.

"Why?"

"Because we've been going on like demented creatures for half the night, and you need your rest for the Grand National. You're going to be risking your life in just a few days."

Through the moonlight streaming in from the window, Nick smiled down into Kate's eyes. "Then be charitable and allow the condemned man to enjoy his last free nights in your arms. It's the least you can do."

But she was not amused. "Must you race again, Nick? Couldn't you withdraw now before it's too late?"

His eyebrows drew together and he pulled away from her slightly. "Of course I must race. What a question. I couldn't possibly back out now. Listen, you refused a drink before. But maybe you'd like one now. How about a glass of wine? There's even an unopened bottle of champagne out there."

"A glass of white wine would be fine." She watched him get up, pull on his pants and then, with a smile and a salute, walk out of the room. When he was gone, Kate pushed herself up against the headboard and drew the sheet up around her breasts.

She'd been so beside herself when she'd come into this room with Nick that she hadn't even seen it, except to notice where the bed was. Now she glanced around, noting her hastily abandoned clothes lying piled atop a costly oriental rug. Then she surveyed the other fine antiques that lined the walls.

There was a handsome armoire and a very beautiful inlaid desk. Directly across from the bed stood a dressing table with a large oval mirror. In the light from the hallway it reflected back her image. Naked, with her hair adrift around her head and her face flushed from lovemaking, she looked like a decadent stranger to herself. Suddenly uncomfortable with her nakedness, Kate reached down for her underwear. She was just pulling her lacy satin slip over her head when Nick came back into the room carrying a tray.

"What are you doing that for? I like you better with your clothes off."

"I daresay, but once the glow of passion has died down, it's a bit chilly in this room."

"Speak for your own glow. My glow is still red-hot." Leering outrageously, he leaned forward and smacked his lips at her.

"I'm just not the sort of girl who's really comfortable lounging around in the nude," she continued, batting him away playfully.

Giving his head a mock-doleful shake, Nick uncorked the bottle on the tray and poured Kate a glass of wine. Then he opened a bottle of mineral water for himself.

"No wine for you?"

"Can't. I'm in training."

"Oh, yes. How could I forget?" Kate frowned, her mind returning to the argument that had just begun between them when he'd left the room.

"How did you amuse yourself while I was gone?" Nick asked, sensing where her thoughts lay and wanting to steer her onto a different subject.

"Oh well, since I didn't have you to look at anymore, I just glanced around and admired the antiques." Kate ran a hand up the length of the finely carved mahogany bedpost. "This place with all its velvet and silk is quite a change from Newride."

"Yes, Newride is still in a pretty primitive state, I'm afraid. What money I've had to spend has gone for stock and equipment, not fancy decorating." He regarded her. "I've just realized how little I really know about you. I've no idea what your taste is, whether you like antiques, for instance, or prefer rooms with a modern look."

"Is it important?"

"I don't know." He took a sip of his mineral water, his eyes never leaving her face. With his free hand he stroked her ankle, which peeked out from beneath the sheet.

Very conscious of his caressing hand, Kate drew the sheet up a little higher. "Well, I don't know all that much about my tastes, either. With the wandering life I've led I've never had a home of my own to decorate, or even an apartment that wasn't borrowed or sublet already furnished." She rubbed her thumb along the rim of her glass. "I know, of course, when I see something I like. Doesn't everyone? But I'm not sure what I would choose if I were given money and a free hand."

"Would you like to find out?"

She glanced up. "What?"

"Kate, my offer is still open. After you've finished your engagement at the Red Candle, you could come back with me to Ireland. If things go well in the National day after tomorrow I should be carrying a fairly heavy purse. You could do all the decorating you cared to.''

Her heart seemed to turn over. She wanted so much to fling her arms around his neck and say yes. *Oh Nick, Nick,* she thought, *I've never met anyone like you and I probably never will again. I'd love to go away with you and hide from the world, just the two of us.* If only it were that simple. But it wasn't.

''Is that why you're riding in this race, for the purse?'' Kate asked carefully.

''Money always comes in handy, but there's another reason. Marchmant has agreed to lend Seasonwine for stud. Right now I'm badly in need of a superior stud.''

''There's Misalliance.''

''Yes, but he hasn't got any reputation except one for misbehavior. Seasonwine's colts won't have to prove anything. They'll be valuable just because they're his.'' Nick frowned, obviously wondering why she'd deviated on this tack rather than giving him a straight answer to his question.

''This Marchmant you're riding for must be a very wealthy man.'' Pointedly, Kate glanced around at the rich furnishings.

''He is, very. But then anyone in a position to race horses has got to be pretty well-fixed. It's an expensive sport.''

''Does he ride, himself?''

Nick grinned. ''He likes to think he does, but he's only just learned and won't get up onto anything but the gentlest nag in the stable.''

''Then he doesn't ride his own racehorses?''

''Lord, no!'' Nick laughed at the idea. Then his amusement fled and his expression became serious. ''Kate, why are you asking about Marchmant? What's he got to do with us?"

"Oh, Nick, don't you see?" She set her still untouched glass down on the side table. "This rich man is only using you. Racing horses is just an amusement to him. What does he care if they or their riders break their necks going over these dangerous steeplechase jumps? He's using you like a spoiled little boy might a toy soldier. And if you get broken again . . ." She shrugged. "Well, it won't matter to him, will it? He can always buy a replacement."

Nick's mouth turned down slightly. "Well, that's one way of looking at it. But that's a jockey's life, Kate. You ride to earn a living, and you take risks."

"But you don't need to ride to earn a living. You've established yourself as a horse breeder."

"Hardly. Newride has a long way to go before it's truly in the black. I'm just a fledgling trying to set himself up in a very tough and expensive business. Right now Seasonwine's stud service would make a fantastic difference."

"Is that the real reason you agreed to ride him in this race?"

"What are you getting at?"

Kate took a deep breath. "I think it has more to do with ego and with your childhood than with winning money and getting a fancy stud for your mares."

Nick's back stiffened and then he got to his feet and stood looking down at her. "Now where does that come from, I wonder?"

Kate plucked at the bedclothes. "After I left Newride I thought about you all the time. I kept remembering things you said, things people like Adelina told me. Then, too, I kept seeing that footage on TV. Oh Nick, it's so horrible! You were literally trampled by a pack of horses. Why, I asked myself, would he risk his life in a crazy profession like that when he not only knew it killed his father but actually saw his father die before his very eyes?''

''We're certainly getting very deep here, aren't we? I hadn't realized you were an amateur psychologist,'' Nick said tightly.

''It doesn't take a psychologist to figure out that there's a connection between your father and the way he died and your obsession with risking your life on the back of a horse.''

Abruptly, Nick turned so that his back was to Kate. He raked a hand through his thick hair while he apparently attempted to collect himself. As the silence lengthened between them, Kate observed the tightly clenched muscles in his shoulders, the rigid set of his spine. Nervously, she drew her knees up to her chest. She hadn't expected to say any of the things that had just come tumbling from her lips. But she was afraid for Nick. These ideas about what motivated him had been building inside her and she hadn't been able to hold them back. Now she had set something in motion that she had to see through to the end.

An instant later, Nick pivoted to face her. ''In the first place, I do need the money I'm hoping to win in the National, and I wouldn't have agreed to chance breaking my neck in the race if I didn't. In the second place, horses and riding are in my family's blood, and not just on my father's side, either. My mother's people are the same, so I come by it naturally. I haven't built my life on some sort of twisted reaction to my father's accident, and I must say I find the suggestion rather insulting. And in the third place, what has all this got to do with my invitation? I know there must be a connection, but I've yet to figure out what it is.''

Kate clasped her knees to her chest more tightly yet, but her green gaze met Nick's steadily. ''You're asking me to put my career on hold and I . . . I guess I'm willing to do it because, obviously, I'm crazy about you. But you have to do something for me.''

"And what's that, pray tell?''

"Nick, please, don't do it. Don't ride in the Grand National.''

His jaw set. "But I've committed myself. The horse has been training for months. It's all arranged.''

"Marchmant can find another jockey. You know he can.''

"Kate, I've signed a contract. Would you back out on a nightclub deal you'd committed yourself to?''

"That's totally different.''

"How?''

"I don't risk getting killed when I walk out on a stage. I don't have someone like Lou LaFiore gunning for me. This very minute the man may be plotting to make sure you don't come out of that race in one piece.''

"I told you I'd made a deal with him. He agreed to back off.''

"All right, you have his word on it. But what good is that man's word? Oh Nick, please!'' Kate pressed her hands together prayerfully.

Slowly, Nick began to shake his head. "You're saying that the only way you'll come back to Ireland with me and give the two of us a try is if I'll back out on my contract with Marchmant. Have I got it right?''

"Yes. Yes, you have.'' Her voice was constricted.

"Kate, I can't do that. Don't you see? It's a matter of honor.''

Kate's pleading expression went stony. "Honor? What good's honor if your back is broken?'' She uncoiled herself and pushed away from the spot where she'd been huddling. Then she reached for her blouse. But as her fingers closed around the silk fabric, Nick seized her wrist.

"Now it's my turn to play psychiatrist. I know what this is all about. You never intended to give me a positive answer. Commitment probably isn't even possible for you."

"What? What's that supposed to mean?"

"You were abandoned as a child, Kate. You never had a proper family when you were growing up. A solid relationship is something you've never known, so you're afraid of it."

"That's crazy!"

"Is it? I don't think so. I think that after our lovemaking just now, you had to gloss over your real reason for turning me down, so you just concocted this excuse about my riding."

"That's not true."

"Oh, yes it is." In the uncertain light Nick's eyes were bleak. "You agreed to come with me to Ireland and then put an impossible condition on it. You did that because you're afraid to give our relationship a try."

"There's nothing impossible about my asking you not to risk your life in a stupid race, for God's sake."

His jaw hardened. "So now my profession is stupid," he snapped. "Is it any more ridiculous than yours?"

"Mine!"

"At least I don't earn a living in sleazy bars making a half-naked spectacle of myself playing songs about love to an audience too drunk to care!"

Kate jerked away from him and said through gritted teeth, "Please call me a cab. By this time it must be obvious to both of us that I won't be taking a trip to the Emerald Isle anytime soon."

CHAPTER THIRTEEN

"KATE, Kate!"

At the sound of familiar childish voices, Kate paused and turned. The high-pitched squeals reverberated above the noise of the well-dressed crowd that milled around a bar in the Members' Enclosure at Aintree where port and salmon sandwiches were being sold.

"Rudy and Randy?"

The twins spurted out of the crowd in the enclosure and galloped across the turf toward Kate. "Grandfather has brought us to see Nick race," Randy exclaimed.

"And Mother's here, too, only she went off to talk to someone," Rudy added breathlessly.

"How nice!" Neither boy asked Kate what she was doing here on the day of the Grand National, though it was a question she'd frequently put to herself in the last twenty-four hours. Smiling, Kate looked up to see the boys' grandfather hurrying toward them. With his distinguished silver mustache and in his tweeds and cap and carrying a shooting stick, Sir Cedric looked like the quintessential English country gentleman.

"Well, well, I say, happy to see you here, Miss Humphrey," he puffed. "But you should have let me know you were planning to come down for this event. I would have sent my car 'round for you."

Kate clutched her trench coat closed at her throat. The April day was blustering and overcast. No one else in the milling throng making merry with beer and ale and happily downing such treats as cockles, whelks and jellied eels, seemed troubled by the weather. But Kate hadn't yet accustomed herself to the English idea of a fine spring day.

"I didn't decide to come until the last minute," she told Sir Cedric. "It was what we Americans call a spur-of-the-moment decision."

That didn't begin to describe the emotional wringer Kate had been through since her argument with Nick. After leaving him, she'd spent the rest of that night and the next day in turmoil. She'd told herself she never wanted to see him again. But gradually, as she'd paced the floor of her room at Mrs. Brasswell's or lay staring sleeplessly up at the cracked ceiling, she'd acknowledged the truth. She was in love with Nick, and she was terribly, terribly worried about him. Late the previous afternoon she'd realized she had no choice but to cancel her evening performance at the Red Candle and buy a train ticket to Liverpool.

"Are you trying to get yourself fired?" the club's manager had demanded when she'd called in to ask for the night off.

"No. I'm sorry." Kate had tried to explain. "It's a personal matter. There's just someplace I have to be tomorrow."

It had been the stark, irrefutable truth. There was no way Kate could do the sensible thing and sit home in Mrs. Brasswell's parlor to watch the Grand National on television. She had to be there. Even if Kate never saw Nick again, she had to see him make it through this thing all right. Then, perhaps, she could start working to forget him and get on with her life, she told herself.

"Quite a spectacle, isn't it?" Sir Cedric commented, waving an aristocratic hand at the scene around them.

"Oh, yes," Kate agreed. Having spent the night at a down-at-heels bed and breakfast in a murky area of Liverpool, she was finding Aintree's seven hundred acres of manicured open turf all the more impressive for being in the midst of England's most heavily industrialized area. It was as if Never-Never Land had been plunked down in the center of a strip-mining operation.

"Our Grand National is the world's most famous horse race," Sir Cedric was saying a trifle pompously as the crowd, dressed in everything from mink coats to waterproof parkas, surged around them, "and you can see why."

Kate looked around in bewilderment. "Well, no, not really," she admitted. "I'm afraid I don't know much about horses or horse racing. For example who is that man over there and what is he doing?"

Sir Cedric squinted. "If you mean that fellow waving his hands about, he's a 'tic tac.'"

"A tic tac?"

"Yes, he's semaphoring the changing odds to a partner on the rail, that smallish fellow over there who's setting up to take bets."

"Oh, I see," Kate said, though she didn't really.

Sir Cedric shot her a good-natured smile. "I suppose it's all a bit confusing for you, m'dear, but if you'd like to walk the course with the boys and me, perhaps I could explain some of it." He indicated Rudy and Randy, who were dancing ahead of them along the fence.

"Oh, I'd love that," Kate said gratefully. Since arriving at Aintree an hour earlier, she'd never felt so lonely and utterly at a loss. She had no idea where Nick was or where she should station herself to see him. It was a relief to be taken under Sir Cedric's grandfatherly wing.

"There are really three courses," Sir Cedric informed her as they began to stroll along after the pirouetting twins. "The hurdle with jumps over light wooden panel is the least severe. Next is the Mildmay, where the fences are the usual British steeplechase sort—birch boughs tightly packed on end to a wooden frame." He paused to point through the barrier nearest them. "The Grand National course, which must be covered twice, has jumps over century-old blackthorn hedges dressed with spruce, and for obvious reasons they're considered the most awesome obstacles in steeplechasing."

Kate stared at a wicked-looking construction. She couldn't even imagine being on the back of a horse who had to jump that thing. And then there was the fact that while making the jump, Seasonwine would be wedged in amid a thundering pack of other four-legged, half-ton animals. She'd read that of the forty who started the four-mile race, several horses always lost their lives and usually only ten finished the ordeal at all. A little shiver ran down her spine and she asked in a slightly strangled voice, "How many jumps are there?"

Sir Cedric proved to be a fund of knowledge. "There are thirty, and with the exception of the water jumps, all are, using your American yardstick, five feet high and at least three feet wide. Many have ditches six feet wide on either the takeoff or landing side. So you can see, in the heat of action it can get a trifle dicey."

Sir Cedric seemed to relish his understatement, but Kate felt horrified. It had been one thing to worry about Nick's danger in the abstract. Now that she'd actually seen what he was going to be up against, she almost wished she'd stayed in London with Mrs. Brasswell's 'telly' where the danger might have seemed less immediate.

"That fence in the distance," Sir Cedric said, again waving a casual hand, "is called Becher's Brook after a captain who took a spill there early in the last century. It's famous for spectacular crashes, actually, and I daresay we'll see some at that spot later on today."

"Oh." Kate clenched her hands into fists. "Yes, I can imagine." It was Becher's Brook where Nick had fallen before and almost been trampled, she recalled.

As they continued to walk the course, Sir Cedric went on chattily pointing out dangerous jumps. There was Valentine's, named after a horse who'd corkscrewed over the fence to make an unlikely jump in 1840, and the Chair where a riderless horse standing in the ditch in front of the fence was jumped and cleared by the animal behind him.

But after Becher's Brook, Kate had really stopped taking it all in. She felt numb with terror for Nick and slightly ill. A few minutes later she couldn't even go on listening to Sir Cedric's good-humored history lesson about what seemed to her a suicide mission for horses and riders bent on self-destruction.

"I . . . if you all don't mind, I believe I'll go get myself something to drink," she said.

"We'll go with you, we'll go with you!" Rudy and Randy chorused.

But their grandfather shook his head. "Now, now, we're supposed to rendezvous with your mother back at the Members' Enclosure in just a short while." He gave Kate an inquiring look. "Would you care to join us there for a spot of champagne? It's not too bad, actually."

Kate shook her head. "No, thank you. You're very kind, but there's someone I have to meet, too."

It had been a polite fib to excuse her hurrying away, but a few minutes later she did bump into an old friend. "Mario!" Kate cried. Magically, Nick's uncle, dressed in an English tweed suit that looked all wrong on him, had materialized from a knot of spectators in front of the grandstand.

"Ciao, bella!" he exclaimed joyously. Beaming, he hurried forward and seized Kate's hand.

"I had no idea you'd be here," Kate said, shaking her head with wonder and pleasure. It seemed so strange to behold Mario under gray English skies. Yet she could have kissed his smiling face. "How long have you been in England?"

"I arrive since yesterday." He held up a forefinger. "This is big day for Nico. I couldn't miss."

"Is Adelina here with you?"

Mario shook his head vigorously. "No, she no like to travel. But me, I come. Something, eh?" He gestured around at the crowds and at the racecourse.

"Yes, it's all very impressive," Kate agreed. "But those jumps. They look horrible."

"Sì, that Nico. He always was a crazy one. I hope he don't break his neck." Mario shook his head. Then his expression brightened. "You know, I wonder if maybe I don't meet you here. Nick, he say no. But me—I say yes, maybe Kate she come."

Just knowing that Nick had discussed her with his uncle made Kate flush. What exactly had they said, she wondered. Had Nick told Mario about their quarrel? "I guess I couldn't stay away, either."

Mario gazed at her thoughtfully. "Nick, he know that you here?"

"Why, no. I just thought I'd watch. I just wanted to see that everything came out all right," Kate answered lamely.

Mario nodded and then patted her arm. "Kate, listen to me, *bellissima.* You go see Nick so he know you here. He not say much about you, but me, I can tell, he very de-

pressed. It not good for him to race when he depressed.
You go see him, give him a smile, a kind word. You know
what I mean, eh?''

Kate took a step backward. "Oh really, I . . ."

But Mario refused to release her arm. "You don't need
to say nothing. Just a smile is enough. You just give Nick
a smile. That's not too much to ask." Mario patted her
encouragingly.

"All right," Kate finally agreed with a weak smile. "But
I don't even know where to find him."

"Nick in the jockeys' changing room now. But soon he
mount up in the paddock. Go there and wait. He bound to
see you." Mario pointed and then gave Kate's hand another squeeze. "You just smile for him, that's all."

IN THE JOCKEYS' CHANGING ROOM, valets had been clean-
ing boots and working on a rainbow of colored silks since
early that morning. Navy-blue sleeves, pink dots, black
hoops, yellow chevrons, cerise hearts, white diamonds,
French blue sashes littered the tables. The air was thick
with jokes and nervous gossip. Every rider was aware that
he might finish this race in glory or in a hospital bed.

After Nick pulled on his paper-thin leather boots, his
valet made a final adjustment on his red-and-white lightweight silks.

"Looks right good, yes, sir."

"Thanks, Mike." Nick gave the man a pat on the back,
picked up his helmet and crop and then walked out to the
weighing room where the hooded scales had been un-
cloaked and the Clerk of the Scales was at his desk. As
Nick stood waiting his turn, he visualized the jumps.

First two ordinary fences, he told himself. Nothing to
worry about—and then there was Becher's, which felt like

jumping over the edge of a quarry. Nick shook his head and whistled silently between his teeth.

Though he had spent the night before lying awake thinking about Kate and feeling rotten about their parting, he didn't allow himself to think about her now. He was going into battle and, as always before a race, his mind was clear of everything but the task before him. His gaze was turned inward, and he felt light, lithe, agile, fit and sharp as a razor—and he felt ready.

Outside, the horses were parading in the paddock. When Nick was up on Seasonwine, the powerful animal jigged and danced in place beneath him.

"Whoa there, whoa there boy. It's all right. We have a job of work today, so you'd better save your energy."

In wordless communion, Nick let his palms rest on the animal's warm hide. Gradually, however, his attention was unwillingly dragged from Seasonwine and he became conscious that his name was being called.

"Nick, hey, Nick! Over here!"

Frowning at the intruding voice, Nick turned his head and spotted Jillian LaFiore. As usual, she was dressed like something out of a fashion magazine with ridiculous pink high heels to match a wide-brimmed hat that looked in danger of blowing off and spooking the horses. Reluctantly, Nick guided Seasonwine over to where she stood.

"Jillian, how's show biz and what brings you out in this weather?"

Jillian pouted. "My tour was a disappointment, and I'm here for the same thing that's lured all these hordes of other people out in this filthy weather. I brought the boys to see your moment of triumph, what else?" With one gloved hand she held onto her hat to keep it from sailing away. "What was wrong with you, anyway? I must have been shouting at you for at least five minutes before you noticed.''

"Sorry, when I'm getting myself up for a race I don't see or hear much outside of what's going on in my own head. What do you want?''

Jillian rolled her eyes. "You needn't look so suspicious, you know. I'm not here to try to take up where we left off.''

"We didn't leave off anywhere.''

Jillian made a teasing little moue. "Oh don't be such a prig. You know what I mean. Maybe were were never actual lovers, but there was definitely something between us. Sparks were flying.''

Nick opened his mouth to deny that, though he knew it was energy wasted. Jillian was a beautiful woman, so maybe he'd felt some physical attraction to her—though he'd certainly never acted on it. But now that he'd met and made love to Kate, all that seemed like ancient history.

"I just wanted to thank you,'' Jillian hurried on. "Lou told me what you did for the boys and I'm very grateful.''

Nick's gaze sharpened. "Is Lou here?''

"Are you joking?'' Jillian gave a brittle laugh. "Right at the moment he's in hiding. The people he testified against play rough and tend to be sore losers. But he did send me a message for you.''

"What is it?'' Nick eyed her warily.

"He said to tell you, 'Don't worry, be happy.''' Jillian looked puzzled. "I know it's from a song, but I have no idea what Lou meant by it.''

Nick hoped it was Lou's way of saying that he intended to keep his part of their bargain and forget any revenge plot he might have been hatching. *Either that, or he wants to put me off my guard,* Nick thought grimly, remembering Kate's warning. In the heat of their argument, he'd dismissed what she'd said about Lou, but it nagged at him now.

"Listen, good luck to you," Jillian said.

"Thanks, and same to you and Lou," Nick answered. Then he touched his crop to his cap and turned Season-wine away, his mind once again fully occupied with the race. Ahead of him the only thing he noticed was an ambulance driving down the track toward Becher's Brook, where it would wait to receive the fallen and wounded. Nick sincerely hoped he wouldn't be among them.

A few minutes later at the post the horses swayed like the sea, the line forming and then breaking and reforming. While the starter gave his instructions, jockeys cursed and muttered under their breaths. Nick steadied Seasonwine. Around them the other horses' eyes gleamed and the men's eyes hardened into stony resolve.

Then the flag dropped and, with Seasonwine's pent-up nervous energy surging beneath him, Nick was off.

KATE HAD BEEN hanging around the paddock for close to twenty minutes when she saw Nick come out. In his jockey's helmet and silks and lightweight white pants and tall leather boots, he seemed a stranger. The formfitting uniform emphasized his sleek muscularity. Almost, he looked as if he belonged to another order of beings.

Was this frowning, abstracted man the same who had made passionate love to her only the night before last? She could hardly believe it.

After talking with Mario, Kate had decided she wanted Nick to know she was here and that she was sorry for the harsh words between them. She hated the thought of his feeling depressed when he was about to put himself into danger. What if something terrible happened? The rest of her life she'd wonder if she were to blame. The thought made her stomach clench into knots of anxiety.

Should she call out to him? she asked herself. Kate hadn't imagined she'd need to make an effort to attract Nick's attention. With her red hair, she wasn't exactly inconspicuous, so she'd thought that Nick would see her and that when he did she'd be able to gauge his mood well enough to know what she should say to him. But when he'd come out he'd just walked right past without even glancing her way.

Clasping her hands, Kate watched as a trainer brought up the beautiful chestnut horse that must be Seasonwine. Once Nick had vaulted lightly up into the tiny scrap of leather that served as a saddle, he seemed even more remote. What was it like to look down at the world from that height? Kate wondered. He must feel like a god up there. Again, she considered calling his name and forcing him to notice her. But another voice called out to him, and he turned away.

Kate stared down the length of the fence. Looking gorgeous in a pink color-coordinated hat, dress and coat ensemble, Jillian LaFiore teetered in the muddy turf on three-inch heels.

As Nick leaned down to talk to her, she propped one of her gloved hands on the top of the rail and gazed up at him earnestly. What were they discussing? Kate wondered. Her brows drew together. Instinctively, she recognized that there was something more than mere acquaintance between Nick and this woman. A spark of jealousy streaked through her. Was Jillian the real reason behind the enmity between Nick and the twins' father? Had they been lovers?

Kate took a backward step. Suddenly she no longer felt so keen on trying to mend the rift between herself and

Nick. But it wouldn't have made any difference what she felt. When Nick finished speaking with Jillian, he trotted his horse away without even glancing in Kate's direction. For several minutes she stood gazing after him, so confused by her spinning emotions that she lost track of time and didn't hear or comprehend what was going on around her. Then, as people shifted back toward the course and excitement began to crackle in the atmosphere, she became aware that she was standing alone and that the race was about to start.

"Oh, my God!" Kate began to hurry after the flocks of spectators. In the distance she heard an announcer's voice. Then a roar went up from the crowd and her heart lurched. It must mean that the race had already started.

She began running, dodging. But the crowd was suffocating and she could see nothing. "Are they off?" she asked a woman in a raincoat and then the man standing next to her with mist coiling around his houndstooth-check hat. But nobody bothered to answer.

Muttering frightened little exclamations under her breath, Kate headed toward Becher's, which Sir Cedric had pointed out as the most dangerous of the jumps. But there the throng of spectators was so thick that she couldn't get close enough to see anything.

The ground vibrated with the thunder of hooves and she heard a horrified gasp rise from a thousand throats. Craning to see, she caught sight of the tips of several caps going up and over.

"What's happened? Oh, please, what's happened?" Frantically, Kate pushed at a wall of backs.

The pack of horses had flashed past like a jet plane roaring into a takeoff. How could Nick survive in the midst of such chaos? How could anyone?

"Well, that's two down," she heard an old man mutter to his companion.

"Which two, which two?" Kate cried out. She would have been better off to watch the race on television, she thought with desperation. "Who's hurt?" she demanded hysterically and somehow pushed through until she could get a view.

A horse had fallen and was being dragged out of Becher's before the pack zoomed past again for the second lap. But it was a white horse, not Nick's Seasonwine. Meanwhile, horrified screams and exclamations were going up from jumps farther along the course. Kate wrung her hands. Becher's wasn't the only dangerous hurdle. They were all dangerous. A rider might break his neck on any one of them.

Rain had started to fall and a thick mist had begun to settle over the ground. A riderless horse appeared in the distance, approached Becher's and then veered off around it. The animal was some shade of brown, but the mist was so thick that Kate couldn't tell whether or not it was a chestnut like Seasonwine. As she gazed at it, her heart was in her mouth.

Then once again the ground began to shake. Two other horses pounded along the wet turf through the writhing snakes of mist. They both bore riders lying so flat to their backs that they seemed part of the straining animals and not separate human beings at all. As they leaped up and over Becher's, the crowd strained and muttered.

Everything happened so fast that Kate couldn't even tell if one of the leading jockeys had been Nick. She blinked and saw another riderless horse veer off to the side with its stirrups flying. A half dozen more equines still bearing their jockeys flashed past like an express train.

Exclamations flew through the crowd. Kate heard Nick's and Seasonwine's names, but couldn't make out what was being said. Whoops of excitement from thousands of throats echoed along the fence and back to the spot where Kate stood.

"Well, that's it," a gentleman standing alongside her told his companion. "Sounds to me as if Conti and Seasonwine must have taken it."

A FIGURE IN A TRENCHCOAT, a hat and dark glasses slipped a coin into the public phone and dialed a long-distance number. "She just bought a ticket for London. She's going to be all alone in that train. I could do the job now."

There was a long pause on the other end of the line. "You're quite sure she's alone?"

"Absolutely. I followed her down. I tailed her all during that race. I even considered pushing her under one of the horses. But it would be just as easy to push her off the train and make it look like an accident. What do you say?"

Again there was a pause. "No."

The caller's eyebrows jerked up. "No!"

"I've reconsidered. There's just too much attention focused on Kate Humphrey now. It's too risky. Better to wait and see what develops."

"You may regret that decision."

"I know," the person on the other end of the line said crisply. "But it's my decision to make, isn't it."

"You're the boss." The caller let the receiver fall into place. Then, with collar pulled up high against the damp weather, the figure in the trench coat walked outside where travelers stood waiting for the train to pull in.

Kate Humphrey stood among them. She was shivering and her face was pale. Nevertheless, the eyes of the observer in the trench coat, as they focused on her, held no sympathy.

"You get off this time, lady," the observer muttered in a voice so low that no one could hear. "But unless I miss my guess, there'll be a next time. And then your luck is going to run out."

"HAVE A NICE CUP OF TEA and tell me all about the Grand National," Mrs. Brasswell urged.

Kate accepted a pretty painted cup and took a comforting sip. She'd left Liverpool and arrived back in London very late the previous night. Though Mrs. Brasswell had obviously been bursting with curiosity about her trip, Kate had been too exhausted and depressed to talk about it. After stripping off her travel-stained clothes, she'd fallen into bed like a dead weight and slept for twelve hours straight.

Now, after a hearty breakfast of bacon and eggs accompanied by thick slabs of buttered toast, she sat in Mrs. Brasswell's homey kitchen and gazed gratefully across the oilcloth-covered table at her motherly landlady.

"There's not a lot to tell. I didn't actually see much of it because of all the people."

Mrs. Braswell *tsk-tsked*. "I daresay Eddie and I were better off than you just being home nice and comfy in front of our telly."

"You watched it, then?"

"Oh, yes, my Eddie wouldn't miss it. You know how he is about horse racing. And we saw it start to finish, too. Such a lovely dress the Princess had on, though I must say I didn't care for the Duchess of York's hat."

Kate managed a wan smile. "You really did get a better look at things than I had." Her smile disappeared and she frowned. "I didn't see any serious accidents, but I heard there were several bad ones."

Mrs. Brasswell clucked and shook her head. "Oh, it was dreadful. One poor animal fell right over on his head, he did. He had to be shot. And there were four others that broke their legs and shoulders and had to be destroyed, too. Such a shame it is. They're such beautiful animals and to lose their lives that way all for a silly race—" Again, she shook her head.

"Yes," Kate agreed seriously. "I'm glad I didn't see that part of it."

"Oh, but Nick Conti was wonderful. What a rider he is. My husband said he outshone them all. He really deserved to win."

"I'm sure he did." Kate gazed at Mrs. Brasswell wistfully. "I couldn't get close enough to see him accept the cup. Were you able to see it on television?"

"Indeed, I was. I wouldn't have missed that."

"How did he look?"

"Oh, tired and a bit bruised, you know, with dirt all down one side of his face. But my, he's a handsome man. A little too thin for my taste, but still— When the Duchess of York gave him a kiss on the cheek, I wished I were in her place."

Kate sighed and put down her cup. "Yes, well I suppose he must be very happy now."

"Oh I'm sure. It's quite a thing to win the Grand National, you know." Mrs. Brasswell observed Kate curiously. "What's wrong, dear? You've been looking a bit peaky the last few days. Things not going well for you on the job?"

Kate laughed ruefully. "I'm not sure I even have a job anymore."

"Why ever not?" Mrs. Brasswell's eyes rounded. "I thought your piano playing had started turning a profit."

"Well..." Kate bit her lip. "I took these two days off to go down to Liverpool rather suddenly, and I got the feeling that Mr. Diger, my manager at the Red Candle, was rather annoyed with me."

"Oh, my, I'd no idea! Well, then p'raps you'd better ring him up right away and find out what the lay of the land is, if you know what I mean. P'raps his feathers just got ruffled up and he only needs a bit of soothing down."

Kate thought it might be rather more serious than that, but she nodded. "Yes, I think you're right. If you don't mind, I'll just go into the hall and use the phone."

"Oh, go right ahead, dearie. Don't mind me. I'll just stay in the kitchen and give these dishes a rinse."

Out in the hall, Kate sat down next to the rickety little telephone table and leaned forward to dial. But even as she reached to lift the receiver, the phone started to ring.

"Brasswell's Bed and Breakfast."

"Could I please speak to a Miss Kathryn Humphrey," a cultivated woman's voice queried.

"This is Miss Humphrey." Who in the world might it be? Kate wondered.

"I'm with Byrnside Recording, Miss Humphrey. Hold just a moment while I put Mr. Winston Deeping on the line."

At the name Byrnside, Kate stiffened. In all the chaos between her and Nick, she'd almost forgotten about the Byrnside situation. In retrospect it seemed even more bizarre than it had when she'd first been told about it—and it had seemed plenty peculiar then.

However, Winston Deeping's name was familiar. Everyone in the music business knew that he was the head of the recording branch of Byrnside Enterprises and that he could make or break the career of any musician he chose. Kate clutched the receiver.

A moment later a man with an elegant English accent came on the line. "Ah, Miss Humphrey. I'm so glad I was able to catch you at home. We haven't met, but I'm a fan of yours."

"You are?"

"Oh, indeed. A few nights ago I heard you play at the Red Candle, and I was most impressed."

"Really?" Kate wondered what night that had been. Surely if someone as important as the CEO of Byrnside Recording had been in the audience she would have heard rumors.

"So impressed, in fact," he continued, "that I'm eager to have you represent our label, and I'm eager to offer you a contract."

"You are?" Kate almost fell off her chair.

"It's a very lucrative deal that I'm proposing, Miss Humphrey, and very much to your advantage profession-ally. But it will mean going back to the States. Would you be willing to meet me for lunch tomorrow so that we can discuss the details?"

CHAPTER FOURTEEN

"NICK, DARLING!" Priscilla Simpson threw her pretty arms around Nick and kissed his cheek enthusiastically. "You were wonderful at the National. Honestly, I felt like one of those medieval ladies in pointed hats watching a warrior knight ride into combat. It was ever so thrilling!"

"Thanks, Priss. At the time I was feeling fairly thrilled myself." Nick took a sip of Scotch and cast an amused glance over his cousin Colin's pretty blond fiancée. She was wearing a strapless gold sheath gathered at the hip and dipping dramatically low in back. "I like your outfit."

Behind her long eyelashes Priscilla's eyes gleamed with mischief. "I like yours, too. Black evening clothes suit you. Make you look all mysterious and broody. You are the most deliciously sexy man. Those blue eyes of yours give me goosebumps. If I weren't already engaged to Colin—"

"Say, what are you two up to?" Tall, fair and handsome in a bluff, open-faced fashion, Colin Crestwell came shouldering his way through the roomful of slightly tipsy partygoers.

Though Colin and Nick had the same grandparents on their mother's and father's sides respectively, no one would have guessed the fact. Physically and temperamentally, they were opposites.

It wasn't just that they'd been sired by two very different men, but it was also a reflection of their upbringing. Where Nick had been orphaned young and shunted aside to foreign boarding schools by his wealthy British relations, Colin has been the apple of their eye and denied nothing. Yet both men wore an air of assurance. It was just that where Nick's had been hard-won, Colin's had been bestowed at birth and was therefore different in quality—softer, more relaxed.

He slapped Nick on the back. "Flirting with all the pretty women in the room, I see. Well—" he glanced around at the well-dressed crowd, the women in jewels and gowns, the men in dark suits and dinner jackets "—it's the conquering hero's right, I suppose. How many parties have you been feted at so far this week?"

Nick shrugged. "To be honest, I don't really know. The last few days have been chaos."

Since winning the National, Nick had been dragged through a continuous round of publicity events. It seemed as if every group in England even remotely connected with the sport of horse racing wanted to throw a party featuring him as guest of honor. And then there had been the newspaper, magazine and television interviews and the obligatory appearances at various other public-relations functions. Though Nick did not regard himself as a party person, he also knew that the publicity reaped from winning the National would be an invaluable boost to his fledgling breeding and training business. He'd had to be a good sport and go along with all the hoopla.

"Well, what you pulled off at the National is going to make you a fortune," Colin declared. "Half the people in this room own stables filled with fancy nags. Now that you've made such a splash, they're bound to want to buy horses from you."

He glanced meaningfully at the expensively outfitted women in the room and shot Nick a salacious wink. "And, with your looks, I wouldn't be a bit surprised if a goodly

portion of your clients belong to the gentler sex, old chap."
He threw a possessive arm around Priscilla's bare shoulder. "But this one is taken—which should present no problem since, as always, you'll have a harem of other eager beauties to choose from. So hands off!"

Giggling, Priscilla shot her intended an affectionate glare. "Silly! Your gorgeous cousin could have me if he wanted, but he's just not interested."

Shaking his head with wry amusement, Nick surveyed the happy couple teasing each other and then took another swallow of Scotch. Thankfully, it was an indulgence he could, with the race finally over, allow himself.

There were other things he could allow himself now that the future was stretched out before him, he mused. A lot of decisions needed to be made. One thing he already knew—there would be no more racing for him. His jockey days were definitely over.

How would Kate feel about that? Nick wondered. A shaft of pain ripped through him so viciously that to hide its effects he looked away from Colin and his pretty fiancée, who were still gazing besottedly into each other's eyes. With the ordeal of the race before him Nick had managed to keep thoughts of Kate at bay. But now with the future settling down into a predictable landscape, it was impossible not to agonize over their disastrous love affair.

The night before the National he'd still been so angry about the things she'd said to him that he'd told himself he was glad they'd called it quits before they became any more embroiled. When she'd accused him of choosing racing as a profession because of some twisted connection with his father's death, it had made him furious.

But all during the National he'd found himself, at odd moments, mentally stepping aside to analyze his own reactions. Even when he'd been accepting the winner's trophy, part of him had been distanced from the event analyzing and observing. It had been unsettling, yet, it had also been revealing. And now . . .

"I say, Nick, do you intend coming down to Beechwold while you're in England?" Colin queried, referring to the family estate in Dorset where their grandparents still presided over the countryside like petty feudal barons.

Nick's brief laugh was ironic. "I think not. Somehow I don't believe Grandmother and Grandfather Crestwell are waiting with bated breath for a visit from me."

Colin frowned. "That's where you're wrong, you know. They're quite proud of you. And after this—well, they'll be puffed out like courting peacocks. A visit from you would mean a lot."

Still Nick shook his head. "You're their pride and joy, Colin, not me. I represent the blot on the family honor."

"You're wrong, old man, I swear you are. Maybe it used to be that way. I know they were vile to your mother and treated you pretty coldly in your youth, and that when you were a kid the only warmth you ever got was from your Italian relatives. But you've turned the tables on them, haven't you? You're the big cheese in the family now. I mean, what am I?"

"For heaven's sake, Colin! You're a lawyer in a very fine old law firm," Priscilla exclaimed. "Stop putting yourself down!"

The tall blond man shrugged. "Yes, by the skin of my teeth I managed to get a degree from Cambridge and now, because of the family influence, I'm comfortably set at Barrows, Perce, Bostwick and Curtis. But there's not much glamour in that, nor much real achievement, either. You, on the other hand," he said, gazing at Nick, "are Mr. Glamour. While you were winning the National, Grandfather was glued to his television set, and so was Grandmother. They feel guilty as hell about the past. I know they do. And they'd like to make amends.''

"The trouble with the past is that you can't change it and you can't make amends for it," Nick muttered and then gulped down the last of his drink.

"I know you can't," Colin agreed. "But what's the use of holding a grudge? I know the grandparents would love to see you. Priss and I will be motoring down there in a fortnight. Join us, Nick. What do you say?''

"I'll think about it and let you know," Nick finally conceded.

THAT NIGHT when Nick returned to Marchmant's apartment, he had a lot of things to think about. For hours he paced back and forth in the living room, glancing from time to time at the door to the bedroom where he and Kate had made such glorious love. He hadn't been able to bear sleeping alone there since and had spent all his succeeding nights on the couch in front of the fireplace.

Kate. He ached when he thought about her. And it was simply no longer possible to put her out of his mind. Mario had told him that she'd been at Aintree.

"Did you see the *bella* Kate?" he'd demanded. "Did she do what I asked?''

"What was that?" Nick had answered cautiously.

"I tell her you depressed and she should give you a smile before you race. Did she?" Mario had looked hopeful.

"No," Nick had answered gruffly and then walked away because he wasn't sure he could control the expression he knew had come over his face. So she hadn't even been willing to come up and say hello. That hurt. Why had she come to Aintree, anyway? he wondered. Just to scoff at what she considered the mixture of brutality and pompous silliness that was his life?

Nevertheless, he'd half hoped he might run into her at one of the parties or other public-relations affairs that had followed the National. It would have been easy enough for her to attend—if she'd wanted to. But though he'd kept an eye out for her bright hair and piquant face, she hadn't shown.

Once again Nick found himself reviewing their argument. Of course, he couldn't have done what she'd requested. There was no way he could have pulled out of the race so late. That was a matter of honor and professional pride. But there were other things in what she'd said, things that disturbed him.

He had thought of his father while he was riding, and when Seasonwine had jumped that last fence and come in first, Nick had had a sense of satisfaction, of completion. And again, he'd been aware that it was somehow tied in with his father. Eduardo Conti had been a handsome, warmhearted man who'd been utterly devoted to his sport. Whenever Nick tried to remember the day his father had been killed, all that came to him was a black iciness. He had no clear images, only feelings of horror.

Kate's idea that there was anything self-destructive in his racing was wrong. But perhaps there had been something to what she'd suggested. Perhaps, Nick acknowledged, it had been a point of honor to master the sport that had ultimately destroyed his father. And perhaps winning the Grand National was a thing he'd felt he had to do for his father—as well as for himself. But now that it was done, he had to think about the future. The trouble was that it depressed him to think about a future without Kate Humphrey in it.

The next morning Nick looked up the address of Brasswell's Bed and Breakfast in South Kensington, where Kate had mentioned she was staying. Determined to see her and work things out between them, he took a cab to the house and rang the bell. The little woman who answered widened her eyes at him.

"You look awfully familiar. Say, you wouldn't be—"

"My name is Nicholas Conti and I'm here to see Miss Kate Humphrey. Is she at home?"

The woman blinked. "Nick Conti. Kate mentioned that she'd met you in Italy. If that doesn't beat all. And you look even better that you did on the telly. My mister will think I'm daft when I tell him this." She shook her head. "Well, you're out of luck, Nicholas Conti. Kate's gone."

"Gone? Gone where?"

"Back home to America, she has. Some big company, Byrnside I think it was, offered her a big recording contract and she decided to take it."

KATE SAT with her hands folded in her lap, looking out the window while the big car purred along a tree-lined road. Riding in monster luxury vehicles was getting to be a regular thing, she reflected in amazement. First Sir Cedric's and now Owen Byrnside's. Only Kate was a lot more nervous about this trip in the black Cadillac stretch limousine than she'd been about driving to London in Sir Cedric's Rolls Royce.

Kate leaned forward and tapped the window that separated her from the uniformed chauffeur. "Can I help you, Miss Humphrey?" he responded through the intercom.

Kate felt ridiculous using a phone to speak to a man who sat only a few feet away. Nevertheless, she activated the speaker and said, "I was just wondering how much farther it is to Mr. Byrnside's estate."

"We should be arriving in another twenty minutes, Miss Humphrey."

"Oh. Thank you." Kate leaned back against the plush cushions and smoothed the fabric of her pleated white-linen skirt. It was a fine April day. The oaks and maples were budded out and beds of daffodils and tulips brightened the yards of the occasional houses they passed.

The weather in New England was quite an improvement over Merrie Olde England, which had been cold and overcast the morning of her departure, Kate reflected. Hoping that boded well, she folded her hands together more tightly.

The decision to fly back across the Atlantic had been very sudden, but then so had Winston Deeping's offer of a juicy recording contract, including her very own album. She would have been crazy to turn it down. Not only were the Byrnside people prepared to launch the album with an advertising budget that would have impressed even Madonna, they were also going to arrange a concert tour for her at all the best spots up and down the East Coast.

After all, what had there been to stay for in London? She would miss Mrs. Brasswell, but nobody else—except Nick. Kate's nails dug into her palms. Now that she knew Nick had won the National and was safe and sound, it was best to put an ocean between then. His world was so different from hers. Going to Ireland with him would never have worked out. It was best to make a clean break before they caused each other any further pain.

Kate sat very still, aware of an icy feeling spreading through her arms and legs. If only the pain she was in now would go away. Eventually it would, she told herself fiercely. She'd fallen for Mr. Wrong before and she'd recovered. She would recover again.

The car turned and paused in front of a pair of massive wrought-iron gates until a guard in attendance nodded it through. Once cleared, the limousine cruised silently up a winding drive surrounded by parklike grounds and lined with rhododendron bushes.

Meeting Owen Byrnside had been a condition of Kate's contract. Spending an hour or two with a sick old man who had delusions about her being his granddaughter had seemed a small enough return for a contract that had to be the opportunity of a lifetime. Still, now that the moment was upon her, Kate felt nervous.

When the limousine pulled into a circular drive and stopped in front of what looked like a gray stone castle, Kate stared in awe. The windows were mullioned, heavily leaded and jutted out into angled bays. Pointed leaves of creeper screened the lower walls, and at the top of the stone front steps, huge mahogany double doors, decorated with a black falcon's-head knocker that Kate recognized as the Byrnside logo, gleamed in the afternoon light.

With excruciating politeness, the chauffeur opened the passenger door, helped Kate out and escorted her to those doors. The bell he rang clanged through the house with great power. When the doors opened Kate was greeted by a uniformed butler, who then turned her over to a tall, thin, dark-haired woman who introduced herself as Loretta Greene, Owen Byrnside's private secretary.

"I would offer you a drink after your journey, only I thought you might take some refreshment with Mr. Byrnside," Loretta told Kate with a cool smile and then led her toward a magnificent curving staircase. As Kate followed, she looked around curiously. A portrait of a pretty woman in a blue dress hung over the fireplace that dominated the entry. A very old-looking refectory table made of some dark wood glowed in the broken light from the windows.

As they climbed the stairs, Kate ran an appreciative hand over the carved bannister and then turned her attention to Miss Greene. Though she was not a pretty woman, her nose being disproportionately large and her eyes slightly too close together, she was so meticulously groomed and tastefully dressed that she projected an aura of varnished attractiveness that Kate rather envied. Kate's gaze lingered on her dress, a beautifully cut floral silk shirtwaist that had surely cost a small fortune. Owen Byrnside's secretary must be extremely well paid.

At the top of the stairs Miss Greene turned toward Kate, her dark eyes flicking over Kate's linen suit and apple-green silk blouse assessingly. "I must warn you that Mr. Byrnside's health is fragile. He's been looking forward to your visit very eagerly, of course. But the excitement may be too much for him. If he becomes overtired, I may have to ask you to leave. I'm sure you understand."

"Of course." Kate gazed into Miss Greene's carefully mascaraed eyes curiously. Was that a faint note of hostility she detected? Well, perhaps it wasn't surprising. The woman was obviously very protective of her boss. She probably considered Kate some sort of scheming charlatan who'd come here to prey on an old man's fantasies.

The abrupt realization unsettled Kate. Was she a scheming charlatan? As she followed Miss Greene down the corridor and through a door on which the woman tapped and then opened tentatively, Kate's stomach fluttered with nerves.

"Owen?" Miss Greene called softly.

"Who else? Don't talk to me as if I were a sick infant. I may be bedridden, but I'm not senile," a raspy voice answered. "What is it? Has she come yet?"

Behind Miss Greene, Kate's brows lifted and the hint of a smile began to twitch at the corners of her mouth. Suddenly she hoped Miss Greene really did receive a good salary. Clearly the poor woman deserved every penny of it.

"Miss Humphrey is right behind me," Miss Greene answered composedly. "See, here she is." She stepped out of the way so that Kate could walk in.

Owen Byrnside's bedchamber was a huge room lit by a bank of sunny windows flanking French doors that led out to a terrace. However, it needed all the natural light it could get, because everything else about it was dark. The floors, covered by an enormous, faded ruby Oriental rug, were almost black, as was the paneling. Stained-glass Tiffany lamps and heavy mahogany furniture completed the rather medieval effect. The large bed occupied by Owen Byrnside had thick, carved posts and a canopy of watered red silk.

"A redhead!" the hawknosed old man exclaimed from the mountain of pillows where he sat propped with his arms outspread like an eagle preparing to launch itself into flight. "Well, I'll be damned! Come here and stand in the light, girl. Let me get a good look at you."

As Kate crossed to the foot of the bed, Byrnside waved an imperious hand at Miss Greene. "You can go now. We won't need anything more for the next couple of hours except coffee and a tray of decent eats. And I do mean decent," he added warningly.

Kate stood studying the hawk-nosed old man, noting the high-domed forehead covered by only a few strands of thin silver hair, the thick, beetling silver eyebrows and the deepset blue eyes beneath them. Despite his age and infirmity, Owen Byrnside looked every inch what he was—the shrewd and ruthless businessman who'd turned a small-town newspaper into a multimillion-dollar international communications octopus.

"Well, well, so here you are, at last," he muttered, casting his proprietary gaze over her, "the first of my three missing chicks. I didn't expect you to be so pretty. You're quite the looker."

"Why, thank you."

"Pull up a seat, pull up a seat. I know it's awkward holding a conversation with an old wreck like me, so you might as well hunker down and make yourself as comfortable as you can."

"You're not an old wreck," Kate said politely. She picked up a tufted chair that had been in front of a desk, placed it next to the bed and sat down on it.

"Oh, of course I am. I'm a wasted old hulk and I'm not one to mince words about that or anything else. You don't get anywhere in this world by pretending things are what they aren't. But it's not me you're here to discuss. Tell me about yourself. Jake says that he had a devil of a time running you to earth. Rolling stone, are you?"

Smiling, Kate replied, "I'm afraid in my line of work, I don't have much choice about that."

"Explain your line of work to me. How'd you get into it? I'm all ears."

Shrugging, Kate began to describe her rootless years as a traveling musician. As she spoke, Owen Byrnside studied her with sharp intelligence, interrupting every now and then to ask a pointed question.

"Sounds as if you've had a rough row to hoe."

"Yes, but then I guess most people don't have it easy."

"Oh, I don't know. I could name a few who've floated through life on a layer of whipped cream. But it's you I want to figure out." Again and again Owen's sharp gaze flicked over her. "In all this talk about nightclubs and piano-playing, you haven't said word one about men. A pretty girl like you is bound to have a few lovers hanging about, especially in this day and age. Anyone special?"

Kate thought of Nick and felt a warm flush begin to rise up from her neck. She opened her mouth to issue a quick denial, but at that moment Miss Greene walked in bearing a tray with a silver teapot, china cups and a plate filled with an assortment of tiny sandwiches.

"Tea!" Owen exclaimed with a scowl. "That dishwater is for the English. I wanted coffee and brandy."

"You know what your doctor says," Miss Greene replied coolly. She leveled a tilt-top table with a piecrust rim and set it close to the bed beside Kate. Then she placed the tray on top of it.

"And what is that plate of nonsense?" Owen pointed a clawlike finger at the heaped triangles of crustless bread.

"Cucumber sandwiches, very light and healthful."

The old man let out a string of expletives that made Kate sit up and blink. Miss Greene, however, remained unmoved. Calmly, she filled two cups, added two lumps of sugar to her irritable employer's beverage and then, with a decorous smile and nod, walked out of the room.

When she was gone, Owen scowled suspiciously at his tea and then took a sip. "Like drinking from a lukewarm birdbath," he groused.

"It's good, actually," Kate replied, sipping her own gratefully. "While I was in England I learned to like tea." She picked up one of the cucumber sandwiches and bit into it. "And these are very tasty. Try one."

"Oh, all right. What choice do I have? Stuck in bed like this, I'm about as free to do as I please as the Prisoner of Zenda." Owen fished up one of the sandwiches and bit it in half as if he were a hungry piranha making short work of a hapless angelfish. Then he eyed Kate narrowly. "You said you'd learned to like tea in London. What else did you learn to like. Did you, for instance develop a taste for a fellow named Nicholas Conti?"

Kate almost dropped her teacup. "How did you—I mean, how could you—"

Owen gave a raspy chuckle. "Oh, I have my sources, even contacts that Jake Caine, the attorney on this case, doesn't know about. But, as a matter of fact, Jake's had a detective on your tail for the past month." The old man tapped a manila folder that Kate hadn't noticed before because it was half-covered by the quilt. "I received his report only yesterday. Had quite a time of it in Italy, didn't you?"

"Why yes, yes I did."

"You're lucky you got out of that situation in one piece. I know a thing or two about the men you were trying to hoodwink." Owen shook his head. "A bad bunch." He cleared his throat. "This Nicholas Conti, on the other hand, seems to be quite an interesting fellow. You might as well know that since your, ah, association with him was so close, I had him researched, too."

Kate was beginning to feel like a laboratory specimen wriggling under the microscope of Owen Byrnside's powerful organization. She didn't care for that at all, especially when it came to her failed relationship with Nick, which was still a fresh wound deep within her. On the other hand, it was difficult to be angry with Owen Byrnside himself. He might be rude, imperious and high-handed, but he was also a helpless, sick old man who was offering her the career she'd dreamed of on a plate—and something else besides, something she was beginning to sense might be even more important.

"What did you find out about Nick?" she asked.

"Only that he's a loner, very appealing to women and hell on the back of a horse. I've seen his picture. Most gals would be bowled over by the fellow. You weren't, I gather?"

Kate looked away from Owen Byrnside's piercing eyes and down at her cup. "Nick saved our lives, and I think the world of him. But we're so different. His interests and mine..." Her voice trailed off and she struggled with the wayward tears that had suddenly begun to burn at the back of her eyes. She'd thought she was all cried out over Nick. "It was just one of those things," she finished lamely.

"Women are different from what they used to be," Owen ruminated. "In my day women were romantic and fell in love young. That's how it was with my Alice. We met when she was seventeen and were married within the year." He pointed at a portrait on the wall opposite his bed, and Kate, glad of an opportunity to look away while she blinked back her tears, turned to study it. As her vision cleared, she saw a painting of a woman with soft brown hair and a sweet smile. It was the same woman whose portrait she'd seen down in the hall.

"She's lovely."

"Yes," he said and then cleared his throat. "You don't look like her."

"No, I don't."

"That doesn't mean diddlysquat, though. My son didn't resemble Alice, either, and neither did Gloria Dean."

Gloria Dean again, Kate thought. She was going to have to do a little research of her own on this person.

Owen reached to set his cup down on the table. When his trembling hands couldn't quite make it, Kate gently took the cup for him.

"Well, what do you think of the possibility that you might be my long-lost granddaughter and in line to inherit a big pot of money?" he asked gruffly.

"I think it sounds like a fairy story, and I also think I'm not the girl you want."

Shooting her an angled gaze from under his sparse gray lashes, Owen slowly straightened. "You might be, though. There's a good chance. How would you feel about it if you were?"

"I don't know," Kate answered truthfully.

"You've grown up an orphan, Kate," he probed with razor-sharp penetration she found impressive and more than a little intimidating. "Haven't you ever wondered about your real family, about where you really came from?"

"Of course I have. But what was the use? There were no records, and after my adoptive parents were gone, no one claimed me or wanted me. I was on my own in this world, and I just had to accept the fact."

"But you could have made a family for yourself. Most women do, and you're old enough to have had time."

Kate stiffened and her red hair seemed to flame as it trapped and magnified a ray of afternoon sunlight. "Marriage, you mean? I guess I've just never met the right man. Musicians tend to be a wild and crazy bunch. And other men, well they just don't understand the life I have to lead."

Owen gazed at her thoughtfully. "No, I imagine most wouldn't. Is piano-playing really so important to you?"

"Yes," Kate answered fiercely. "Music and the career I hope to make out of it is all I've ever really had. I couldn't give it up, not for anyone or anything. It would be like giving up myself."

Owen continued to study her, taking in the small, set white face, the incandescent hair, the rigid set of her shoulders. "Well, my dear," he said, "no matter how Jake Caine's investigations turn out, you're alone in the world no longer. You've got me—whether you want me or not."

"I have?" Her green eyes widened.

"Yes, and I hope you really mean what you've just said to me because though I may not look like much stuck here in this bed, believe me, I'm no mean ally. I'm going to give you your heart's desire. You'll have to supply the talent, of course. But if you've got what it takes, I'll provide the opportunity. If success at this music business is what you really want, Kate Humphrey, hold on to your hat!"

CHAPTER FIFTEEN

THREE MONTHS LATER and an ocean away, Shug O'Reilly exclaimed to his boss, "Damn, but Miss Peach is a little beauty!"

"Yes," Nick agreed. "Sounds as if Seasonwine thinks so, too."

"Oh he does, all right." Shug chuckled. "Just listen to him. Practically battering down his stall to get at her, he is."

Nick glanced over his shoulder. The big stallion, temporarily at Newride on loan from Marchmant, was working himself up into a frenzy. As soon as Nick had led Miss Peach in, Seasonwine had begun to dance, snort, whinny and kick with anticipation.

"Hold your horses, old boy," Nick murmured as he stood back to admire the roan filly. She was the fastest and most promising of all he'd raised so far. She had a beautifully modeled head set off by a white blaze between eyes of unusual intelligence. Right now, however, sensing what was up, she looked nervous and frightened.

"Now, don't worry," Nick whispered into her flattened ear. "He's not as bad as he sounds, and while it may not be much fun for you, this spring, if all goes well, you'll have one heck of a colt to show for it."

Miss Peach looked unimpressed, and Nick stroked her flank sympathetically. As far as he could tell, sex for horses was enjoyable only to the male. It was like that in most of the animal world, and too often for humans as well. With that, he found himself thinking yet again of Kate.

All summer he'd been desperately trying to forget her. He'd told himself it would be easy, what with the enterprising new turn his life had taken. Good old Colin had been right about business picking up. Since Nick's Grand National win and all the publicity surrounding it, he'd been deluged with training requests and his sales had been phenomenal. Newride was solidly in the black, for a change, and financially it and its owner's future of training and breeding prime horseflesh looked bright.

As he ruminated on this, Nick quieted Miss Peach and then handed her reins to Shug while he went to fetch Seasonwine. When Nick opened the gate, the stallion fairly burst out of his stall. "Whoa boy, whoa, take it easy. She's not going away. She's staying right here for you."

How much simpler life was for creatures like Seasonwine and Miss Peach, Nick mused a trifle bitterly as he led the eager stallion toward the nervous, quivering filly. When they had mated, Seasonwine would walk quietly back to his stall and begin to munch oats, the incident forgotten.

Apparently, Nick mused bitterly, it had worked that way for Kate, too. She'd walked out of his life without a backward glance. To be fair, he'd been able to do that with all the other woman he'd known, too. But not this time—not with Kate. She'd left her mark, and it went deep.

After Seasonwine and Miss Peach were safely back in their stalls, Nick left the barn and strode back to the house. On the porch he stood for a moment, surveying his property. Much of the money he'd won had gone toward fixing up Newride and the place showed it. That should have given him a sense of satisfaction. Instead, he felt restless, irritable. What good was a place like this if you had no one to share it with?

He turned back toward the front door. Only the house hadn't been touched. Somehow Nick couldn't bring himself to remodel the kitchen or embark on any of the other improvements the house sorely needed. Those were all things that needed a woman's touch, things he'd once hoped Kate would take a hand in. Only she hadn't wanted to be buried in Ireland on a horse farm.

Inside Nick went to his stereo cabinet and picked out a CD entitled *Rare Finds* which he'd acquired only very recently. It was Kate's, her first Byrnside release. For a long moment Nick stared down at the glamorous photograph of Kate on the CD jacket. He recognized the dreamy expression in her eyes because he'd seen her look at him that way the first time they'd kissed.

It was a form of self-torture, yet he'd been playing that CD over and over every night. And tonight wasn't going to be any different, he realized as he inserted the disc into the CD player and then set down on a comfortable old lounge chair and put his feet up.

As the sophisticated piano jazz filled the room, he steepled his fingertips and frowned thoughtfully. He wasn't going to forget Kate Humphrey, he acknowledged to himself once and for all. He was in love with her. And that meant only one thing. He couldn't let her get away. He had to do something.

"THIS LOOKS LIKE what you want," the librarian said, pulling out a tall, brightly colored volume from the shelf just above her head.

Kate squinted at the title. *Rock Sisters of the Sixties*. "That does look like the sort of thing," she agreed.

"There are articles on Mama Cass, Janis Joplin, the Supremes, Joan Baez. Yes, and here's a piece on Gloria Dean. She's the artist you were interested in, right?"

"Right," Kate said, accepting the volume and putting it on top of the stack of other books on female musicians the librarian had found for her. "Thanks. This ought to do me for a while."

"Well, I hope you find what you're after." Looking mildly curious, the librarian pushed her wire-rimmed glasses back up her nose and dusted off her hands.

"I'm sure with all the help you've given me, I will," Kate answered politely.

Hesitantly, almost fearfully, Kate opened the volume on sixties women singers and turned to the article the librarian had pointed out. Gloria Dean's photograph struck Kate immediately. The woman had had vivid red hair and catlike green eyes. As Kate gazed down at those eyes, she felt as if all the breath had been knocked from her lungs. My God, she thought, could this actually be my mother?

It was Owen Byrnside who'd forced Kate to take this question seriously. The old man had been as good as his word, and in the past months he and his money and influence had set Kate's world spinning at a mad rate.

There had been recording sessions in the glamorous, state-of-the-art Byrnside studios, meetings with publicity people, and, finally, a complete make-over, which had included a stunning new wardrobe. Then, synchronized with the release of her first album, Owen's recording executives had arranged television, magazine and newspaper interviews to go along with a twelve-city tour. As part of that tour, Kate was just now completeing an engagement at the Pier Six Pavilion in Baltimore's glittering Inner Harbor.

At first Kate had been reluctant to accept Owen Byrnside's largesse. His generosity had made her feel guilty, as if she were taking what didn't belong to her under the worst kind of false pretences—an old man's pathetic hope that he wouldn't die without leaving an heir.

But Owen had been impatient with this attitude. "In the first place, I didn't make my fortune by investing in lost causes. My people are always on the lookout for new young talent. They agree that you fill that bill. And another thing—why are you so all-fired determined to think that it's not possible we're related?"

"I just can't believe it," Kate had answered lamely. Then more forcefully, she'd added, "Why won't you have me tested now, so we can get that information answered for both of us?"

A mulish look had settled around the old man's mouth. "I'll do the testing when I've got all three of you under my roof, then and not before. But we were talking about your attitude, not mine. What you really mean is that you don't want to believe I'm your grandfather," he'd shot back. "You know, girl, I get a lot of time to think in this nasty nest of pillows." Owen had actually been sitting in an armchair next to his bed with his feet propped on a footstool. He beat a gnarled fist at a silken cushion wedged at his side. "And I've developed some theories about you."

"Oh, really?" Kate had gazed at her crotchety mentor with amusement.

While she'd been recording her album he'd demanded that she visit him often, saying, "I get lonesome. I'll send my car around for you." At first she'd been ill-at-ease in his gothic-style mansion, which looked to Kate like a set for a horror movie. But gradually she'd gotten over that, and she and Owen had developed a camaraderie, even a sort of intuitive understanding of each other.

"Yes, really. You make a big thing out of being a poor little orphan girl. But you know what I think? I think you actually like it that way. Now be honest, you do, don't you?"

Kate's jaw had dropped. "That's crazy! What are you talking about?"

"I'll tell you what I'm talking about. The way I see it, being all alone in the world has become a point of pride with you. Maybe you can't think of yourself any other way. Anyhow, I think you're afraid to admit you might not be so alone, that you might actually have a family." Fiercely, Owen had stared at her, his pale gaze direct and challenging.

Kate had floundered for an answer. "I...I...that's silly. Why wouldn't I want to have a family?"

"Because it changes who you are, because it gives you some responsibilities you never had to accept before and also takes away a lot of excuses."

He'd narrowed his eyes. "You know, now that I think of it, I bet that's why you've never nabbed yourself a husband. And don't tell me you never met the right fella. For a pretty girl like you, the world is full of the right men. You're just too afraid to pick one out of the crowd.

"I know how it is," he'd continued while Kate stared at him in outrage. "Naturally a person's most comfortable with how they were raised, even if the way they were raised could use a lot of improvement. You grew up thinking of yourself as a loner. It's what you know and what you're familiar with, and you're scared to try anything different. So you tell yourself that this music career you're so hell-bent on is all you really care about. Well, you may live to regret that, my girl. Mark my words."

At the time Kate had flushed bright red, thought of Nick, and retorted angrily, "It's not true!" But now, as she gazed down at the image of Gloria Dean, she recalled Owen's accusation and rubbed the pulse throbbing in her temples. It was so much like what Nick had said that last night after they'd made love in London. "You're afraid of commitment!" he'd accused.

With a sigh, Kate began to scan the article on Gloria Dean. It read:

Though one of the turbulent decade's most beautiful and charismatic singers, Gloria Dean burned out her talent by setting herself on a drug-riddled course of self-destruction. Gloria made a point of making a splash at high-living parties from Los Angeles to London, Paris and Rome, but she was essentially a loner. When she died of a drug overdose, no one mourned. Her fans had forgotten her, and she had no close friends.

A horrified tremor rippled up Kate's spine. Could this pathetic woman with her empty shell of a life have been her natural mother? It was not a welcome thought. Yet, like Kate herself, Gloria *had* been a green-eyed redhead with a career in music.

With a snap, Kate closed the book. Then she stood and gathered up her purse and jacket. Checking the new gold watch that Owen Byrnside had given her to commemorate the release of her album, she saw that it was getting late. It was time she caught a cab back to her hotel so that she could take a leisurely shower, then eat and dress before her evening's performance.

An hour later, Kate stood in the marble shower stall in her hotel's luxurious bathroom. As rivulets of hot water beat down on her slim, naked body, all she'd read about the sad life of Gloria Dean still simmered in her head.

"So, okay, the woman had red hair and was musical," Kate muttered aloud over the drum of the pelting spray. "But she and I have nothing else in common. I'm not a drug addict, nor is my life an aimless round of wild parties. I know what I want and where I'm going."

But do you? a nagging little voice inside her queried while she rubbed soap up and down the length of her bare arms. Do you really?

Again Kate's thoughts returned to Nick. Try as she might to forget, she kept remembering his invitation to give their relationship a trial and the way she'd rejected it. That had been a decision point, perhaps the most important one in her life. Now Kate felt as if she'd been offered two prizes, and like the fool who couldn't tell the difference between brass and true gold, she'd picked the one of lesser value.

Suddenly Kate slumped against the marble tile and covered her face with her hands. For many minutes her hot tears mingled with the streaming water. But gradually she straightened and then wiped her reddened eyes with the back of her wet hand. "It wouldn't have worked," she muttered fiercely and then snapped off the water and yanked at a towel. "It just wouldn't have."

TWO HOURS LATER, Kate sat at her dressing table applying her stage makeup and mulling over a few changes she intended to make in her act. A rattle of knuckles on the other side of the door interrupted her thoughts.

"Who's there?"

"A face from your deep, dark past," a familiar male voice answered through the thin wood.

Kate blinked and then, as recognition dawned, she smiled and threw open the door. "Billy Rockland, as I live and breathe! What are you doing here?"

"I'm down the street at Max's," a young man with a devastating smile and the face of a fallen angel said, naming a popular jazz club in Baltimore. "So, as long as I was in the neighborhood, I just thought I'd drop by to say hello to my favorite pianist." He folded his arms across his chest, leaned his willowy body against the door frame and looked Kate up and down appreciatively. Then he gave a low whistle. "Say, aren't you something in that dress. I like the tapestry jacket."

"Why, thank you, sir." Kate gave a mocking little curtsey. "It's terrific to see you again."

Billy Rockland played the horn like a saint and broke hearts like a devil on a spree. Although Kate had briefly fallen prey to his glamorous looks and easy charm, she'd soon realized that love was just a game to Billy and that the sweet promises he made to her had about as much substance as sugar in water.

She and Billy had parted ways and he'd gone on to new conquests. But musicians inhabit a small world. Ex-lovers were bound to meet and had to learn how to get along. Kate and Billy had been working together again in London and Billy had been trying, unsuccessfully, to renew their affair when the gig had fallen apart and he'd had to leave.

"You're not exactly an eyesore yourself," she told him now. "Who are you working with at Max's?"

When Billy named the trio with which he was playing, Kate's brows lifted. "Hey, pretty nifty. I guess you did all right after you got back from our European disaster."

Billy studied her, a little half smile quirking his sexy mouth. "Oh, I'd say you're the one who's landed on her pretty little feet. I've been reading about you, girl. Since London you've taken off like a hot rocket. Tell your old pal Bill, what's the secret of your success?"

"Beauty and talent," she replied with a cheeky grin. One of the conditions of Owen Byrnside's patronage had been that she tell no one of his search for a lost granddaughter, and Kate could certainly see the sense of that. If word got around there would be an avalanche of false claims and the quest would turn into a three-ring circus.

"Well, that certainly explains it," Billy said, eyeing her speculatively. "You were always a beauty, and there's never been any doubt in my mind that you're up to here in talent." With his forefinger he drew a line across his throat. "Are you traveling alone by any chance?"

"Yes," Kate admitted warily, guessing where this was leading.

Billy straightened. "Me too. Listen, how about we get together after our shows—you know, have a few drinks, a few laughs, talk over old times? I can catch you up on some of the latest gossip."

She cocked her head, suddenly tempted by Billy's invitation. Lately she'd been feeling so lonely and isolated in her chain of hotel rooms. Billy could be an absolutely spellbinding companion, and it might be good to shoot the breeze with a colleague who happened to be a very attractive member of the opposite sex. Maybe that was the kind of thing she needed to help her stop thinking about Nick. "Okay," she said. "After things are all wrapped up here, I'll grab a cab down to Max's."

Later on that evening Kate regretted having accepted Billy's invitation. She always put everything she had into her performances. When she finished up at Pier Six she wanted nothing more than to fall into bed and close her eyes. But she'd promised, and Kate was not one to back out of promises easily.

When she finally got to Max's, however, she was glad she'd made the effort. The place had a friendly, low-key atmosphere and relaxing over a well-earned glass of wine and talking shop was fun. As wickedly charming as ever, Billy entertained Kate with stories about their many mutual acquaintances.

"Had you heard that Bert Rouse and Ellen Carrell are an item now?" Billy asked, lounging back in his chair as he named another pianist and a pretty young woman who'd lately begun to make a name for herself as a singer.

"No, I hadn't heard that." Kate shook her head. "What an unlikely couple!"

"Now why do you say that?" Billy demanded, gazing at her through his lashes—a trick that had once devastated her and was doubtless still wreaking havoc on a lot of other poor unsuspecting females.

"Oh, I don't know. He's always been such a quiet steady type of guy, and she seems kind of flighty."

"Sort of the reverse of what you and I were," Billy responded, flashing Kate his most melting smile.

Kate stifled a laugh. "Sort of," she agreed.

Billy reached out and took her hand, which had been laying on the table. "I know you think I'm just one big line, Kate girl," he said, beginning to toy with her fingers. "But believe me, this comes from the heart. I've been thinking a lot about those days when you and I were together and asking myself if I didn't make a big mistake by not treating you right."

"Oh, really?" Merely amused, Kate removed her hand from his. "Actually, I think you probably never made a mistake in your life, Charming Billy. I mean, why should a handsome guy like you deprive the rest of the female population by sticking with only one woman? It wouldn't be kind," she said with a laugh, and then changed the subject.

But Billy proved to be more persistent than he'd been in the old days. Then, like a honeybee, he'd simply buzzed off to another flower at the slightest hint of rejection. Now, when Kate began to yawn and look for her purse, he insisted on seeing her home in a cab and then walking her through the hotel lobby and coming up in the elevator to her door.

"Well, this is it," Kate said, pausing in front of 602 and beginning to dig for her keys.

"Nice digs," Billy commented, gazing down at her with sleepy eyes.

"Yes, it's very comfortable." *And cold and lonely,* Kate thought as she finally found her room key.

"They must think pretty darn well of you to put you up at a fancy place like this. Not like a couple of years back when you and I played that dump in Florida. Remember our rooms?"

It had been four years back, actually. "Sure I do. Battalions of cockroaches the size of toy trucks." Kate gave a delicate shudder. "How could I forget?"

"I sure haven't forgotten." His gaze was fixed on her face, and Kate, who'd been suspecting that their goodnights might turn complicated, became certain of it. "We had some good times together, you and me," he murmured huskily.

"Yes, but I was awfully young and that's all water under the bridge."

"You were an awfully sweet kid, too, Kate. And I was a jerk. I didn't deserve you."

No, he hadn't deserved her, Kate thought. Yet, she felt a bittersweet tug of nostalgia as she remembered that period in her life. She had been so full of her plans for her future, so determined to make good despite all odds. Even her ill-fated fling with Billy had been but a momentary setback. She'd picked herself up and plodded on, determined to make a name for herself all on her own. And here she was, suddenly and unexpectedly at the place where she'd dreamed of being, on the threshold of a really thrilling career.

So why didn't it mean more? Why did her routine of hotels, planes and performances seem so empty? If she'd accepted Nick's invitation, she'd be at his farm in Ireland now, Kate found herself thinking. Perhaps they'd even be lying in that big old bed of his together, making love. Kate could almost hear his intimate laughter, feel the warmth of his arms around her, the sweet, stirring excitement of his kiss. Suddenly her head whirled, and she felt a burning sensation in her chest.

"Is it really too late?"

"What?" Dragged from her confused thoughts, Kate stared up at Billy blankly.

"Is it really too late for us, Kate girl? I know it's been a long time, but maybe that's what we've both needed— time. We've both had a few years to do some growing up, figure out what's important in life. I know one thing I think is important." Without further ado, he reached out, pulled her into his arms and began to kiss her.

If there was one thing Charming Billy Rockland knew how to do, other than play a mean and masterful trumpet, it was how to kiss a woman into submission. He'd certainly had plenty of practice.

Perhaps it was Kate's loneliness and the memories of Nick that had been plaguing her for months, but Kate, who'd always admired expertise no matter what the arena, began to respond. Billy wasn't Nick, but he wasn't bad, either, and she'd been feeling so lost. For just a moment it felt good to find a safe harbor within the circle of masculine arms.

"God, but this feels good, Kate," Billy murmured into her ear. "You're a sweet bundle."

Kate blinked, surprised and then angry at herself.

"What do you say?" he went on huskily. "I can't walk away now. Why not open that door and invite me in? I promise you won't be sorry."

"I already am," Kate declared, giving her head a little shake to clear it and then flattening her palms against his chest and pushing. "I know I just gave you the wrong idea, kissing you that way."

"What wrong idea? What do you mean?"

"Billy, I really am sorry. I don't want to resume our relationship."

He scowled. "I suppose you're going to tell me there's someone else?"

"'Fraid so. That was stupid of me. I apologize." She watched the expressions chase themselves across his handsome face: first anger, then irritation, then a tightening of the mouth and an expressive lift of the shoulders. "Well, I deserved that, I suppose," he clipped. "'Hell hath no fury—'"

"Billy, it's not that, really. I'm telling the truth. There really is someone else."

He smiled crookedly. "Okay, if you say so. He's a lucky guy, whoever he is."

"Maybe." Kate had no intention of talking about Nick. Nor did she want to unlock her door until Billy had gone away—over the years she'd learned a thing or two about dealing with men who hadn't gotten what they wanted.

Fortunately Billy was one of the more easygoing members of the species. He walked off in the direction of the elevators and left Kate in peace.

With a sigh, she unlocked her door, and closed it behind her. When she'd flicked on the overhead light and put the chain in place, she heaved another sigh and then stepped back. Paper rustled beneath her high heels, and she glanced down. Someone, probably a hotel clerk had slipped a brown manila envelope under her door.

Kate picked it up and, after kicking off her shoes and draping her coat over the bed, walked with it over to the club chair by the window. For a moment she sat gazing out at the lights of the city, the ripple of blue neon on the aquarium across the harbor, the flare of cloudy red from the smokestack of the sugar factory. Then she pulled open the flap of the envelope and shook out its contents.

It contained a note from Owen and her booking agent, a collection of reviews from her clipping service and a square white envelope addressed in a spidery hand and with what appeared to be an Italian postmark.

Kate stared down at it. Then her heart began to thud. She didn't remember ever seeing Nick's handwriting. What if it were from him? But the invitation inside the envelope had been sent by Adelina, not Nick.

"Adelina and Mario," Kate murmured, gazing down at the indecipherable Italian script and then rereading the awkward translation that had been included along with a brief personal note from Adelina. "Please come to our wedding and wish us happiness," it pleaded. And then, in a sly afterthought, "Nico will be there and so, too, Rudy and Randy. We all miss you, *bellina*!"

EXACTLY TWO WEEKS LATER Kate stepped off a jet at the Rome airport, caught a cab and checked into the elegant hotel where she'd been booked. That evening she sat at a round marble table sipping a cappuccino and gazing out a restaurant window at the Fontana di Trevi across the way.

How different this arrival in Rome was from her last, she mused. Instead of the thrift-shop vest and anxious air she'd sported on that memorable occasion, this morning she'd stepped off the plane wearing a designer suit and a veneer of well-traveled sophistication. But that's all her surface composure amounted to—a veneer. Beneath it, Kate's stomach fluttered with the uncertainty of a teenager trying her luck at her first mixer.

"The *signorina* is all alone?"

Kate looked up to see a handsome, dark-eyed man gazing down at her speculatively. His smile was suave and he wore a fashionably rumpled white linen jacket over expensive bisque-colored pants. A wide gold watch gleamed on his tanned wrist and another gold ornament shone in the patch of hairy chest at the V of his cream silk shirt.

"For the moment, yes," Kate said, "but I was just leaving." She opened her clutch purse and fished out a bill.

"You are an American." His charming smile widened appreciatively. "A woman so lovely as yourself shouldn't be alone in a strange city. If you have time and would like some company, I would show you some of the beauties of Roma."

"Thank you," Kate answered politely, "but I'm afraid I haven't the time." She signaled the waiter, who came hurrying over. "I have something very important to do, and I'm on a very tight schedule, you see. So, if you'll excuse me—"

His face fell, but he could obviously recognize a woman who really wasn't interested when he saw one, so he shrugged and turned away in defeat. "Good luck with your thing of importance, *signorina. Ciao.*"

THE NEXT MORNING Kate picked up the car she'd hired and drove north toward the picturesque little village where Mario and Adelina were to be married. According to Adelina's note, she had already sold her house, so after the wedding ceremony the reception was to be at Mario's farm.

"I'm going to be late," Kate muttered, glancing repeatedly at her watch as she sped along. Everything had taken more time than she'd counted on. The car had had to be serviced before she could take it, the traffic snarls in Rome had been horrendous, and she'd veered off on a wrong turning that had cost her at least an hour.

Fretting because she'd missed the ceremony itself, Kate turned into the dusty road that led up to Mario's house. As her rental car bumped along the familiar track, her head swam with conflicting emotions, and her hands trembled on the steering wheel.

Vividly, she remembered how fearful she'd been when Nick had first driven her here—and how relieved to find benevolent Mario and his harmless pigs and chickens at the end of their journey. And then there had been Nick's first kiss after their trip to Viterbo. Her stomach tightened as she recalled the feel of his lips on hers and her runaway response. From the first moment she'd looked into his eyes she'd wanted him. Distrusting him at first, she'd tried to fight that attraction. But it had been a hopeless battle. And now that she knew what a fine and honorable man he really was—oh, how could she have walked away from him?

"Nick!" she murmured aloud. Was he here now? she wondered. Would she be seeing him in the next few seconds? And if she did, what would they say to each other?

The square white house came into view along with a line of cars that had been parked off to the side of the lane. As she had suspected, the day's festivities were already well under way. The house had been spruced up with a fresh coat of whitewash. New plantings and bright pots of chrysanthemums sat on the long porch. Above them, colored streamers fluttered from all of the windows.

To one side of the house, a line of tables covered with white cloths, wine jugs and platters heaped with food had been set out. Around these, groups of wedding guests dressed in their Sunday best milled, laughing and talking with great spirit.

Kate pulled in next to a Fiat exactly like her own, only much older and rustier. Then she got out of the car, straightened the skirt of the taupe silk suit she wore, retrieved the wedding gift she'd brought from the passenger seat and hurried toward the house.

Adelina spotted her first. With a cry of joy, she came hurrying forward and kissed Kate on both cheeks. "Kate, Kate, I no believe my eyes! You come all this way!"

"Of course! You didn't think I'd miss your wedding, did you? I'd have come if I'd been in China. Oh, Adelina, you're a vision of beauty!" Kate leaned back and ran an admiring eye over the older woman. Adelina's dress was of rose silk, overlaid with pale pink lace that looked handmade. Around her throat she wore a string of fat pearls and her dark hair had been piled high and studded with matching pearl-trimmed silver combs. But it was the glow on her face that made her beautiful. She radiated happiness.

Suddenly Mario appeared at her side wearing a gorgeous silk shirt and a broad smile. "See, Kate come just like I say," he declared and then leaned forward to hug Kate and kiss her noisily on both cheeks. "You fly all this way to see me get tied up like a pig for market." He rolled his eyes mischievously. "Is a fine sight, no?"

Playfully, Adelina slapped his shoulder. "*Buffone!* She come to see you finally, at last, become a happy man!"

"Sì, cara mia," Mario replied, giving his new wife's plump cheek an affectionate peck. Then he turned back to Kate. "Come, come! Eat, drink! Meet your old friends!" He pointed toward a spreading tree where Rudy and Randy, neatly combed and dressed in matching suits, were taking turns being pushed on a tire swing by their mother.

At the sight of Jillian LaFiore, looking gorgeous in a long-sleeved blue velvet dress with a tulip skirt and white lace at the throat and cuffs, Kate's stomach clenched. She remembered how jealous she'd felt when she'd spotted Nick and Jillian together at Aintree. Why had Jillian taken the trouble to come to Adelina and Mario's wedding, she wondered. Was it because of Nick? And where was Nick? Kate glanced around, but she didn't see him anywhere among the throng of guests.

As Adelina relieved Kate of the small, prettily wrapped box she'd brought and Mario led her toward the tables, the happy couple answered both Kate's questions.

"When we invite Rudy and Randy, we never expect them to say yes," Adelina said. "But *sì*, their mother fly all the way to Italy with their grandfather."

"Not just for our *matrimonio*," Mario interjected in a conspiratorial voice. "See, over there?" He nodded toward the front entrance to his house where two dark-suited men had just emerged.

One was Nick. The other—Kate inhaled. "That's Lou LaFiore!"

"*Sì.* He here to meet with his wife and *bambini*."

"But is it safe?" Though she was asking about Lou, Kate's gaze lingered on Nick. He was deep in conversation with the other man, his face turned away. But the sight of his familiar, lean form sent tingles of bittersweet excitement down Kate's spine.

At that moment Rudy and Randy, trailed by their mother ran up to Lou. Squatting, he hugged each of them. Then he put an arm around Jillian and together the four walked away to a nondescript black car.

Kate watched until Lou got in by himself and drove down the lane, leaving his wife and children behind. Then Kate's gaze swiveled back to Nick. He too had been watching Lou's departure. At that moment, however, he looked up and his gaze meshed with Kate's.

Like a startled creature poised for flight, Kate waited, her nerves quivering. Now that Nick knew she was here, would he come over to her, speak to her? She felt shattered when, instead, he turned away, stepped off the porch and began to chat with a small knot of guests from the village who stood eating cake and quaffing cups of homemade wine around one of the tables.

During the next hour things went on in that frustrating manner. Though Kate's hungry gaze followed Nick, she couldn't bring herself to approach him. Instead, she played with the twins and asked their mother about her theater tour.

"Oh, it was a dreadful bore, I'm afraid. The play simply wasn't right for me." Jillian cocked her head. "The boys tell me you were quite a heroine here in Italy. They talk about you constantly. But I must say, I didn't expect we'd be seeing you again at this wedding."

"While I was at the farm with Rudy and Randy, I became very fond of Adelina and Mario," Kate replied.

"Oh of course, everybody loves Nick's uncle," Jillian exclaimed, casting a jaundiced eye at the twins, who were digging into the cake with both pairs of hands.

While Jillian rushed away to drag her offspring from the food table, Kate glanced around again for Nick. Instead she found Mario, who brought her a piece of cake, which he insisted she eat along with a cup of his wine. Then it was time for Adelina to open her presents. After that the bride tossed her bouquet, and Kate astonished herself by catching it.

"You be the next *sposina*, you be the next!" Adelina shouted joyfully while the twins hopped up and down like jumping beans and Jillian LaFiore smiled tightly.

Flushing with embarrassment and unable to think of an appropriate response, Kate's gaze once more snagged Nick's. He stood next to Mario, apart from the little knot of women around Adelina, his arms folded across his chest, his expression impassive. Yet his gaze wasn't indifferent. It touched her like a living thing. Beneath her suit jacket, Kate felt goose bumps rise on her arms.

Now is the moment when we should speak to each other, she thought. She took a step toward him, but again, he pivoted away. Stuffing his hands deep into his pockets, he strolled through the crowd and off in the direction of the barn.

Kate stared after his departing figure. Suddenly she was angry, both with herself and with him. This was ridiculous. She hadn't come all this way to see him and not speak. They were intelligent adults who needed to resolve in some way the feelings that still vibrated between them. If he wouldn't make the first move, she would.

"Kate," Adelina cried, rushing up with a huge smile on her face. "Your present is a dishwasher, truly?"

Kate nodded. "It's a gift certificate for a freestanding one. All you have to do is call the store and they'll deliver it to the farm and show you how it works."

Adelina shook her head in wonder. "A dishwasher. *Che miracolo!*" She kissed Kate's cheek and then tugged at her hand. "Come meet my cousin Arafina. I tell her all about you, and she dying to say hello."

"Sure." With a last rueful glance at the barn into which Nick had now disappeared, Kate allowed Adelina to tug her through the crowd. As they went, Adelina started making introductions on all sides, each of which seemed to involve ten minutes of staccato conversation.

It was at least another three-quarters of an hour before Kate could disentangle herself. At the edge of the crowd of wedding guests, some of whom were now dancing to the strains of music from an old record player, she looked around for Nick. Not seeing him, she walked out to the barn where she guessed he might still be.

As Kate picked her way through the weeds and hard-packed dirt she rehearsed what she wanted to say. Unfortunately, though, she wasn't sure exactly what that might be. *Nick, I've missed you? Nick, is it too late for me to re-think my position on living with you?*

Kate shook her head. How ridiculous her feelings sounded when she tried putting them into words. Perhaps she had been a fool to come, hoping that somehow when they saw each other things would fall into place. Obviously, Nick hadn't missed or longed for her. Nick wasn't shy. Surely if he felt as she did, he would have sought her out and told her so instead of avoiding her as he'd done all afternoon.

Nevertheless, Kate walked around to the barn's entrance and stepped inside. Immediately, she stopped short. Nick was down at the far end in front of Cesare's stall, but he wasn't alone. Jillian LaFiore was in his arms, her face buried in his throat while he stroked her long blond hair.

Instantly, Kate stepped back and turned away. The sick, jealous feeling at the pit of her stomach was hideous. *I have to get out of here,* she thought. It was a mistake ever to have come.

CHAPTER SIXTEEN

BACK IN HER HOTEL ROOM that evening, Kate paced in front of the bed for what seemed like hours. Finally she opened the French doors and stepped out onto the tiny balcony overlooking the square.

Outside, Rome beckoned like a ripely beautiful woman dressed for seduction. Making the most of the fine autumn weather, pigeons floated in the evening sky, lovers promenaded arm in arm, exquisitely fashionable young people kibitzed in the squares, and a vendor with a push-cart full of trinkets called out his wares in a melodic tenor that would have rivaled an opera singer's.

In the distance Kate could see empty tables in the restaurant where she'd eaten the night before. She glanced at her watch. Though it was past dinner time, she was far too upset to feel hungry. After making hurried excuses to Mario and Adelina, she had driven back to Rome in such a depressed state and so blinded by tears that she supposed she was lucky to have made it back safely at all.

Now that she'd turned in her rental car and confirmed her morning flight back to the States, the evening stretched before her like an accusation. I should be out walking or taking in the opera, she thought. How eager she'd been to do those things on her first, ill-fated arrival in Rome. Now none of it seemed to hold any appeal.

Yet Kate knew she couldn't stay cooped up in this room pacing back and forth and brooding. Abruptly, she left the balcony and grabbed up her purse and jacket. Outside the hotel she took a table at the outdoor café nearby in the Piazza Navona and ordered an *acqua minerale* to sip while she made some plans for using up the hours ahead.

But as she sat pretending to admire the Bernini fountains across the way, no plan came into Kate's head. Try as she might, all she could think about was the image of Nick and Jillian LaFiore together. And, despite the lime flavoring her mineral water, all she could taste was her own bitter disappointment. She'd had such high hopes that when she and Nick saw each other they could somehow mend the breach between them. Now those hopes were crushed.

"Kate."

Her head jerked around. "Nick?"

He was standing just behind her, one hand in his pocket, a tentative expression in his blue eyes. "I went to your hotel, but they said you'd left. Then I saw you over here."

"Yes, I—I wanted to get out." Her voice was thin and strained.

"It's a perfect evening for it. Mind if I sit down?"

"No, no, of course not. Please." Kate's heart beat in her throat. Nick was the last person she'd expected. For a crazy second she almost wondered if she were imagining him.

When he'd pulled out a chair, he leaned back and looked at her. She looked back, drinking him in. At the wedding she hadn't been able to study him closely. Now her eyes feasted. "Are you getting ready for another race?"

He shook his head. "No. Why do you ask?"

"You haven't gained any weight. In fact, if anything, you look thinner."

He shrugged. "Things have been hectic. I've been very busy. The same for you, I gather. I see your album everywhere."

"Really?" She managed a little nod. "I haven't seen any sales figures, but as far as I can tell it seems to be doing well."

"*You* seem to be doing well. Congratulations."

"Thank you."

The waiter brought Nick a Campari and he picked it up and sipped it, all the while gazing at her steadily. "It's wonderful to see you again, Kate."

"It's wonderful to see you." She hesitated just a beat. "I've missed you."

"Have you?" He set his drink down as if he didn't like the taste. "Then why did you leave the wedding so quickly? Why didn't you stick around so we could talk?"

Kate's jaw dropped. "Talk? Nick I didn't know you wanted to talk to me."

"Of course I did. In fact, I asked Adelina when she sent you that invitation to mention particularly that I would be there. I thought that if you came it would have to mean you wanted to see me. I was so glad when I spotted you out on the lawn with Mario, I felt like throwing my hat up in the air."

Kate was flabbergasted. "Then why didn't you come over and speak to me right away? I was hoping you would."

"I had no way of knowing that. You didn't look as if you were dying for a conversation with me. And anyway I was with Lou who'd just been telling me some of his problems, which are very heavy. I couldn't just walk off and leave him."

"But later on . . ."

"Later on the time never seemed quite right. Adelina was opening presents and tossing bouquets. There were people everywhere." Nick lifted the palms of his hands. "I thought I'd wait until the crowd thinned and we could have a little privacy. But when that started to happen, you were gone." He frowned. "After coming this far for the wedding, almost halfway across the world, I don't understand why you left so quickly." His blue eyes searched her green ones. "Why, Kate?"

Her gaze dropped to her fingers, which clenched her glass tightly. With an effort, she loosened them. "I was upset. I walked out to the barn to find you and saw you with Jillian LaFiore. The two of you looked so..." Kate's voice trailed off.

Nick placed both his palms flat on the table and leaned forward. His eyes seemed to drill into Kate's like lasers. "My God, you must know I'm not interested in any other woman but you, and haven't been for months. I think I made that pretty clear when we were together in London. You're the one who walked out on me, who left England without even bothering to say goodbye."

"I was at Aintree and saw you win," Kate blurted. "I couldn't go until I knew you were all right."

"If you felt so concerned about my well-being why didn't you stop by to say hello or wish me well? It would have meant a lot to me, more than I can even tell you."

"Oh, Nick, I did, but when I went to the paddock, you didn't even notice me. You saw Jillian LaFiore, though. You stopped to talk to her."

He looked astounded. "You mean you were there and didn't try to catch my attention?"

"I—I—"

"For God's sake, Kate, when I'm getting ready for a race, I'm concentrating on what I have to do. If I didn't seem to notice you, it's because my mind was on the jumps, working out my strategy. And as far as Jillian LaFiore is concerned, I have no interest in her."

"Out in Mario's barn, you had her in your arms."

Nick's chiseled mouth twisted with impatience. "Jillian was crying on my shoulder because of Lou. The man's going to need to be in hiding for months, if not years. All I was offering his wife was sympathy, nothing else, Kate. Nothing else."

Across the table they stared at each other. Then Kate's eyes filled with tears. "Oh Nick, I've missed you so much! I really have!"

"I've missed you, too," he answered raggedly. "Everything has been going my way these last few months, but without you it hasn't meant much. Without you I've been lonely as hell."

"It's been the same for me." Her voice broke and she dabbed at her eyes with the small paper napkin that had come with her drink. "I said such stupid things to you back in London. I'm so sorry! Can you forgive me?"

Nick pushed his chair back. He slapped several bills down on the table and then took Kate's hand. "C'mon, let's get out of here. We'll take a walk and discuss it."

"Oh, yes." Kate let him pull her out of the chair. Such a mist had swum into her eyes that she could hardly see. But Nick put a firm hand around her waist and guided her through the maze of round marble tables and out onto the cobbled paving lining the piazza.

Night had fallen. The lights of Rome glittered around them, and throngs of people out for an evening stroll crowded the pavement. Itinerant musicians circulated among the tourists. A young girl in a tie-dyed dress played the flute. A bearded young man strummed a guitar and sang. Outdoor artists sketched quick portraits and flapped them enticingly. But Kate and Nick were oblivious to all this. As they meandered with the crowds in the direction of the Pantheon they concentrated solely on each other.

"Not all you said to me that night in London was wrong, Kate," Nick murmured gruffly. His arm tightened around her waist. "I've been thinking a lot about it. In some ways you hit the nail on the head."

"I've been thinking a lot about what you said to me, too," she replied huskily. "It made me angry when you said what you did about my being afraid of commitment, but maybe you were right. Maybe I've been alone so long that I'm afraid of being any other way. Maybe I'm just a coward."

With his free hand, Nick caressed Kate's shoulder. "You're no coward. You're the gutsiest woman I've ever met. That's one of the things that made me fall in love with you. And I am in love with you, Kate. But you already knew that."

"No. No, I didn't." She stopped and faced him. Ignoring the Roman pedestrians streaming around them and shooting openly curious and amused looks, they stood gazing into each others' eyes. "I love you, too, Nick. If you still want me, I'm willing to do anything, try anything to make it work for us."

"If I still want you?" Nick's fingers locked with hers. "Let's go someplace where I can show you just how much I want you!"

"Oh, yes, yes!"

Because Nick had driven directly from Mario's without bothering to check into a hotel, they went back to Kate's room. For all its luxury, it had seemed like a bleak prison when she had left it. Now when she switched on the light and led Nick inside, it appeared snug and inviting, a perfect haven for lovers. The heavy apricot hangings at the windows and the matching velvet upholstery on the antique chairs glowed warmly against the polished parquet floors. The crystal chandelier suspended above the four-poster bed twinkled from the high inlaid ceilings like a shower of diamonds.

The carved door swung shut and instantly, as it latched behind them, they turned into each other's arms. Both their mouths sought the other's, brushed and clung. With soft, urgent groans, they burrowed into each other. For long minutes the only sound was their rough breathing, the fevered silken rustle of Kate's skirt against Nick's woolen slacks, and the distant hiss of traffic on the street below.

At last Kate pulled away, moaned faintly and then, with her hands relaxed on Nick's shoulders, let her forehead drop forward to rest against the ticking pulse at the base of Nick's cleft chin. He stroked her hair, murmuring something deep in his throat. At last, with hands that trembled slightly, he slipped her jacket off. When it fell to the floor, he began to undo the buttons of her white silk blouse. After a moment, her fingers found the buttons on his shirt as well.

Sensuously, almost dreamily, they removed the garments on the upper halves of each other's bodies. Then, when all that remained was Kate's skirt, shoes and panty hose and Nick's slacks, he sat her down on the bed and knelt before her.

"You have beautiful legs," he murmured, running his hand down the swell of her calves and then exploring the delicate structure of her ankles with the pads of his thumbs. "Every part of you is beautiful." As he slipped her shoes off, he leaned forward and lovingly kissed each of her knees.

Why this should have such an overpoweringly erotic effect, Kate had no idea. All she knew was that her entire body seemed suddenly electrified. With her palms flattened on the bed at her sides, she leaned back and closed her eyes. "Nick!"

"Yes, darling. I've been waiting all this time for you, too." He rose, slid next to her on the bed and took her into his arms. Tightly locked in each other's embrace, they kissed and kissed. Like parts of the same being that had been separated but were now whole at last, they rolled from side to side, exploring the flawless fit of their new union.

Then, needing to forge that bond more perfectly yet, they began to remove what remained of each other's clothing. Nick undid the waistband on Kate's skirt and slid it down over her hips. His slacks followed. And then, while he watched with eyes that smoldered like molten sapphire, she slithered out of her panty hose.

"Oh Kate, oh Kate my darling! I was so afraid we'd never be together like this again!"

"I was afraid, too. Nick! Oh, please!"

There were no more words, only caresses and sighs and then gasps of excitement and mute pleasure. Though they were both on fire with longing, Nick insisted on taking the time to adore each part of Kate, her throat, her breasts, the quivering softness of her belly.

Ardently, she kissed and caressed him back. His tough, sleek body seemed so utterly beautiful to her. Lovingly, she ran her hands and then her lips over his muscled chest and shoulders, the hard contours of his narrow hips and steely horseman's thighs.

At last they came together, and it was slow, and deep and satisfying. "I love you, Kate," Nick whispered as he climaxed inside her.

But Kate was beyond words. All she could do was clasp his lean waist tight and arch her back as she, too, found a release that for a moment seemed to send her spinning out into the starry night that now shrouded the windows enclosing their hideway.

For a while after that, they simply held each other and whispered love words, nonsensical sounds that at that moment seemed to hold more meaning than a roomful of dictionaries. Finally, however, Nick got up off the bed and dialed room service.

"I think this calls for a celebration," he said, shooting Kate a roguish grin.

"*I* think you'd better put something on before you answer the door," she shot back at him with a laugh. All the while her eyes caressed the naked masculine beauty of him. His body was like sculpture. As she gazed at him she thought of the Michelangelo David in Florence, except that Nick's body was tougher, less boyish. And it was very, very sexy.

Half an hour later they sat together in bed drinking champagne and finishing off bowlfuls of half-melted chocolate *gelato*.

"Did you have dinner?" Nick queried as he licked a spoon clean and then set down his empty dish.

"No."

"Would you like to go out and get some?"

"No." As she scooped up the last spoonful of her ice cream, Kate shook her head. "I don't want to go anywhere. I just want to stay here with you like this."

Nick filled both their glasses and then slipped his arm around Kate's shoulders and leaned back on the feather pillows heaped up against the carved headboard. "It's nice, isn't it? Just the two of us like this."

"It's wonderful," Kate agreed fervently. "I don't want it ever to end. I'd like to stay here like this with you forever."

"That's a pleasant fantasy, but I'm afraid it won't work," Nick replied, suddenly serious. "Tomorrow the sun will come up, and you'll fly back to the States and your career."

"Oh Nick . . ."

"No, hear me out. That's why we need to talk, Kate. We have to work things out between us." He turned slightly so that he could more easily look into her face. "Let me start by telling you something."

As she watched him take a sip of champagne, Kate waited fearfully. She didn't feel ready to face the reality of their problems. Not yet.

"I'm retiring from racing. From now on I'm strictly a breeder and trainer of horses."

Few things he could have said would have pleased her more. But she had to wonder what had brought the decision on. Did it have something to do with her?

"I've decided that winning the Grand National is a very good stopping point," he said, as if reading her mind. "I had to run that race, Kate," he continued in a level tone. "Maybe you were right and it did have something to do with my father. I can't say. But I do know that it had a lot to do with proving something to myself about my courage. After an accident like the one I had, I couldn't help but wonder if I'd lost my nerve."

"Nick—" Kate started to protest.

He held up a hand. "I know you think that's a silly macho hang-up, but to me it seemed important. Anyhow, it's over and I'm ready to rest on my laurels."

"Well, they're very fine laurels to rest on," Kate replied gruffly. It was so good to know that she'd never have to worry about Nick going through something like Aintree again. Impulsively, she reached up and kissed his cheek.

"I take it you approve?"

"Very much! I nearly died when I saw Becher's Brook."

He grinned. "I hope you'll approve of what I'm going to tell you next. Kate, I'm flying to the States myself in a couple of days."

"You are?"

"To Virginia, as a matter of fact. I'm going to look at some property there, a farm."

Kate's eyes widened with astonishment. "You mean a horse farm?"

Watching her face intently, he nodded.

Kate blinked, trying to understand, but what had come into her head seemed too incredible. "You mean you're thinking about buying it, about settling there?"

He nodded again. "It's a possibility I've been considering seriously."

Kate's breath caught and she flattened her hand against her throat. "Oh, but Nick, it would be such a drastic change. To you the United States would be like a foreign country."

His lips quirked. "It *is* a foreign country, actually. But not all that foreign. My career has been international, so I've spent quite a bit of time in the States. I know my way around. Besides, I make myself at home wherever I happen to be. I told you once that I'm a chameleon."

Kate nodded. She even remembered the moment when he'd made that remark. It had been in Viterbo while they'd been eating lunch and just making the first tentative moves toward understanding each other.

"I meant that I've never really belonged anywhere," he began to explain. "We're alike in that respect—only, since you've no family at all, your situation is a lot more straightforward. I've learned to be good at changing my spots to fit a new environment because one way or another, all my life I've been an outsider."

"Not here in Italy with Mario and Adelina. They adore you."

"And I adore them. I'm fond of all the Italian side of my family, but my background is so different from theirs. I'll always be a bit of a cuckoo in their nest."

"That's not true."

He shrugged. "It's the way I feel, and in the end feelings are all we have to go on, aren't they? I'm even more of an outsider with my English family. For years they rejected me outright."

"They don't reject you now, do they? How could they? Now that you've won the National, you're famous, a regular British hero. They have to be proud."

Nick rotated the stem of his champagne glass between his thumb and forefinger. "Before coming here for Mario's wedding, I stopped in Dorset and spent some time with my grandparents." His lip curled slightly. "You're right, their attitude toward me has changed. And it's not just me. They even have regrets about the way they disowned my mother. We reconciled, so I feel better about all that. Still, you can't change the past, can you? It's always there behind you."

Kate smiled and stroked his knuckles, admiring as she did so the fine-tuned strength of his sinewy hands. "Maybe that why it's a comfort to know that the future's always there ahead of you."

A warm light came into Nick's eyes. "It's the future I want to talk about, plan for. That's what this trip to see a farm in Virginia is all about."

"You really are serious, aren't you?"

"Very." He nodded emphatically.

"But you'd have to sell your place in Ireland, and you love Newride."

He kissed the satiny skin of her naked shoulder. "I love you more."

Kate's heart seemed to go still in her breast and then start up again with a lurch. She clasped her hands together so tightly that her knuckles went bloodless. "You're doing this for me? Oh, Nick! But how could you live permanently in the States? You're not a citizen."

"That wouldn't be a problem if I married someone who was."

"Marriage?" For a moment Kate couldn't breathe. She looked at him with her heart in her eyes. "Nick, I'm willing to do what you asked before. You don't have to sell your farm or marry me. I'm willing to go to Ireland and live with you."

"That would make it difficult for you to carry on with your career, wouldn't it?"

"I'm willing to take a chance on that. I don't want to live without you. I love you too much."

For a moment he gazed at her, his blue eyes alight. Then he unclasped her hands, lifted them to his lips and caressed each palm tenderly. "It's mutual, Kate," he murmured deeply. "That's why it's best for me to cross the Atlantic. If this place in Virginia is all the estate agent makes out, it will be an ideal spot for me to conduct my business. I'll be close to the important tracks and breeders."

His brow wrinkled slightly. "Maybe it won't be quite so perfect for you, but it won't be bad, either. You'll be within easy driving distance of Washington D.C., and no more than an hour by plane to New York and most of the other major cities on the East Coast. What do you say?"

She gazed at him doubtfully. "You're sure about this? Remember, my offer's still open. I'll come and stay with you in Ireland."

"No." He shook his head. "When you refused me before, your head was screwed on very tight, wasn't it? Music is your life, Kate. It sustains and nourishes you, and you can't give it up. And now that you're beginning to achieve such success..." He shook his head so emphatically that a black curl tumbled loose over his forehead.

Kate couldn't resist reaching out and smoothing it back. "I wouldn't have offered to live with you at Newride if I hadn't meant it."

"I know that, Kate. But I'm not so unimaginative that I can't picture what would happen if you tried to turn yourself into a milkmaid there for my sake. No matter how much we started out loving each other, it would be a disaster. I don't want you making any big sacrifices for me that you'll later regret. I want to give us the best chance possible. Somehow we have to both compromise enough to make this work." He looked at her questioningly, the pulse ticking at his temple the only indication of just how anxious he was about her reply.

Kate took his glass away, set it down and then hurled herself at him. "Oh, Nick, of course I'll live in Virginia with you." She wrapped her arms around his neck and rained kisses on his cheeks and forehead.

"You haven't seen the place yet, and neither have I. You may not like it," Nick managed to exclaim. Chuckling at her enthusiasm and obviously delighted, he held her away slightly.

"If you like it, I'll love it. I'll even learn to love the beautiful horses you'll train there. I'll even take riding lessons!"

"Whoa! I said we should each compromise. That's a major concession."

Kate's green eyes glowed with love and happiness. "Darn right it is. But you wait and see. Before a year is out I'll be Dale Evans to your Roy Rogers."

"Now that is an interesting promise, isn't it! Oh Kate, Kate my love! To make me happy, you don't need to do a thing but be there. That's all, just be there."

He cupped her chin with the palm of his hand and studied her glowing, upturned face. Then, his blue eyes darkening like a purpled sea at sunset behind their thick fringe of black lashes, Nick groaned softly and claimed her mouth with his. Soon the kiss turned into a far more passionate embrace and then a union even more complete and fulfilling.

All that night they made love, first with their bodies and then with their minds and souls. As the moonlit hours passed, they lay in each other's arms, stroking an arm or breast, caressing a palely gleaming leg. All the while they talked in sleepy whispers. Nick told Kate about his difficult days in boarding school and tried to explain some of his feelings about riding. "When you get up at dawn and climb onto the back of a horse and ride out, suddenly you've set yourself free. There's no other feeling like it."

"Oh, I don't know. Sometimes I feel that way when I'm playing the piano. There's just me and the music and nothing else. During those moments I feel truly free."

He kissed her ear. "You see, we have a lot in common."

"More than you know. It's possible that I might have a rich grandfather, too."

Nick raised an eyebrow. "How is that? You told me that you were abandoned at birth and that both your adoptive parents died."

"I was, and they did. But there's been a new and rather strange development." Admid many incredulous interruptions from Nick, Kate described Owen Byrnside and his quest.

"You mean I might be marrying an heiress?"

"Not likely. I'm sure it's going to turn out to be one of the other two orphans who's his true granddaughter, and he won't test until he's found all of us. But in the meantime he's been wonderful to me, and I couldn't love him more if he really were my grandfather."

Nick shook his head. "That's quite a story." He kissed her deeply. "But right now, as you can see, I'm more interested in our story." For a while their conversation became physical rather than verbal. But at last Nick whispered in Kate's ear. "When we get back to the States, will you come with me to look at that farm? I can't buy unless you approve."

"Of course I'll come."

"But aren't you supposed to be performing someplace?"

"Yes, but I'll cancel."

"I don't want you canceling anything for my sake. That's not the way for us to begin."

"Then I'll think of something else. Anyhow, I'll be there." She threw her arms around his neck and drew him to her. "That's something you can count on, Nick Conti. From now on, I'm going to be there."

EPILOGUE

ONCE AGAIN Jake Caine guided his Mercedes through Owen Byrnside's tall wrought-iron gates and up his long curving drive. Outside Jake's car windows autumn had begun to turn into winter. Brilliant leaves carpeted the rolling lawn and a brisk wind blew through the barren treetrops.

Yet at the head of the drive, the gray stone facade of Taleman Hall, softened by the late-afternoon light, looked less forbidding. For a moment, after turning off the motor and climbing out of his parked car, Jake Caine stood gazing up at it. Then, shifting his briefcase from one hand to the other, he walked up to the entrance and announced his arrival with the heavy brass knocker that decorated the studded oak door.

Owen Byrnside's secretary, Loretta Greene, answered. As usual, she was immaculately groomed and beautifully garbed in a black-and-white print dress with a deceptively simple cut. "Here you are at last," she said as she stood aside so that Jake could walk past. "For the past hour he's been asking if you've come every five minutes."

"Sorry. I was delayed in traffic," Jake answered truthfully. He'd never liked Loretta Greene. There was something too careful and calculated about her—which, as he was well aware, seemed a strange reaction for a lawyer to have since he was, by profession as well as inclination, a careful person who liked to think things out beforehand himself.

"Well, I hope you've brought good news. He's all ruffled up and needs some soothing down."

Jake patted his briefcase. "I think Owen will be interested to hear what I have to say."

Miss Greene shot him a curious look. "Does that mean you've found another one of his missing orphans?"

Jake was Owen Byrnside's lawyer, not Loretta Greene's. "You'll be hearing soon enough."

Miss Greene pursed her carefully painted lips, but was far too well-mannered to continue her probing. "Very well, then let me take you directly up to him. He's waiting with bated breath."

Upstairs Owen Byrnside sat propped up in a chair, swathed in blankets. He held his thin arms crooked stiffly out at his sides like crippled wings, and his gnarled hands were clenched so that the blue veins stood up on their mottled surface. The strong afternoon sun streaming through the windows picked out the deep lines etching his ravaged visage. But it also showed the indomitable spirit and intelligence still alight in his pale blue eyes.

"At last!" he cackled as Jake strode into the room. "I'm not paying you a king's ransom to keep me waiting, young man!"

"Sorry, sir. It was unavoidable, I'm afraid." Jake set his briefcase down and pulled up a chair. As he did so, his eye fell on two silver-framed photographs prominently displayed on the adjacent tilt-top table. He picked one up and studied it. It showed Kate and Nick Conti dressed in their formal wedding clothes and standing in front of the massive fireplace in Taleman Hall's east parlor, where they'd been married a month back.

"They certainly look like a happy pair," Jake commented. The photographer had caught Kate and Nick toasting each other with champagne and gazing adoringly into each other's eyes.

Owen smiled reminiscently. "Yes, that was the first wedding this old heap of a place has seen. I thought it went fine."

"It did."

"And I like Kate's young man. Seems a fine, smart fella with a good head on his shoulders."

Jake laughed. "Well, it isn't as if you didn't do a complete background check on him. You probably know more about Nick Conti than he knows about himself."

"I wasn't going to take a chance on Kate marrying a crook or a fool," Owen snapped. Then, ruefully, he shook his head. "It was a happy day. I only wish my Alice could have been here for it," Owen added a trifle wistfully.

Jake glanced at the lovely woman in the portrait opposite the bed. "How do you know she wasn't?"

Owen's gaze followed Jake's and his expression softened. "You're right, I don't. In fact, I actually do believe she was. Sounds daft, I guess, but lately I've been feeling her presence very strongly. I think Alice knows what I'm doing, and approves."

He looked back over at Jake, who'd set down the first photograph and picked up the second. It, too, was of Kate and Nick—only it showed them dressed in jeans and fleece jackets standing in front of a white rail fence. Kate was feeding an apple to a horse while Nick looked on.

"That's a nice place they've got down in Virginia," Jake commented.

"Wish I could see it for myself," Owen answered. "But from what Kate has to say, she seems happy there. And she's sure looking good."

"How's she keeping up with her music?" Jake queried, setting the second picture down and taking a seat.

"She's not doing so much nightclub work. Doesn't want to travel, you know. So it's mostly albums and local stuff.

But that's all right. As long as she's happy, that's all that counts."

Jake nodded. "Ah, happiness. It's what we all want, and most of us can't find no matter how hard we look."

Owen gazed at his good-looking young lawyer shrewdly. "You speaking from experience?"

"Experience and observation. But I didn't come here to talk about myself." Jake studied his employer. It hadn't escaped his notice that Owen now talked about Kate exactly as if she really were his granddaughter—a development which might prove dangerously disappointing. "You know," he said carefully, "there's no reason why you couldn't have Kate tested now."

Instantly Owen's smile was replaced by a scowl. "And what would that prove?"

"Whether or not she's really related to you."

"Young man, we've already been through this. But since you brought it up again, let me ask you something. What if the test proves Kate isn't related to me at all?"

"That's a very real possibility."

"Of course it is. I'm not such a fool that I don't know that. And what if I never find the other girls? Then where would I be? I'd be nowhere with nothing and no one to call my own, isn't that right?"

Jake nodded, beginning to really understand. The old man wanted a granddaughter so badly that he was actually afraid of finding out that Kate wasn't the one. "Well, then, maybe I've brought some news that will change your mind," Jake answered sympathetically. He picked up his briefcase, positioned it on his knees and snapped open its brass locks. "We've finally got a line on your second orphan."

Owen's hands clenched on the pillows. "Well, it's about time," he said gruffly. "I was beginning to wonder if that bloodhound you've got working on the case is all he's cracked up to be."

"Actually, it wasn't our detective but my new executive assistant, Miss Bonner, who got the job done."

"Miss Bonner? Hmm." Owen rolled his eyes. "I don't believe I've met this Miss Bonner. What's she like?"

"Organized, efficient, very, very businesslike."

"Young?"

"Yes, middle twenties I would guess."

"Pretty?"

"Passable." Jake pictured the attractive blonde with the poised smile and oversize horn-rimmed glasses who'd become such a fixture in his office. At first he hadn't paid much attention to her. But in the past few months she'd begun to intrigue him. He wasn't exactly sure why. Maybe it had something to do with the way she looked at him, so utterly cool and self-possessed. Last week he'd even asked her out to lunch. She'd refused, which had intrigued him even more.

"Well, I'll have to arrange to take a look at her. But she's not what interests me right now," Owen commented. "Tell me about my orphan."

Jake withdrew a file from his briefcase and handed it over to Owen, who seized it eagerly and flipped it open. "There's not much to tell. As yet, we haven't made contact, but I don't anticipate that will be difficult. As you can see from her file, her name's Maggie Murphy, and she's a nurse."

"Another looker," Owen said, gazing down at the photograph in the file, which showed a sweet-faced young woman with expressive gray eyes. He glanced up at the portrait of his gray-eyed wife and then back down at the picture. A new, suppressed excitement came into his voice. "Don't dangle your toes on this one, Jake! Find her for me! Find her right away!"

COMING IN 1991 FROM
HARLEQUIN SUPERROMANCE:

Three abandoned orphans,
one missing heiress!

Dying millionaire Owen Byrnside receives an
anonymous letter informing him that twenty-six years
ago, his son, Christopher, fathered a daughter. The
infant was abandoned at a foundling home that
subsequently burned to the ground, destroying all
records. Three young women could be Owen's long-
lost granddaughter, and Owen is determined to track
down each of them! Read their stories in

#434 HIGH STAKES (available January 1991)
#438 DARK WATERS (available February 1991)
#442 BRIGHT SECRETS (available March 1991)

Three exciting stories of intrigue and romance by
veteran Superromance author Jane Silverwood.

Harlequin romances are now available in stores at these convenient times each month.

Harlequin Presents
Harlequin American Romance
Harlequin Historical
Harlequin Intrigue

These series will be in stores on the 4th of every month.

Harlequin Romance
Harlequin Temptation
Harlequin Superromance
Harlequin Regency Romance

New titles for these series will be in stores on the 16th of every month.

We hope this new schedule is convenient for you. With only two trips each month to your local bookseller, you will always be sure not to miss any of your favorite authors!

Happy reading!

Please note there may be slight variations in on-sale dates in your area due to differences in shipping and handling.

HDATES

HARLEQUIN'S "BIG WIN"
SWEEPSTAKES RULES & REGULATIONS

NO PURCHASE NECESSARY TO ENTER OR RECEIVE A PRIZE

1. To enter and join the Reader Service, scratch off the metallic strips on all your BIG WIN tickets #1–#6. This will reveal the values for each sweepstakes entry number, the number of free book(s) you will receive and your free bonus gift as part of our Reader Service. If you do not wish to take advantage of our Reader Service but wish to enter the Sweepstakes only, scratch off the metallic strips on your BIG WIN tickets #1–#4. Return your entire sheet of tickets intact. Incomplete and/or inaccurate entries are ineligible for that section or sections of prizes. Not responsible for mutilated or unreadable entries or inadvertent printing errors. Mechanically reproduced entries are null and void.

2. Whether you take advantage of this offer or not, your Sweepstakes numbers will be compared against the list of winning numbers generated at random by the computer. In the event that all prizes are not claimed by March 31, 1992, a random drawing will be held from all qualified entries received from March 30, 1990 to March 31, 1992, to award all unclaimed prizes. All cash prizes (Grand to Sixth) will be mailed to the winners and are payable by check in U.S. funds. Seventh prize will be shipped to winners via third-class mail. These prizes are in addition to any free, surprise or mystery gifts that might be offered. Versions of this sweepstakes with different prizes of approximate equal value may appear at retail outlets or in other mailings by Torstar Corp. and its affiliates.

3. The following prizes are awarded in this sweepstakes: ★ Grand Prize (1) $1,000,000; First Prize (1) $25,000; Second Prize (1) $10,000; Third Prize (5) $5,000; Fourth Prize (10) $1,000; Fifth Prize (100) $250; Sixth Prize (2,500) $10; ★ ★ Seventh Prize (6,000) $12.95 ARV.

   ★ This presentation offers a Grand Prize of a $1,000,000 annuity. Winner will receive $33,333.33 a year for 30 years without interest totalling $1,000,000.

   ★ ★ Seventh Prize: A fully illustrated hardcover book published by Torstar Corp. Approximate retail value of the book is $12.95.

   Entrants may cancel the Reader Service at anytime without cost or obligation to buy (see details in center insert card).

4. This Sweepstakes is being conducted under the supervision of an independent judging organization. By entering this Sweepstakes, each entrant accepts and agrees to be bound by these rules and the decisions of the judges, which shall be final and binding. Odds of winning in the random drawing are dependent upon the total number of entries received. Taxes, if any, are the sole responsibility of the winners. Prizes are nontransferable. All entries must be received at the address printed on the reply card and must be postmarked no later than 12:00 MIDNIGHT on March 31, 1992. The drawing for all unclaimed sweepstakes prizes will take place May 30, 1992, at 12:00 NOON, at the offices of Marden-Kane, Inc., Lake Success, New York.

5. This offer is open to residents of the U.S., the United Kingdom, France and Canada, 18 years or older, except employees and their immediate family members of Torstar Corp., its affiliates, subsidiaries, and all other agencies and persons connected with the use, marketing or conduct of this sweepstakes. All Federal, State, Provincial and local laws apply. Void wherever prohibited or restricted by law. Any litigation within the Province of Quebec respecting the conduct and awarding of a prize in this publicity contest must be submitted to the Régie des loteries et courses du Québec.

6. Winners will be notified by mail and may be required to execute an affidavit of eligibility and release, which must be returned within 14 days after notification or an alternative winner will be selected. Canadian winners will be required to correctly answer an arithmetical skill-testing question administered by mail, which must be returned within a limited time. Winners consent to the use of their names, photographs and/or likenesses for advertising and publicity in conjunction with this and similar promotions without additional compensation. For a list of major winners, send a stamped, self-addressed envelope to: WINNERS LIST, c/o Harlequin Reader Service, 3010 Walden Ave., P.O. Box 1396, Buffalo, NY 14269-1396. Winners Lists will be fulfilled after the May 30, 1992 drawing date.

If Sweepstakes entry form is missing, please print your name and address on a 3" × 5" piece of plain paper and send to:

In the U.S.	In Canada
Harlequin's "BIG WIN" Sweepstakes	Harlequin's "BIG WIN" Sweepstakes
3010 Walden Ave.	P.O. Box 609
P.O. Box 1867	Fort Erie, Ontario
Buffalo, NY 14269-1867	L2A 5X3

Offer limited to one per household.

LTY-H191R